THE DEADLY DEEP

THE DEADLY
DEEP

JON MESSMANN

CUTTING EDGE

ISBN-13: 978-1-970848-03-8

Published by
Cutting Edge Books
PO Box 8212
Calabasas, CA 91372
www.cuttingedgebooks.com

" ... and [Elijah] said to his servant: 'Go up now, look toward the sea.' And he went up, and looked, and said: 'There is nothing.'

And he said: 'Go again seven times.' And it came to pass at the seventh time, that he said: 'Behold, there ariseth a little cloud out of the sea, like a man's hand.' "

I Kings 18:43-44

CHAPTER ONE

AP July 6, 1975
CHARTERED CABIN CRUISER SUNK.
SOLE SURVIVOR SAYS WHALE ATTACKED
BOAT. AUTHORITIES INVESTIGATE.

The girl could feel the sun baking through her, warm and caressing, as she stretched herself out on the mat atop the roof of the boat. She could also feel the dark eyes of the young mate on her and she wished she dared to unsnap the top of the red bikini. *That'd give him something to stare at,* Candy Nolan told herself. Her breasts were her best asset, full and round and smooth as whipped cream; "terrific boobs," as Harry always put it in his own inimitable way of putting things. His voice, coming up from the stern deck, broke into her thoughts, the steel-file rasp of it cutting the still air.

"This spot's no goddamn good. Move this tub someplace else," Harry growled.

"Patience, Mr. Owens." She heard Tom Peterson's voice, calm and low from the wheelhouse. After a dozen chartered trips with Harry, the captain had learned how to handle his arrogant explosions. In some ways better than she had in three years as his mistress, Candy admitted to herself. But then, Peterson was a professional charter-boat fisherman, used to dealing with men whose wealth made them feel they owned everything and everyone. Candy opened her eyes and sat up and knew the young mate's eyes watched her breasts balloon up from the wisps of material. Ralph, his name was, Ralph Gunnetta. She glanced down the length of the boat to the stern where Harry sat in the big swivel chair, holding on to the thick, big-game rod, the butt of it firm in the gimbal of the chair. The fishing cap protected Harry's head from the sun but the back of his thick neck was red over tan, she saw. Harry always got red on the back of his neck. His skin was sensitive there. It was perhaps the only sensitive thing about Harry Owens, she reflected.

Candy took the plastic bottle of lotion and spread some of the viscous substance along her legs and wondered what was wrong with her lately. It was becoming harder and harder for her to stand Harry, in bed or out of bed. She wondered idly which was worse. In bed, at least, his self-centered boorishness was a private thing with no other eyes observing his behavior, his total disregard for her or what she felt. One night, in bed, she'd given voice to that, saw his sharp blue eyes grow hard as he pulled his head back from her breasts.

"All that counts is that I want it. Just remember that, honey," he had rasped. She had remembered the warning and a lot more. Three years of more. At the beginning, Harry had told her that he loved her, she reflected, as he cascaded presents on her. She'd been anxious to indulge in that self-deception. It made the term *mistress* more acceptable. Of course, she'd always known better, and yet for six months, she'd almost been able to make herself believe differently. But that ended soon enough and she kept reminding herself of all those times as a carhop, waitress, department-store clerk, cocktail-lounge hostess—then Harry Owens, and more material comforts than she'd ever been able to get any other way. Hell, everybody exchanged something, didn't they? Candy put the cap back on the bottle, heard Harry's sudden shout.

"Something's hit," he cried out from the stern of the boat, and she felt the sudden fluster of quiet activity. The young, dark-eyed mate managed to take his eyes from her and scan the sea behind the boat. Candy rose, swung down from the cabin roof, holding on to the handrail as she made her way aft to where Harry was reeling in furiously.

"Shit, it's no sword and it's no sail," she heard him growl, and then saw the fish leap half out of the water, twisting and wriggling, blue stripes on a faintly yellow belly. "Christ, a skipjack," she heard Harry cry out in disgust. "Who the hell wants that?"

Tom Peterson had moved down from the wheel. "Bring him in closer and I'll cut him loose," the captain said.

"And leave the hook in him?" Candy heard herself say, felt the distaste curling her lips back.

"That's right," Harry flung back. "Shit, it won't hurt him."

"Says who?" Candy snapped. Harry continued to reel in the line with angry impatience.

"Scientists, that's who, goddamnit," he roared as he yanked the reel back. "They made tests and all that shit."

"Shit is right," Candy flung in return. "Tests on pain, on whose yardstick? Anybody ever ask the fish if he hurts? Look at him twisting and trying to get that thing out of his mouth. Don't tell me he doesn't hurt awful."

Harry half-turned in the chair as he held on to the rod, his eyes shooting blue fire at her. "Fuck off, goddamn it," he yelled as Peterson leaned over the transom of the cruiser and cut the line with a small ax. Candy turned away, climbed back up along the side of the deck and back to the cabin roof, refusing to watch the fish swim away with the metal hook sticking out of its mouth. It had to hurt, she repeated silently. Not that Harry could give a damn if it did or didn't.

She sat down on the mat and held contradictory thoughts. She hoped Harry didn't catch a fucking thing all day. She hoped he didn't even see a swordfish or a sailfish. At the same time, she hoped he got his catch. Otherwise, he'd take it out on her all damn night. He'd play her as he wanted to play his fish, putting her through every goddamn thing he could think up. Yet where in this world could she do any better, Candy asked herself. She knew many who'd give anything to be in her place right now, enjoying the Caribbean sun and sea. They'd take Harry anytime. But then they didn't really know him.

The sudden movement cut into her thoughts and she saw the dolphins first, then heard Harry's growl of displeasure. He had eyes only for his sword or sailfish. She watched the two dolphins sail into the air, then dive back into the sea to reappear again, the same two. Or perhaps two others. She couldn't tell. They shot out of the water, as if yanked on unseen strings, in an effortless, parabolic curve, then plunged into the seas and repeated the maneuver, this time ahead of the boat. She turned, watching as they circled the cabin cruiser with their almost magical cascades of form and grace, and then, as suddenly as they'd appeared, they were gone.

She looked away, her glance meeting the mate's hungering eyes. He'd be all lean sinew in bed, all electricity, quick and almost effortless, like the dolphins, she mused. She toyed with the thought. Jesus, it was time she enjoyed getting laid again. She wondered if she had ever enjoyed it with Harry, wondered and decided that she must have at the beginning. Or maybe that was just part of the self-deception, too. She let her eyes drift to the young mate, saw the brazenness of his glance. "You've worked for the captain long?" she asked idly. He would understand the question was merely a signal.

"Almost three years," he said and she almost laughed. Three years, the magic number. It was Harry's voice, a note of awe in it, that made her turn her eyes to the water.

"Jesus, look over there," she heard him say, and her eyes scanned the sea and there, not more than fifty yards away, an island seemed to be rising up out of the water. Gray-blue, smooth on the top, the island lifted itself out of the sea with majestic slowness as she stared, transfixed, and suddenly the island shot a stream of water from its top.

"Goddamn, look at that bastard," Harry rasped.

"It's a blue," Tom Peterson said. "Jesus, he must weigh a hundred tons." Candy, sitting up straight now, suddenly felt a chill under the hot Caribbean sun, and frowning, she watched the huge whale move still farther out of the water. Slowly, as she watched, the whale turned until its great head faced the boat. It began to move toward them, only the huge bulk of it masking the speed with which it came through the water.

"What the fuck is it doing?" she heard Harry exclaim.

"I don't know," Peterson answered, apprehension in his voice. "They don't usually come this close."

"Christ, it's coming for us," Candy heard Harry shout. "It's going to ram us," he cried out. She'd never heard fear in his voice before. It was nice to hear, she found herself thinking, incongruously. "Get the goddamn engine on," she heard him scream.

The sounds, the voices, the whirring cough of the engine turning on, all came to her as if from a distant sphere. All her senses were riveted on the huge form that bore down at them, was, in fact, almost upon them. It seemed some kind of joke, she thought, something ridiculous even to contemplate as, hypnotized, she could only stare at the tremendous bulk that neared the boat. It was close, now, terribly close, the gray-blue skin marked with scars and scratches; she heard Harry screaming, Peterson cursing, the young mate's frenzied shouts. The boat vibrated, started to gather itself, but it was too late. The tremendous form loomed up and Candy's hypnotic trance suddenly shattered. She heard herself scream as she leaped to her feet. She half-dived and was half-catapulted as the whale rammed into the cabin cruiser; the hundred deadweight tons of it slammed into the boat as an ocean liner would plow into it. Candy, flying through the air, heard the sound of wood splintering, planks shattering over the tremendous thudding crash.

She twisted, managed to get her legs up under her as she struck the water. She hit and went under at once, struck out, and fought back to the surface. Shaking water from her eyes, she saw the cabin cruiser collapsed in the center, looking like a mis-shapen egg that had been pushed in, with its insides running out the middle. She couldn't see Harry or Peterson, but she picked out the young mate clinging to the side of the flying bridge and then, her eyes sweeping the water, she glimpsed Harry's head, and to his right, Peterson. As she watched, her eyes widening in horror, she saw the huge form of the whale begin to rise, moving straight up out of the water as if it were standing on its tail fin, higher and higher until it blotted out the sky itself. She watched the sea drop down from its tremendous sides and then, twisting, the whale came down onto the boat like a gigantic sledgeham-mer, smashing the craft in two, plunging everything down into the water under its terrible weight.

Candy saw Harry, then Peterson, disappear as they were pulled down into the water after the whale by the huge suction it created as it dived. She felt the pull of the water reaching out to her and she backpedaled as hard as she could, managing to draw free of the suction. She halted, rested, watched as bits of debris floated to the surface. Nothing but the scattered debris came up. Everything else was gone: Harry, the boat, Peterson, and the young mate. And the huge whale was gone, too. There was nothing in any direction but the blue, silent sea. It was as if nothing at all had happened, and only the water enclosing her body was proof that she hadn't imagined it all.

A piece of the boat's deck floated by and Candy reached out, caught hold of it, pulled herself onto it, and rested. It wasn't big enough to carry more than half of her and she lay there feeling not so much lost as disembodied, as though she had witnessed a movie with herself as part of it. She let her eyes move across the water, expecting to see the huge form of the whale rise up again, but there was only the slow roll of the sea. She shifted her weight on the piece of wood. Strangely, she didn't think of sharks. She was a survivor and, as such, she would survive. Candy Nolan was neither a philosopher nor an environmentalist. All she knew of whales came from reading *Moby Dick* in school and an occasional newspaper article. But she knew, in the dimness of her scant knowledge, that whales didn't do things like this. And yet she had just witnessed and lived through it, and she could only wonder why. What had made the huge whale attack the ship? What had made it come up out of the depths to destroy the boat? She shifted again on the piece of deck and the Gulf-stream currents carried her along and she felt the heat of the sun and finally she could think no more, wonder no more. Finally she could only lie there and pray.

Candy Nolan was picked up by another boat just before night and rushed to the hospital at Key Largo. The police questioned her after she was treated for shock and she told them what had happened. They called the Coast Guard, who sent up a young, shore-based lieutenant to interview her the next day. His name was Jack Matthews and he was very polite, listened to everything she said, but Candy was too much a product of the streets not to catch the deprecation just under the pleasant patience.

"Miss Nolan, whales don't behave in that manner," he said finally as she stared at him. "Even harpooned whales seldom turn and attack."

"Are you calling me a liar?" Candy snapped. Lieutenant Matthews smiled politely, soothingly.

"No, but I must wonder if perhaps you saw a whale, then lay down to enjoy the sun and the boat exploded and you woke thinking it was the whale. Strange thoughts do occur to people under stress," he said.

"The whale attacked the boat," Candy said slowly. "He attacked the goddamn boat on purpose."

The lieutenant shook his head again and kept his patient smile. "It's just not done, Miss Nolan. Whales just don't behave that way," he said.

"Well, this one did. Maybe he's a crazy, I don't know. But I damn well know what happened. He attacked the fucking boat and sank it, goddamn it. I was there," Candy spit back.

The lieutenant backed off, thanked her, took her story down, and made it part of his official report as he wondered exactly what did happen. He had to wonder more when, later that day, he got the wire-report on another fishing cruiser, the *Roberta II,* with four men aboard, that never returned to port. A search found a piece of her transom with half the name on it. According to the plans of her skipper, which he had left with the dockmaster before putting out of the Keys, the *Roberta II* had been fishing less than twenty miles from where Candy Nolan had been picked up.

Lieutenant Matthews put the two reports in one file and added another page to his original report. He sat frowning at the finished report. He'd never heard of a berserk whale, though there just conceivably could be one. It was strange, he conceded. No, weird, he corrected himself. He thought about returning to question Candy Nolan again, decided against it for now. He didn't want to go off chasing wild stories as though they were credible and make a damn fool of himself. The Coast Guard wouldn't appreciate that. He put Candy's statements into the file and turned to more routine business.

INS JULY 8, 1975
LOBSTERMAN KILLED AT HIS
TRAPS IN BIZARRE INCIDENT

The citizens of Chittam, just north of Booth Bay, Maine, between Elkins Light and North Reef, weren't terribly upset about Efrem Getz personally, but they were very bothered by the incident itself. They couldn't understand it and a collective shiver went up and down their spines, perhaps an exercise in mass precognition. It was "mighty strange," they said and, for the last time, shook their heads over Efrem Getz. They'd certainly done it often enough while he lived. "Odd people die in odd ways," one man said in a moment of lean philosophy.

Efrem Getz was unquestionably the most thoroughly disliked man along that section of the Maine coast. He told summer visitors it was because his traps were at the choicest lobster grounds and because he was the best damn lobsterman on the coast. He was that, most everyone admitted. He had an uncanny knack of knowing just exactly where to drop his traps and consistently brought up the finest, fattest lobsters caught on that part of the coast.

But Efrem Getz wasn't disliked for that and he knew it. Efrem Getz was a man with a sour soul, a man in whom nastiness flowed the way blood flows in other men. No one in Chittam, or North Reef or Elkins Light, for that matter, had escaped his temper or his tongue over the years, and some had met with his huge, hammerlike fists. He was often feared, as well as disliked, for his terrible tempers. He lived in a small, plain house on a rocky ledge where the wind never stopped blowing and where, in winter, it took sheer physical strength just to open the front door. Efrem seemed to enjoy letting nature as well as man do its damnedest to buffet him.

One day, Efrem went down to Portland, stayed for a week, and returned with a young girl to keep house for him. She was pretty, not much over twenty, and black, and some said they'd heard he'd taken her out of a jail-house, but nobody ever knew. She went into town once a week, did the shopping, kept pretty much to herself, and was quiet and polite, all of which the townsfolk appreciated. In fact, some much preferred her coming into town to shop than Efrem. It soon became obvious that she was doing more than simply keeping house for Efrem Getz and soon, as was the nature of his temper, he took to beating her regularly. One day in April, when the wind was cold and wet and sharp as needles. she walked into the office of the chief of police in Chittam.

"Mr. Getz fell and hurt himself," she said simply. "You better get up there with a doctor or an ambulance."

Chief Crowder called Doc Hansen and they rushed up to Efrem's house. They found him lying halfway in the kitchen and it was plain that his head had been split wide open by the cast-iron skillet on the floor next to him with blood on the edge of it. The girl simply walked out of the police station, disappeared, and no one ever saw her again. Efrem's head was patched up and he was back at his traps within a month. The incident didn't make him any less nasty but he did become more of a recluse, which no one minded.

No one might have known just what happened to Efrem Getz on the morning of July eighth if it hadn't been for Billy Hoggins.

Billy, just turned fourteen, had rowed out to do some crabbing, saw Efrem appear in his outboard to empty his traps. A good wind was blowing, as it always did in the early morning off North Reef. As Billy told it later, he was some fifty yards from Efrem and he almost didn't believe what he saw.

Efrem pulled up to his first marker and began hauling up the line and his trap. When the trap came out of the water, there were maybe fifteen lobsters clinging to the top and sides and the cork markers of the line. Efrem, quick to take advantage of this unexpected windfall, swung the trap with all the lobsters on it into the boat. As he swung it, two of the lobsters came loose and landed on him. One seized Efrem by the collar with his crusher claw, then ripped with the pincer. Billy Hoggins heard Efrem's cry of pain as he yanked the lobster from him. The other had caught hold of the back of his thick jacket and clung there.

The other lobsters, instead of scuttling around the floor of the boat defensively, came at Efrem with their big claws waving. One ripped into his ankle and Efrem cursed a cry of pain, bent down to shake it loose as another sunk its ripping claw into the calf of his leg. Another seemed to go under his foot, causing him to slip and go down onto the floor of the boat. Two more of the crustaceans struck at his face instantly. One sank its claws deep into Efrem's neck along the side and the spurt of blood from the severed arteries drenched its shell with red. The other ripped a tearing gash that left Efrem's right eye hanging. Billy Hoggins heard Efrem's screams of pain and yanked his crabbing net up, took up his oars, and began to row to the lobsterman's dory. Efrem was wriggling, twisting, fighting, and screaming on the floor of the dory as the lobsters swarmed over him, ripping and tearing at his hands as he struck at them, tearing through the clothing to his skin. When Billy reached the dory, Efrem's face was no longer a face but a torn, bloodied mass, without a nose, eyes, hardly a mouth, blue-black crustaceans hanging on to it, others boring into his body, one dug deep into his lower abdomen. Efrem's screams had become low moans as Billy's boat nosed against the dory. The soft bump nudged the dory and Billy drew back as the crustaceans turned toward him. They began to scuttle toward him, clambering up the lobster pots to the gunwale of the dory, waving their claws wildly, threateningly. He heard the clicking sound of their claws hitting against each other and he backed his boat away, spun it around, and rowed for shore with terror moving his arms like pistons.

He ran when he reached the small wharf at Chittam, shouted his story to the first person he met, which happened to be Roger Taylor, the postman. Roger took him to Chief Crowder's office, where Billy stopped sputtering and trembling long enough to repeat what he'd seen. The police chief rounded up his deputy, and with Roger Taylor, went out to where Efrem's dory bobbed in the Atlantic. There was nothing in the boat when they got there but Efrem's torn, gouged, and bloodied body. Ashore, they had hardly believed Billy's story, but there was no disbelief now, only revulsion and stares of consternation. They towed the dory and Efrem Getz back to shore and Chief Crowder sent in a report to the State Police.

It was there that the wire services picked it up, sent a reporter to interview Billy Hoggins. The reporter tried interviewing a few other people but got no place. The people of Maine are noted for their tight-lipped attitude toward outsiders and they kept their feelings about Efrem Getz and the strange incident to themselves. The reporter went away with his basic story and it received wide coverage from the wire services. July and August are always good months for that kind of news item.

The good citizens of Chittam, North Reef, and Elkins Light kept their perplexed reactions to themselves. They also kept their consternation to themselves when, the following day, two more lobstermen were attacked by angry lobsters when they brought up their traps. Once again, the crustaceans were clinging to the tops of the traps and the cork line markers as they were hauled up. Tom Osgood lost a finger before he could drop his traps back into the sea. Sam Dant had one huge fellow almost sever his wrist with his crusher claw, and got back to shore with the crustacean still hanging on to him, though more dead than alive from a blow with a hammer.

When, the following day, every lobsterman's trap lines had been cut—ragged, torn ends left dangling beneath floating markers—an impromptu meeting was called in the schoolhouse. Dick Evans, the mayor of Chittam, was sure the lines had been cut by "some of those nature-lovers that are always hollering about over-fishing." They'd taken advantage of the furor caused by Efrem Getz's strange death to make their point, he expounded. Tom Osgood and Sam Dant weren't so sure. That night, little knots of people gathered to talk more about the odd happenings. But they still kept it to themselves. They weren't about to make their towns seem like places for freak happenings, to say nothing of calling down on their heads a lot of curiosity-seekers and nosy outsiders.

So the wire services carried only the strange story of Efrem Getz. For the moment. That's how it started, just the two bizarre news items, two more strange incidents in a strange world. Nothing. And everything.

CHAPTER TWO

The cottage faced the Atlantic just north of Rehoboth Beach on the Delaware coast. It was sturdy and secure and lay wrapped in darkness with a half-moon spearing a pale, evanescent light through the window. Inside, Aran Holder lay awake, the girl beside him stirring her long, lithe body, catlike, almost purring in contentment. Her moaning screams of pleasure still seemed to echo in the silence of the cottage. She had risen up under him with wild abandon, the exact confluence of wanting exploding together. It had been good, Aran Holder reflected. It was always good with Jenny. They fitted, in all kinds of right ways. They had a chemistry, a rhythm. Their nerve-endings dovetailed.

Suddenly Aran Holder was wide awake. They had left the radio on, as they always did, and a newscaster had come on, pairing the two items, Candy Nolan's story of the attack by the whale and the strange story of Efrem Getz. "Fish stories, indeed," the newscaster quipped as he signed off and the music took over again. Aran Holder lay quietly, staring up at the ceiling while his mind hummed busily along its own pathways.

"You're thinking. I can feel it," he heard Jenny's voice say, and her elbow pushed into his ribs. He turned to look at her. "About that crazy news item just now," she added smugly.

He chuckled. "OK," he admitted. "Anything out-of-the-ordinary, anything unexplainable. Occupational disease, the hazards of being a science writer."

She rose on one elbow to push away thick, black hair that had fallen over his forehead, using her fingers to smooth the unruly strands down on his head and her breasts were smooth against his ribs. She made a face. "It's a confirmation to me," she said.

"What's a confirmation?" he asked.

"That crazy news item," she said almost sullenly. "It confirms what I've always thought. Nothing connects."

"How's that?" Aran asked and she lay back, answered as she stared up at the ceiling.

"The world: it's disconnected, made up of separateness. There really isn't any rhyme or reason. Father Callahan used to tell us that there's an overall master plan, that everything is part of it, and nothing happens except within that great, vast wisdom of a plan. Crap. It's all jigs and jags, bits and pieces. The connections are only local."

"No," Aran said. "I don't know that I'd agree with Father Callahan's interpretations of everything, but it does connect. It's all part of a whole."

Jenny rose abruptly, sitting up straight to look down at him. She shook her head vigorously at him. "No, it doesn't fit," she said. "While we're making love, other people are being killed in weird accidents. While we're experiencing total, absolute pleasure, other people are experiencing total, absolute pain. Where's the balance in that? A farmer spends all year nurturing and nourishing his crops into fullness while right under the ground the larvae is sucking and pulling and growing and comes out as the beetles that destroy his whole crop. Now where's the master planning in that? It's all a jumble of separateness and crisscrosses."

"It connects. It fits in its own way, all of it," Aran said.

"How? Where? You're an award-winning science writer. Explain it to me," she snapped.

"Whoa, now," Aran protested. "That doesn't make me Jehovah." Jenny Vandam grunted and he pulled her against him. "You want someone to make you feel less guilty, that's what you want," he said. Her eyes frowned at him. "That's right," he reiterated. "I know you, Jenny Vandam. You feel guilty because while you're enjoying yourself, someone else is being killed. That offends your sense of justice. It's what makes you unusual, Jenny Vandam. Your instincts are in the right place. You have a connate caring and that's quite wonderful."

"You make me sound like a one-celled creature, something primitive that simply reacts to stimuli," she said with a mock pout.

He leaned forward, kissed her, felt her mouth open for him at once, her body quiver as his hands found the tiny tips of her breasts. "What's wrong with reactions?" he murmured and she shrugged agreement, her hands reaching down his body, caressing, fondling, arousing; and in moments they were entangled again, skin to skin, mouth to mouth, all the sensory organs directed at one pulsating objective; ecstasy sought, implored, demanded, and finally the night erupted once again.

Later, Aran Holder lay with the girl in his arms, slowly succumbing to sleep. *It all connects,* he murmured to himself. *It's not all haphazardness that works out only sometimes.* The night took possession of the little cottage, and outside the surf swept against the beach with measured cadence.

He woke in the sun of morning, opened his eyes to see Jenny seated in front of the small dresser across the room, brushing her long, strawberry-blond hair, her body a long-limbed sea-nymph's body, all of one tanned shade except the narrow band of white that stretched across the dark, mossy triangle, a kind of bathing suit by omission. Her every move was a thing of natural gracefulness and he watched her lift her arms, push hands under her hair and her breasts, not overly large, stretched to point upward with magnificent insouciance. He'd been here for a week at the cottage on the private beach where Jenny spent her summers. Her parents were in Europe as they usually were. It was his first real vacation in too long and he was particularly glad to be away from the university in Washington. He'd agreed to teach the course, after Arthur Hawkins talked him into it. After all, his specialty was taking scientific complexities, especially new theories and discoveries, and reducing them to language understandable and assimilable by the general public. After he'd won the Magnus award for an article, he'd received offers to teach from a half dozen schools.

The course was to be wide-ranging, free-form exploration of the moral aspects of science's headlong plunge into new areas of knowledge: the new discipline of bioethics. However, he found he had trouble keeping to that. The students he faced were a good deal more interested in shortcuts to complex theories they were studying in other courses than in the moral dimensions of modern science. He had found the course irritating and fatiguing and he was glad to get away, to have time to think about and to write pieces of his own.

He'd met Jennifer at a faculty cocktail party where she'd come with Herbert Atkinson; an old family friend, not a date, Aran had been relieved to find out. Atkinson was one of the stuffiest, driest old young men at the university, and Aran couldn't imagine this lively, radiant girl going out with him. More precisely, he couldn't imagine himself going out with anyone who saw anything in Herbert Atkinson and he wanted very much to go out with Jenny from the afternoon of that first meeting. They'd met after that again, in the right way, the only way that counts, the inner, silent communication, the transmissions of pheromones, and the rest had come easily and naturally and had been good from the start.

Jenny, Jennifer ... he called her by both names because sometimes she was definitely Jenny: quietly wanton, full of girl-woman charms and fascinations, a quicksilver spirit; and other times she was Jennifer: poised elegance, echoing the best in private schools, fancy camps, summers in Europe, and all the things her background had given her. When she wasn't soaking up sun during the summer on the Delaware beaches, Jenny taught grade school in Falls Church, Virginia. Aran was sure she was good at it. She had to be, with that instinctive caring inside her.

She turned, and broke off his thoughts, slipped on the bottom part of the blue bikini, and looked sexier for it. "Get up, sloth," she said. "The water looks magnificent."

"Slave-driver," he grumbled, and swung from the bed, made his way into the bathroom and washed sleep from himself and put on his bathing trunks. She was waiting in the doorway for him, the top of the bikini in her hand. It was a private beach, but there were others about, though usually not this early in the day, and she always took it along just in case. They half-ran down to the water. The surf was quiet, only small rollers coming in to spill their white crests onto the beach. The sand was firm underfoot and no one seemed around and Jenny flung the top of the bikini down and dashed into the water. Aran followed more slowly, unable to summon up her explosion of energy. He sank into the surf, swam lazily, watched Jenny a little bit farther out, moving back and forth through the water, turning like a seal, her breasts surfacing occasionally in wet, glistening mounds of loveliness. He turned on his back, floated lazily with the current, heard Jenny's form rippling the water as she surface-dived, came up again. Her first cry was more of surprise than pain, followed instantly by another sharp scream, real pain in it this time. Aran whirled in the water, saw Jenny half-turned, twisting, and then her head spinning around to him, her eyes wide.

"Oh, Jesus. Aran, I'm being bitten," she screamed. He struck out for her, saw her pull for the shore, cry out again. They weren't far from the beach at all and he reached her, saw the darting form shoot away, no fin on it, too small for even a sand shark. Jenny had touched bottom, was half-running, half-swimming into the shore, and he swung in behind her. He saw another darting form whirl and vanish—an ordinary bass. Jenny was out of the water now, falling forward onto the wet sand of the beach, and he was beside her in an instant, his eyes taking in the trickle of blood from her right hip, her thigh, and her left ankle. He held her to him as she trembled, looking up at him with fear in her blue eyes.

"What the hell was it?" Aran asked.

"The fish, they attacked me. Didn't you see them?" she asked.

"I only saw a bass," he said.

"That's right, the bass," Jenny said. "They came at me, first one, then two more. I saw others moving in when I struck out for the beach."

"The bass?" he echoed incredulously. "Are you sure? Maybe you saw the bass but it was something else."

"No, it was the bass," Jenny said adamantly. "I saw them, the first one especially."

Aran examined the wounds: small, sharp punctures, not terribly deep. He had been thinking about a small barracuda close in to shore, but the holes were not the sharp, slicing bite of the barracuda. He rose, pulled Jenny to her feet. "Come on, let's put some antiseptic on those bites," he said. "Can you walk?"

"Of course. They don't even hurt now," she replied. They returned to the cottage and Aran cleaned the blood from each wound, swabbed antiseptic on and then styptic powder, and in a few minutes, Jenny was making breakfast. He stared out the window at the calm sea and realized he was unduly bothered.

"Damnedest thing, if it was the bass. Talk about unnatural behavior," he muttered.

"Hah!" Jenny exclaimed. "I told you, nothing connects." He shot a glare at her and her eyes grew serious.

"You're thinking about that newscast and what just happened, aren't you?" she said. "There are chains of coincidences, you know."

"I suppose so, but I'm always bothered by aberrant behavior. With people, it's usually an after-the-fact thing, an effect, the end-result of the thread unwinding. With animals, in nature, it's more often than not a sign, a before-the-fact warning," Aran said.

"Have your coffee," Jenny said impatiently. "Stop trying to make connections. It was just one of those odd things that'll never happen again."

"Want to go back in?" he asked sharply, saw her lips grow tight, her eyes flash at him.

"That's playing dirty. It just happened. Try me in the morning," she snapped. He pulled her to him, kissed her, and felt the soft-hard pressure of her nipples into his chest. He was coming dangerously close to being in love with Jenny Vandam, he told himself. They had breakfast, made love leisurely later, then went outside and lay on the beach and no more was said about the strange attack. Not until a little past noon, when the harsh sound of ambulance and police sirens interrupted the quiet. Aran sat up, looked down along the adjoining beaches, saw the sand thrown up by the police car as it cut from the road down to the end of the neat beach, half-hidden by a growth of yaupon.

"You go see. You're the nosy one," Jenny said without moving.

"Curiosity, the gathering up of experiences, is the life-blood of the writer," Aran said a little haughtily.

"Uh-huh," Jenny mumbled and he rose, strode off down the beach, crossed to the adjoining beach. A row of small beach houses crested a dune a few hundred yards back from the beach itself and when he reached the far end of the sand he saw the ambulance and one police cruiser just roaring away. A second police car stayed, the young policeman taking statements from some of the crowd. Aran shouldered his way close enough to listen, followed the policeman as he took down more statements, paused to listen to some of the other men and women as they spilled excited words over one another. He felt his frown growing deeper, so deep that his brow finally ached from it and he smoothed it away with his hand. Finally, he turned, began to walk back along the beach, up to where Jenny lay on the sand. She felt his approach, sat up, her eyes taking on graveness as she read his face.

"Something bad," she remarked as he sank down beside her.

"Bad enough, and maybe more than just bad," he said. "A man and his two young sons swimming, all three attacked and badly bitten. They just managed to get ashore, one boy almost dead." He paused, glanced at her as she waited. "They were attacked by a school of bass, the father told the police. They were suddenly surrounded and attacked."

"Jesus," Jenny whispered.

"Some other people swimming nearby were also bitten after they heard the screams of the man and his sons and headed for shore," Aran said.

"God, the same fish that attacked me," Jenny intoned.

"Maybe," Aran said.

"What do you mean, *maybe*?" she snapped. "You think all the bass around here have suddenly turned killer?"

"I don't think anything yet," Aran said grimly. "But something sure as hell is wrong and I am making connections. Maybe

I'm rushing off too fast, but I don't think so." He glanced up at the sun, guessed it was almost three o'clock, time enough for what he wanted to do. He pulled himself to his feet. "I'm going to make a phone call," he said, looking down at the girl severely. "You're going to be a beach bunny until I find out a few things."

Her eyes flashed to the water, back to him. "Don't worry," she said. "You're looking at a newly confirmed landlubber." He leaned down, kissed the top of her head, her sun-blond hair soft under his lips. He strode off to the cottage, sat down by the phone and got information, asked for the number of the United States Fish and Wild-life Service.

"Do you want the Law Enforcement Division?" the girl asked.

"No," he answered. "Fishery Service Division."

"Which regional office?" she questioned with some annoyance. He let his mind pull on memory.

"Boston," he said. Boston covered Maine to Virginia; Atlanta covered from North Carolina to Florida. She gave him the Boston number and he jotted it down, dialed it and asked for Emerson Boardman. A voice came on to inform him that Emerson Boardman was in a conference. Aran left his name and number, asked that Mr. Boardman call him back. He clicked off, went into the bathroom, and showered. Emerson would return the call, he was sure. He'd known Emerson Boardman before he took over as director of the Boston regional head-quarters. They had enjoyed a relationship of mutual accommo-dation. Emerson had helped him in getting to certain facts and figures for his articles and often tipped him onto worthwhile subjects. He, in turn, had written Emerson's last two speeches before the Environmental Safeguards Commission. Publicly, Aran considered Emerson Boardman an able administrator, a man able to see the many sides of complex questions. Privately, he held Emerson to be a typical bureaucrat, cloaked in cautious self-protection at all times. It was that very same self-protection that assured he would return the call. Emerson respected the power of the pen.

Aran turned off the shower, dried himself briskly, and donned slacks and shoes. He was putting things in a small overnight bag when the door opened and Jenny entered, her eyebrows lifting at once.

"Anticipating," he said before she gave voice to the question in her eyes.

"Anticipating what, if I may ask," she said with haughty annoyance in her tone. The phone rang and she picked it up, listened, and handed it to him.

"This call." He grinned at her. He sat down, reached out and pulled her down on one of his knees as he waited for Emerson to come on the line.

"Hello, Aran," he heard the familiar voice say after a moment. "An unexpected surprise."

"I'd like to see you tomorrow," Aran said. By the morning, Emerson would have heard about the attack just north of Rehoboth beach. And probably others, Aran grimly added to himself.

"Tomorrow?" Emerson mused aloud. "About eleven-thirty? Maybe we could get in lunch."

"Fine, I'll be there," Aran said. He put the phone down and looked at Jenny's eyes searching his face.

"This is all because of the attack by the bass," she said. He nuzzled his face into her breasts, pushing aside the bikini top she had put on.

"I'll only be gone a day or two," he said. "I smell a good story here, a real hot article."

Her eyes stayed steady. "It's more than that," she said. "You're not just chasing down a story lead."

He put his head back, met her perceptiveness. He'd seen it before, part of that reservoir of instinctual sensitivity she possessed.

"All right, I'm bothered," he admitted. "Maybe that girl's story about the whale attacking the boat will turn out to be her overworked imagination, and maybe the lobsterman was an old drunk who just fell into his catch and got chewed up. Maybe, but I don't think so. I've a funny, gut feeling that something's very wrong."

"What do you think it is, Aran?" Jenny asked gravely.

He shrugged impatiently. "I've no ideas, no theories, not even a wild guess at this time. But the behavior of those sea bass today—it's got to me."

Jenny stood up. "When do you want to leave? Tonight?"

"No, an early plane in the morning will get me to Boston in plenty of time," he said.

She nodded, relieved, wanting the night together. "I'll drive you to Dover in the morning," she said. "You can get a feeder flight to Philly from there." She paused. "How long will you be gone?" she asked, sliding out the question.

"Two days maybe," Aran said. "While I'm in Boston, "I'll stop by and say hello to my folks."

"That would be nice," she said, suddenly all warm, full of wanting the best for him. He pulled her to him.

"I'll take you out to dinner tonight. Get changed," he said.

"We've food here," she said, but her protest was weak. He patted her firm rear and she went into the bathroom. Aran stretched his legs out in the chair, listened to the sounds of Jenny in the shower: warm sounds, intimate sounds. She came out soon with a towel wrapped around her, went into the other room, and reappeared in an aqua dress that shimmered, looking breathtakingly lovely. He stared at her for a long moment.

"Well?" she said, finally. "What deep thoughts, oh, wise one?"

"I'm thinking that I'm crazy to leave you and go chasing up to Boston to see Emerson Boardman. Maybe I'm the one with an overworked imagination," he said.

"You said you had a gut feeling," she reminded him, and he nodded.

"Yes, but maybe's it's all coming from a personal place. My mother's people were all fishermen, on the Aran Islands; rugged, hard-working, and poor," he said.

"That's why you have the name?" Jenny questioned.

"Mother's bow to heritage." He nodded. "I wonder if maybe that's why this thing has so caught me up in it. Certain things grab you because of your heritage. We're all echo chambers of our origins."

"Ontogeny recapitulates phylogeny," she remarked.

"Something like that." He laughed. He put on a shirt and finished dressing, and the sun was still over the horizon as they went up the sand dune in back of the cottage to where the cars were parked, his station wagon looking monstrous beside her little Fiat. He took his car and drove inland to a place she knew near Federalsburg, in Maryland. It was rustic, served good beef, and had a small combo for after-dinner dancing. They dined leisurely, discussed their respective possibilities for the winter, decided that being near each other was of paramount importance. Dinner over, they danced, had more drinks, danced some more, and finally started to drive back to the cottage. Aran switched on the car radio; the first station he found was steeped in nostalgia of the fifties and he spun the dial. He found a local station with cool, modern jazz that suited their mood.

They were almost at the cottage when the station break came and with it the news report that followed. Aran felt Jenny stiffen beside him as the announcer's voice, full of the intoned urgency of all such newscasters, told of the attack on the father and his two sons, then followed with a list of five other attacks on bathers. Two people, a woman and a man, unrelated, were killed, so severely bitten they couldn't be saved. Four were badly mauled and in critical condition in local hospitals, and a dozen people had been severely bitten. Of the five other attacks, three occurred along the stretch between Bethany Beach and Ocean City, Maryland, one at the beaches of Assateague Island, and one at the shore resort area of Cape May in New Jersey.

"The police departments of all the coastal areas from Cape May to Delmarva have issued orders to close all beaches until a further investigation of conditions can be made," the newscaster said. "A special report has been made to the Coast Guard and to the Federal authorities." The newscaster went on to quote the views of a professor of marine biology vacationing at Rehoboth Beach which amounted to a plea for further study on unusual behavior patterns of all sea life. Aran switched the radio off in disgust, parked beside Jenny's car, and grimly took her hand as they walked to the cottage.

"It's eerie," Jenny said as they undressed. Shuddering, she came over to him.

"It probably has a biologically recognizable answer once it's pinpointed," Aran said.

"You don't think so," Jenny snapped, spearing into his soothing words.

"I told you, I don't think anything. I've no theories," he said. She sat down on the edge of the bed and he came to sit beside her. "I want you to go over exactly what happened this morning, what you saw, anything that was unusual," Aran said.

Jenny's eyes grew thoughtful. "I saw the first bass for an instant, just a darting shape," she recalled. "I didn't think anything about it. They sometimes do come in close to the beach.

You know that. I saw him again; at least I think it was the same one. He darted around me in a circle. I thought it was my movement in the water making him stay away. I didn't see anything else until I felt the first bite. I glimpsed him then, and two more coming in. They started biting, too. I saw others, just shapes starting toward me when I yelled for you. That's all there was to it, that's all I can tell you."

Aran sat silently for a moment, his mind clicking off its own thoughts. "Let's go to bed," he said, pulling her to her feet. She let the dress fall to the floor, stepped out of it, and in moments lay beside him, clinging to him. They didn't make love, content with that particular closeness of body against body, concern against concern. She fell asleep in his arms and he joined her steady breathing a few minutes later. Outside, the surf rolled, an inexorable sound.

CHAPTER THREE

Emerson Boardman sat in his neat office with the large window that let him look across the tip of the city to the harbor and out to Massachusetts Bay, really a local name for the Atlantic. His secretary, Dolly Wojieski, had just brought in another batch of the bizarre reports. She leaned over the desk, arranging them, and her blouse opened enough for him to see the tops of her very round breasts. He wanted to reach in and squeeze them with his hands, cup them in his palms, but he resisted the impulse. These were office hours and he and Dolly were scrupulously correct during office hours. He'd insisted on that.

But he looked forward to the night It was Friday and Friday nights had been his and Dolly's almost since she'd started working for him eight months ago. Most people would call it an affair, a typical office affair, but the word made him squirm in distaste. He disliked the very sound of it. Affairs, as such, were not part of Emerson Boardman's background, his moral roots. He'd always looked down at those men who kept falling into cheap, petty little relationships with their secretaries and assistants. Besides, at forty-five, he wasn't interested in sordid little liaisons. His relationship with Dolly Wojieski wasn't that at all, he kept reminding himself. It was deeper, based on real, meaningful elements, a source of happiness in his life, an oasis of pleasure, and the result of fifteen years of Emily Boardman and her severe, New England, tight-lipped, repressed ideas of human relationships. With Emily, emotions were always held in check, everything structured and kept in its place, no excesses of any kind. Dolly was all excesses. She'd opened up a new world for him, though sometimes he wished she were less occupied with material things such as raises in salary, a better office, promotions.

He sighed silently, leaned forward, and read the last batch of reports she'd brought in. He wished they'd stop coming. The entire morning had been filled with increasing tensions, people reacting badly to these bizarre happenings. The stories had been getting wide news media coverage and an element of fear was definitely creeping into the latest reports. *Damn*, Emerson Boardman swore inwardly. He liked to keep Fridays quiet and calm, to give himself time to anticipate the night in Dolly's bed. But the phones kept ringing, the news media calling from all over. Talk about predators; Christ, they were like sharks on a feeding frenzy when they got hold of something.

He'd better prepare a statement of some kind, he mused. Hell, he didn't know any more than anyone else yet. How the hell could he issue a statement? The phone rang and he almost jumped, picked it up. It was Les Streeter telling him he'd make the early afternoon meeting he'd called. Emerson put the phone down, stared at the reports again. The lobstermen, from Kennebunkport all the way north, were reporting their trap lines cut, and when they found one they could haul in, it was covered with lobsters that attacked viciously. Three more men had lost fingers; four received bad gashes in their hands. A telegram from the Lobster Fisherman's Association told him that the daily catch had dwindled to almost nothing in the last forty-eight hours. There'd been two more attacks by bass on swimmers off the South Jersey coast. He glanced up as Dolly appeared in the doorway, all soft roundness and making him think of Emily's angular, thin-fleshed frame. Do the outsides and the insides always match? he wondered.

"Aran Holder to see you," Dolly announced, and Emerson rose as Aran entered the room, came around the desk with hand outstretched.

"Good to see you, Aran," he said warmly. He saw Aran's eyes sweep the reports on the desktop. "Shall I guess what brings you here?" Emerson smiled.

"I don't imagine you need to; not now, anyway," Aran said. "There are a lot more than I heard about, aren't there?"

"Most of them have come in since the morning," Emerson said. He gestured to the desk. "Have a look for yourself."

Aran sat down, gathered the reports on his lap, and quickly skimmed them, then returned them to the desk. "I was involved in a minor incident with the bass north of Rehoboth Beach yesterday," he said, and Emerson's eyes took on new interest at once.

"What can you tell me?" the director asked.

"Not anything very much. They attacked the girl I was swimming with. It was unprovoked. She wasn't carrying anything to attract them. She wasn't bleeding from any cuts. She wasn't having her period and there wasn't a damn thing nearby that would have brought them into shore," Aran said. "Yet they attacked her; only three bites, actually."

Emerson Boardman listened sharply to Aran. It was the first on-the-scene report he'd had from a trained professional, a scientifically oriented observer. Suddenly he saw a real use for Aran Holder in this matter. It would be one more instance of mutual benefit. Aran would want inside on this story, whatever it turned out to be, Emerson knew, and there'd be a credit marked up for himself for future use. He put a hand on the younger man's shoulder, wished he had Aran Holder's thick, black hair, his steel-blue eyes, and, most of all, the fifteen years of youth between their ages.

"I'd wanted to have lunch, but I have to stick close to the desk now. But you just skimmed the reports. Why don't you have a sandwich sent up for yourself and go over these things carefully and see if you can spot anything? I've called a meeting with some of my people for two o'clock, before I issue any statements. I'd like you to sit in on it," Emerson said.

"Good enough," Aran said. "You know I always like to start at the beginning. That'd be the girl who said the whale attacked the fishing cruiser. May I phone her at the hospital, if she's still there?"

"Go ahead," Emerson Boardman said and smiled to himself. Thoroughness was one of Aran Holder's hallmarks. "See you at two." He smiled.

Aran rose, gathered the sheaf of reports, and went outside with them, asked Emerson's round-faced secretary where he could work undisturbed and she showed him to a small conference room with a table, four chairs, and a phone. The lone window looked out on lower Boston. The city seemed to have a new face every time he returned to it, he thought. He ordered lunch, a tuna fish sandwich, and found himself wondering wryly whether he was ordering what was about to become a very scarce commodity. Sitting down at the table, he leafed through the reports, found the one that contained Candy Nolan's statement and a copy of a Coast Guard interview with her, signed by a Lieutenant Jack Matthews. He read the report three times, felt his lips tightening as he wondered about Candy Nolan. The copy of the Coast Guard report listed the name of the hospital in the Keys and he put in a long-distance call for Candy Nolan there. His lunch arrived as he listened to the operator making her way through a procession of various voices, receptionists, switchboard operators, nurses, and finally the somewhat brassy voice of Candy Nolan.

He identified himself, explained why he was calling, and sensed instant defensiveness on the girl's part. "I'd just like you to answer a few things that'll help me in analyzing all this," he said soothingly, implying total acceptance on his part of her story.

"Why not?" he heard Candy Nolan reply after a moment's thought.

"Had your friends on the chartered boat been fishing that spot for some days?" Aran asked.

"No, but I understand Captain Peterson often fished there," the girl said.

"Did you see only one whale?" he asked.

"Only one. That was enough," Candy Nolan answered. Aran smiled across the miles.

"Have you thought of anything you saw that you forgot to mention to the officer from the Coast Guard?" Aran asked.

"No," she said.

"Could you describe this whale to me?" he asked mildly.

Candy thought back for a moment. "He was big, Christ, was he ever big," she said.

"What color was he?"

"Kind of a grayish blue-black."

"Anything else you can tell me about it?" Aran prodded.

"It was ridged on the underside. I saw that when it stood up in the water and came down on the boat," Candy said. "And its head wasn't square like a picture of a whale I once saw."

"All right, thank you very much, Miss Nolan. If I've any more questions, I'll be in touch," Aran said.

"I'm leaving here tomorrow," the girl said.

"Wonderful. Good luck," Aran said and hung up. He sat for a moment, steeped in his own thoughts, then turned to the other reports as he ate his tuna fish sandwich. He finished the last of the reports a little before two and took them back to Emerson's office. "They don't address themselves to anything we need to know," he commented.

"Exactly. I'd like to take you into this thing as an official investigator. The news media are interested only in the sensational aspects, a good story. They never ask the questions that are important and the police give everything their usual routine questioning. You'd know what to look for and what we need. Hell, you're almost personally involved already. How about it? The usual daily fee plus expenses."

"Good deal," Aran said, aware that Emerson knew that the real payment was in the story itself. It was a typical example of the way Emerson moved, filling up holes in his organization when he needed to do so, covering all the bases, and adding up credits.

The round-faced girl entered to tell Emerson that the others had arrived and were waiting in the conference room. Aran thought he detected a flicker of something in Emerson's eyes as the older man looked at the girl, a kind of silent shrug of apology. He followed Emerson into an oval room with an oval table. Four men were waiting there, two of whom he knew: Carlton Cryder, a marine biologist, and Robert Eakins, an ichthyologist. Both worked for the Fisheries and Wild Life Service, government career men, both solid enough but neither terribly imaginative. Emerson introduced him to the other two men, the first one an oceanographer from the Woods Hole project, and the second, Leslie Streeter, a biochemist Emerson had brought in from Boston University.

"Holder, Aran Holder," the biochemist mused aloud as they shook hands. "Aren't you the chap who did that piece on molecular behavior under stress?"

"I'm afraid so." Aran smiled.

"First rate," Leslie Streeter said. "Great job of explaining the subject. I've used it in some of my classes."

Streeter was a tall man, graying at the temples, handsome, with a slightly condescending tone in whatever he said, Aran noted at once. At Emerson's suggestion, everyone sat down around the table. He turned to Eakins first. "Has anyone come up with anything at all?" Emerson asked, directing the question at Eakins specifically, at them all in general. "I've outlined the problem to each of you."

"There really hasn't been enough time to come up with anything," Carlton Cryder said.

"I know that, but I'm interested in projections, theories, if you will. We have to know which way to point in this thing," Emerson said. Aran heard Eakins, the ichthyologist, clear his throat.

"With what little we know, it appears that two separate groups of marine life have undergone a simultaneous behavioral change. It appears this is related, but that is not necessarily so," the man said.

"Two?" Aran cut in.

"The sea bass and the lobsters." Eakins frowned.

"What about the whale attack on the chartered cruiser?" Aran asked.

"I thought there was doubt about that story," Eakins said. He was a small, thin-faced man who looked perpetually on guard. He looked even more so now.

"Not in my mind. I just talked with the girl," Aran said. "She described a big blue. She knew what she'd seen. And what happened to that other charter boat, the *Roberta Two*? No, I think the whale attack must be included." He saw Eakins shrug, accept the inclusion, and look uncomfortable.

"I've had some of my people bring in three sea bass. They're putting them through lab tests now. Perhaps they will find a chemical or biological change in the makeup of these fish to explain their behavior," Eakins went on.

"Assuming the bass your men caught were part of the same group that did the attacking," Carlton Cryder cut in. "This behavior could be that of a strange, segmented part of the species itself."

"I think we must also consider the location of the bass attacks on swimmers in the waters off beaches where almost everyone is wearing some sort of lotion or suntan oil on their bodies. Something in those commercial preparations could be creating this aggressive reaction on the part of the fish," Eakins volunteered.

"All of a sudden?" Aran asked. "People have been wearing that stuff for years. Besides, the girl I was with had no lotion on."

"I've wondered about a change in water temperature. Large groups of marine life might react in unusual ways to a sudden change in the temperature of their environment. Unfortunately, preliminary water samples taken reveal no sign of vital temperature shifts," Cryder said, a little dejectedly. "But then, such changes could come up from depths beyond our sampling as yet."

Emerson turned to the oceanographer, youngest of those assembled, a serious-faced young man, his glance asking confirmation.

"I've been checking our charts," Roy Waite said. "As you know, the movement of deep-sea currents depends on sun, wind, the rotation of the earth, and two factors within the sea: temperature and salt content. So far we've detected no current changes in the major flows, such as the Gulf and the Humboldt, which could cause any significant temperature change. Even an upwelling would cause no effect this suddenly, or, if it did, a lot more sea life would be affected. Allowing for the Coriolis force, we've pinpointed nothing as yet. Of course, the truth is that with all we know about ocean currents, we really know very little."

Aran saw Emerson growing impatient and annoyed, saw the man turn to Leslie Streeter as the biochemist leaned forward, a warm smile on his face that barely avoided condescension. "I think everyone is in the right church but the wrong pew," Leslie Streeter said. Aran felt himself move forward.

"It's nothing caused by temperature changes nor current flows that might create that kind of environmental change. Nor is it any lotions or oils people might be wearing," the biochemist went on. "There are sixty-one separate elements in every cubic mile of sea water; at least that's all we've isolated so far. There may be others. Oxygen, hydrogen, chlorine, sodium, sulfur, calcium, potassium, carbon, boron, strontium, fluorine, argon, nitrogen, zinc, iron, lead, arsenic, barium; the list goes on and on. Some elements such as krypton, cobalt, tungsten, and mercury are found in minute quantities in any given cubic mile of sea water; but others, such as oxygen, hydrogen, chlorine, magnesium, sulfur, carbon, and sodium, are found in the millions of tons per cubic mile. Any important change in the balance of these major elements, or any of the elements for that matter, could very well upset the environmental climate of the sea. Such a change could certainly trigger strange behavior in life-forms."

"We'd need extensive water sampling analysis to know that," Emerson murmured.

"Exactly. For a crash program, I'd say I'd need at least fifty technicians to analyze the samples brought in," Leslie Streeter said.

"Fifty?" Emerson boomed. The biochemist shrugged.

"If it's top priority?" he said.

"Well, I don't know that it's all that top. Hell, it might just go away by itself. Mutative behavior can do that, you know,"

Emerson countered. "I couldn't put on fifty analysts out of my regular budget. I'd have to clear that through Washington." He paused, cleared his throat, and stood up. "I'll go into this with Washington," he said. "Meanwhile, I'd like each of you to keep on in your own tracks and report in anything you might come across. I'm sending Aran out to talk to some of the people who were actually involved in attacks. There's so much these news reports don't tell us. I'll be in touch with everyone here."

The meeting ended in handshakes, Eakins and Cryder going down to their offices only a few doors away. Aran followed Emerson back to the latter's office, sat down as the director asked that an expense check for travel be prepared for him. Emerson leaned back in his chair, put his fingertips together.

"What'd you think?" he asked. "Especially in Leslie Streeter's approach?" Emerson asked as he took up a yellow notepad.

"It makes the most scientific sense," Aran answered.

"Exactly what I thought," Emerson said, starting to write on the pad. Aran thought again of the biochemist's theory, telling himself that it did hold the best hope for the moment. Yet, for some strange reason, he had reservations about it. Gut feelings again, he acknowledged silently. Leslie Streeter's approach held together best. Ecology was a science of balances and man kept taking those balances for granted, especially in regard to marine ecology. The sea seemed so vast, so inexhaustible, such an endless producer of life-giving properties. It made it entirely too easy for man to ignore the balances that kept it what it was ...

Emerson's voice cut into his thoughts. "How's this sound?" the man called out. "The Department of Fish and Wildlife is investigating the unusual and aggressive behavior of some forms of marine life. Some form of environmental change may be causing this aberrant behavior. Precautions instituted by local authorities should be observed for the time being. The department feels that there is no cause for undue alarm."

Aran smiled at Emerson. "Somewhat of a dismissal, isn't it?" he asked. "I think the public wants comfort, reassurance."

"Hell, anything else would only add to the hysteria that's going around. I'll bet a good part of the attacks on swimmers is nothing more than mass hysteria triggered by somebody who panics at seeing a bass," Emerson said.

"Maybe." Aran shrugged. Dolly Wojieski appeared with his check, a draw against expenses, and Emerson fastened a level eye on him.

"You know the kind of facts we need, Aran. Cut through the hysteria. I blame the news media for a lot of that. They blow everything out of proportion."

"Let's hope so," Aran said, and Emerson shot him a sharp glance. Aran waved a hand at the older man. "Be in touch soon as I've got something," he said, and turned and walked from the office. He glanced at his watch. There'd be no time for a visit with his folks now. A phone call would have to do, he thought. He had ample time to call from the airport as he waited for a flight. Of course, his mother was disappointed he couldn't stop by, and Dad was still nursing an attack of kidney stones that had hospitalized him.

"I'll be back in a day or two. I'll come by then," Aran promised finally, put the receiver back on its cradle, glad for having at least called. He sat down to wait for his flight and thought about Emerson's statement and the air of dismissal in it. He hoped Emerson's somewhat cavalier attitude was in order. He hoped ... but he felt very differently.

In his office, Emerson gave the statement to Dolly to type and send out and pushed his chair back so it faced the window. He was glad he'd set things in motion, had set everyone working on some aspect of the problem. He'd wait till morning to call Washington. He wouldn't ask for fifty analysts unless there were more reports. Good God, there was no use in adding to the hysteria.

But before he left the office to go to Dolly's apartment, another report came in: only a few facts first, then more details following. It was the report on the *Mary Ann.*

The *Mary Ann* had sailed out of Sheepshead Bay, that tip of Brooklyn along the Atlantic, for fifteen years, four times a week. She carried a crew of three besides her skipper, Captain Billy Straub. Like most of the party boats, Captain Billy had his regulars—those who fished from his boat from one to four times a week. The others filled out the usual load, never more than forty. Captain Billy didn't believe in overcrowding his customers, especially those who'd sailed out of Sheepshead Bay with him for years. He appreciated his regulars and they swore by Captain Billy. Over the years, as the social climate changed, more women came to take up the sport and many became regulars. He glanced over the crowd lining the rails of the starboard and port sides and the stern. He looked down at them and smiled as a father smiles over his children.

The daily pool was being organized already, everyone putting in three dollars as fishing talk and camaraderie filled the clean, crisp air. Leaders were being tied; swivels, hooks, and sinkers were made fast, checked, examined, changed. Captain Billy directed his attention to the course of the *Mary Ann*. It would be a good fishing day, he murmured to himself. You got to feel the good days when you'd been at it as long as he had. He'd tuned in on the fishing reports as he waited for the morning tide at the dock. Flounder was running well off Barnegat and weak-fish plentiful from Sandy Hook down to Monmouth. Shinnecock reported in with big white marlin, sixty-pounders, along with fifty-pound school tuna, and a few of the big boys, two-hundred-pounders. His people weren't geared for that kind of stuff. They were heading for the blues and the cod between the buoys off Moriches Inlet.

The captain piloted the *Mary Ann* out into the soft roll of the Atlantic, her solid diesel engine throbbing. When he reached a spot some four miles south and ten west of Shinnecock, he slowed, shut off the engines, and drifted as his boys tossed out a trail of chum and the small sound of anticipation rose up from the railings below him. He looked down from the wheelhouse, waved to Bess O'Neil. She was at her usual place on the stern rail, her gray-haired head wedged in beside Sam Jacozzi's bald head. They made a pair, those two, both widowed. Bess was as good with a rod and reel as anyone aboard; an open, friendly soul with a rough, bluff exterior. Most often she came aboard with a shopping bag full of cookies or brownies or cakes she had baked, enough for everyone on board to share. This morning it'd been apple squares.

Bess caught his glance, waved up at him. "I'm going to win the pool today," she called. "I feel lucky."

"She always feels lucky, but when does she ever win the pool?" Sam Jacozzi said, and received a poke in the ribs for it. Captain Billy heard a cry from the port rail, looked to see a series of leaping, cascading forms emerge from the water, some sixty yards off the port side. The dolphins glistened in the sun as they cleaved the air, putting on a brief but spectacular display of acrobatics. He never watched them but that he marveled at their grace and speed. He'd read how scientists working with them had found that dolphins could learn more quickly, and with more responsiveness, than monkeys. He believed it. Watching them, he always had the feeling that they knew exactly what they were doing, consciously and deliberately, not out of some blind instinctual mechanism that made them leap into the air. They seemed to know that people enjoyed watching their displays, and performed as a sort of gift.

The dolphins vanished in minutes and the boat's passengers settled down to fishing, lines cast out from all sides now. Howie Henderson's voice called out the first strike from the starboard rail. "Christ, he's a big one," Captain Billy heard Howie's voice shout. Others moved their lines, reeled in some. That was when it began.

From the wheelhouse, Captain Billy saw the dark mass slowly rising up from the bottom, moving toward the surface of the water, half-surrounding the boat. At first he thought that it was an oil slick rising up from underneath and he murmured a curse. The dark mass continued to rise, a gelatinous shape spreading. He stared at it, saw movement within its uneven area. Then, suddenly, he heard his voice, a whispered gasp, as he saw the dark mass for what it was: fish, hundreds and hundreds, no, thousands, packed tightly together, coming up under his boat. Automatically, his eyes picked out blues and cod, and now he heard the voices rising from the rails below, the sound of sudden alarm, amazement, consternation. He was reaching to switch on the engine when he felt the *Mary Ann* start to quiver, lifting, being pushed upward at one side. He turned in the seat to see the stern rising out of the water; then his boat started to heel over on the starboard side. He switched the engine on and heard the hollow, whirring sound as the propellers were already half out of the water.

"Holy Jesus. My God, they're pushing us over," he heard himself cry out. He raced to the starboard side of the wheelhouse, looked down. All he could see was the solidly packed mass of fish, many of them twenty-pounders, rising up as a solid mass of flesh and bone. The *Mary Ann* shuddered, suddenly heeled over more sharply, and he felt his feet going out from under him as he slid across the wheelhouse, caught hold of a side, and halted his fall. He heard screams now from below, pulled himself up to see people sliding across the decks, crashing into the rail and going over into the sea, landing atop the water and the less densely packed mass of fish at the port side. This wasn't happening, he told himself. It couldn't be happening. Christ, they were only fish, only blues and cod. But the mind incongruously answers itself and he heard automatic calculations being thrown back at him. A thousand of them at fifteen pounds each, and many were twenty-pounders at least, came to fifteen thousand pounds, over seven tons. He felt the pull of his lips as they drew back. Seven tons of power and thrust, more than enough; and, as if in answer, the *Mary Ann* heeled over till she was on her beam ends. He felt himself thrown clear of the wheelhouse, down against the stern deck, and into the water along with others who had managed to cling on to something. The screams were different now, filled with pure terror, and he reached out, pulled himself back aboard the boat, clinging to the side and lifting himself up onto the stern deck, which was now a perpendicular wall.

He looked back at the water where heads were bobbing up and down. He made out Sam Jacozzi, and Bess O'Neil, still next to Sam. He glimpsed his mate, Fred, and two of his other regulars, Eddie Cochran and Lou Agnolli. Most everyone could swim, but suddenly that was entirely irrelevant. As he watched, he saw the fish attack. From all sides and coming up from beneath, the blues and cods swarmed over the swimmers, biting, ripping, tearing, literally eating their victims alive. In moments, the water had turned a deep red, and the screams filled the air until he wanted to cover his ears, but he couldn't move his hands that held him to the side of the boat. He saw Bess trying to swim toward him as the blues ripped into her, scores of them feasting on her flesh, tearing chunks from her in jagged mouthfuls. He saw her go under a mass of flapping, wriggling bodies. He got his fingers into a place where the planking had come loose, pulled himself up farther, found another broken piece of wood that let him climb up farther until he managed to wrap himself around the broken windowframe of the wheelhouse and cling there.

Looking down, he saw Sam Jacozzi being eaten away by a swarm of cod. He caught Sam's glazed eyes as the man looked up at him as if he were accusing him with his last moment of life, and then he was gone. There were hardly any screams now, and still the mass of fish, not solid as before, spread out more, whirling and moving in small circles. The devouring was over, Captain Billy saw. It had all happened so fast, so unexpectedly, there hadn't even been time to send out a distress call. He felt the *Mary Ann* quiver, begin to settle down into the sea. He estimated that if she didn't turn over completely, she might take a half hour to fill and go under altogether. He'd provide a last morsel then. As he watched, a pack of the fish, a few hundred, he guessed, slipped under the *Mary Ann*, pushed her sideways a dozen feet and the sea rushed into her and the half hour became a matter of minutes. Below where he clung, closer than a moment before, the blues and the cod milled about, the dark mass of them now spread out to stretch hundreds of yards in all directions. Suddenly, almost as one, they began to dive, disappearing into the sea. In less than a minute, the huge mass of them had disappeared completely and there was nothing—only the softly rolling water and a few bits and shreds of apparel floating atop the waves.

Captain Billy Straub clung to the top of his vessel, the last of the *Mary Ann,* his world, his life, a part of his very self. It was only yesterday, he recalled, that he'd listened to the radio tell of bass attacking bathers and he'd scoffed, laughed at the story, dismissed it out of hand. These hadn't been bass, though. They'd been blues and cod, nothing else. Was he going crazy? Was this all some kind of hallucination? Was the world going mad? He reached a hand down, touched the water, drew his fingers back. He stared at the water, hoping to see Bess or Sam Jacozzi or Howie Henderson reappear. But no one came to the surface. No one and nothing.

Strangely, Captain Billy Straub didn't wonder whether anyone would find him. Other party boats would be passing close on their way back to Sheepshead or Great South Bay. He didn't even wonder if the fish would reappear to devour him alive in the water. All he wondered was whether anyone would believe him. He hardly believed himself. The *Mary Ann* somehow stayed afloat on her side, like a dead fish, and it was near the end of the day when the *Sea Fox,* another party boat out of Sheepshead, spotted the floating hulk and rescued Captain Billy Straub.

Later, when he was surrounded by newsmen ashore, there was one, singular fact that stayed in his mind above all else as they pumped questions at him. "Like piranhas," he half-whispered with his eyes staring and stark with burning memories. "I saw a picture once of piranhas stripping a cow to a bare skeleton in less than ten minutes. It was like that. Blues and cod like piranhas. Oh, Jesus."

The scene would stay with Captain Billy Straub until the day he died.

It was late that night that Emerson Boardman lay in bed alongside Dolly. The report on the *Mary Ann* had set all hell loose. Even Washington had called with questions. But one thing had come out of it. He'd received an immediate OK for Streeter's fifty analysts. God, he hoped they'd come up with something damn fast. It was assuming ugly proportions now. If this kept up he'd have to take charge in the field himself. He hated field work, rushing here and there, pressure work, terrible hours in every kind of weather and God knows in what places. Damn, he'd had enough of that years ago. All he wanted now was the comfort of the warm regional offices.

And Dolly. He looked across at her, saw that she was asleep. He made a face. He didn't blame her, though. He hadn't been able to get himself untracked when he finally reached her place. He'd tried, four times, but each time had been embarrassingly unsatisfactory. There was just too much on his mind tonight. Worry killed the sex urge, he had often heard, and had proved that out himself tonight. Idly, he wondered if Emily had been worrying about something all these years.

He turned on his side and went to sleep. He'd have to go into the office tomorrow. There'd be no lazy lounging in bed with Dolly. Christ, God knew what tomorrow would bring, he thought as he fell off to sleep.

CHAPTER FOUR

Aran heard about the *Mary Ann* when he landed at Dover, just as he was about to phone Jenny. The airport newsstand operator had a small table radio on and Aran stood very still at the door to the phone booth as he listened to the newscast. When it was over, he turned from the phone, a terrible heaviness gathering inside him.

"Good God, what the hell's happening?" he heard the man at the newsstand ask of no one in particular. Aran walked from the airport to where a line of taxis waited. There was no time to call Jenny now. That'd have to wait till later. Now the interviews he'd come to get were burning inside him with renewed fire. He found a cab with special long-haul rates and headed for the hospital at Ocean City. As he sat with his head back against the rear of the seat, the newsstand man's question circled before him. Just what the hell was going on? he repeated silently. He thought about Leslie Streeter's educated theorizing and he gave a snort. Theorizing was a fancy word for guessing. A change in the delicate balances of the sea, Aran mused; the biochemist's theory still held the most logic. But the bizarre behavior wasn't confined to two or three species. He'd always felt that and now had been proved right. Whatever it was, it was spreading, taking in more and more forms of sea life. Aran felt an uneasiness ripple through him as the wind ripples the water. For all of Leslie Streeter's approach, there seemed something more to the attacks than ecological reaction. They held an anger and viciousness that seemed to transcend the merely biological. He closed his eyes, played with unsatisfying, random thoughts until the taxi slowed, pulling up before the hospital.

He hurried into the square, gray-white building, surprisingly modern and well-equipped for a small hospital. He spent the following hours, until the visiting hours ended, talking to bathers who'd been attacked and who'd witnessed the attack on others. He made careful, copious notes for himself, listening to each person with penetrating sharpness. When he left, he called a taxi and was driven north to the little cottage. The cab halted on the small road back of the dunes and he walked down to the cottage, saw the light still on and Jenny still up. She opened the door at his knock and was in his arms at once, clinging to him in her shortie pajamas, the sheer, wispy material no barrier at all to the warm softness of her.

"I wondered why you hadn't called," she said, pulling back finally. "But this is better." Her eyes searched his face. "You look tired. Want some eggs? Coffee?"

He nodded. "I am fatigued," he said. "Too much concentrated listening." He slumped into a chair, putting his attaché case nearby, and watched her start to prepare things.

"Have you come on to anything?" Jenny asked. "The news has been full of that Sheepshead Bay party-boat disaster."

"I know," Aran said, and told her about the meeting at the Fish and Wildlife Offices and of the biochemist's theories.

"They sound plausible, at least," Jenny offered as she set down the eggs.

"Nobody's got anything better yet," Aran said, and Jenny's eyes paused on him.

"Yet?" she echoed. "That sounds like you don't completely go along with his ideas. Do you think there's some other cause?"

"I don't know," was all he could say, and directed his attention to the eggs, feeling very inadequate and unsettled. When he finished, still toying with his coffee, Jenny came, put her arms around him, her breasts soft against his face.

"Come on to bed. You need some sleep," she said.

"In a minute," Aran replied. She pressed her lips to his forehead and went into the bedroom. Aran turned the light out in the room, sat in the darkness, and listened to the sound of the surf outside. He rose after a while, opened the door softly, and stepped outside into the night. Slowly, he walked down to the beach to stand at the edge of the water. A nearly full moon silvered the surface of the sea and the vast ocean seemed ominous, a keeper of a million secrets. It always seemed that way to him at night. The sea, he mused, turning the word in his mind, such a simple word for three-quarters of the planet, probable cradle of all life, man's own place of biological yesterdays. Yet of all things modern man took for granted, the sea was perhaps the most so taken, seen only as something to be used with inexhaustible disregard.

Aran half-closed his eyes, squinted out at the dark water and saw more than he could see. With his mind, he speared down into the ocean depths, beginning at the very top and sifting down. Mentally, he moved among the microscopic specks invisible to the naked eye, seemingly nonexistent, yet filling the water—the plankton, a kind of living marine dust, the very life chain of the upper waters. So varied, so vital, so vast as almost to defy comprehension, aptly named from the Greek word for *wanderers,* the plankton drifted aimlessly on sea currents and upwellings of subterranean water. Single-celled algae—diatoms and dinoflagellates, countless billions upon billions of them—each dependent on the minerals and salts of the sea, and in turn furnishing nourishment for tiny copepods and giant whales. The skein of life in the sea builds with its own silent ordination of role, each form of life furnishing food to another form of the bio-logic chain: plankton to copepod to herring to bluefish to tuna and on and on. In the vast domain of the sea, each creature has its own weapons, its own role to play, and the very composition of the sea itself—the iron, hydrogen, and sodium and each of the other sixty-one elements—formed the delicate environment in which all life existed. From giant squid to mammoth whale to tiny starfish and bivalve, every living thing swirled and whirled, swam and crawled, slid and clung within that vast aquatic store-house of energy.

What was happening in those deep and murky depths, Aran wondered, perhaps in the tremendous trenches still unexplored, among creatures still not known to man? Was something chang-ing that powerful yet delicate balance of life within the sea? Was something evolving that would change the oceans, Leslie Streeter's theory of the shifting of balances? Was it a temporary, passing thing or would it change the seas for aeons to come? Aran felt his jaws growing tight. Events supported the theory, and yet why did such an ecological change manifest itself in only this one, visible manner? The question hung, and then he heard the sound of the cottage door being opened, turned to see Jenny coming down to him. She reached his side and her hand folded itself into his.

"It looks so calm, so serene," she half-whispered. "It looks the same as always. But it's different, isn't it?"

"Maybe," he allowed. "I wish I knew more." She stood very close beside him and Aran's wonderings continued and he yearned to be really able to see as a microscope sees, to delve into the molecules that, even as they stared at them, could be chang-ing character. But the questions he'd asked himself continued to cling. Why did the change only manifest itself in these vicious attacks by marine life? Why was there no other, equally visible result? Finally he turned, walked back to the cottage with Jenny still clinging to his hand, little-girl-like. She lay close against him through the night and he slept finally, welcoming her softness pressing into him.

Aran was still sleeping when the commercial tuna boat, the *Sister Rosa,* put out from Providence, Rhode Island. Her skipper, Jacob Elias, had lived his sixty-odd years fishing for tuna. He was no party-boat fisherman and he held no truck with any of the scare stories the newspapers and television had been throwing up. Thirty miles out, he ordered chum of herring and mackerel put out and the lines dropped. They had reached the central waters for the big two-hundred-pounders, some going even as high as five hundred. Jacob Elias, a big, gravel-voiced man, scanned the morning waters, took in his crew at the rails, when suddenly he felt his vessel shake, quiver, grind to a halt. He gave the engine more power and heard the whirring sound of jammed propellers and then the hard grinding rasp of metal grating on metal. He swung the wheel, found the rudder also jammed, and the ship shuddered again.

At that moment, he saw the tuna rising all around the ship and two of the crewmen who had raced to the stern to lean over the transom called out with awe and alarm in their voices. "Jesus, they've jammed the propellers," one man called. "The damn rudder, too." In astonished bewilderment, the two crewmen stared down over the stern where the huge fish had flung themselves into the propellers: suicides, torn and chewed up by the whirling blades, yet their bodies wedged into the props, bringing the blades to a halt. Jacob Elias turned the wheel over to his mate and started back to the stern when the first two- hundred-pound tuna leaped out of the sea to land on the stern deck. A second followed it instantly, then a third, and suddenly the air was filled with the blue-black forms leaping onto the stern of the vessel. Crewmen fell back as hundreds of the big fish leaped onto the stern, filling the afterdeck with their big, thick bodies piled atop each other, flapping and squirming, and still they came, more and more and more.

In hardly over a minute, the stern of the ship was piled high with a hundred of the huge, thrashing forms, each at least two hundred pounds, over ten tons on one small spot, and Jacob Elias saw his boat go down at the stern. He ran forward, shouting commands, suddenly aware of what was happening, but his men were unwilling to move into the hail of two- and three-hundred-pound bodies that still filled the air. The *Sister Rosa*'s prow went up into the air, and in less than three minutes, she was virtually upended by the tons and tons of tuna in one spot on her stern deck. The captain ran forward, tried to kick the nearest of the fish away, ducked one cascading form, and was caught by another. He was knocked backward to the deck, sprawling, looked up to see the *Sister Rosa* going underwater, stern first. The sea flowed over her transom and down the decks, spilling her crew into the water as she went under fast.

Jacob Elias went down with his boat, a man unable to believe what was happening as the waters curled around him. The tuna that had piled themselves up on the stern deck swam away as the sea took the vessel down. The crew was torn to pieces in a matter of minutes by the frenzied, enraged tuna—all but one man, a Portuguese sailor who clung to a section of the mast and was somehow passed over by the milling mass of tuna. He was found only an hour later by a passing coastal tanker and brought to shore where he gasped out his story, his eyes a mirror of the pure terror that would never completely leave him.

When Aran woke that morning and called Emerson Boardman, he was told the story of the tuna fishing boat and a host of other reported incidents. "Christ, there's a panic on," Emerson said. "Commercial fishing skippers are refusing to go out until we can come up with something. Most of the major resorts up and down the coast have been closed by local authorities and the resort operators are screaming financial disaster. There were more attacks on swimmers, off Atlantic City and along the Florida coast. I've called a meeting for tomorrow afternoon, four o'clock. Washington is sending the Navy and a couple of senators will be there along with a hell of a lot of other people representing special-interest groups. I expect you there. Have you come on to anything yet?"

"Nothing that makes a case yet," Aran said. "I'm going to talk to Straub, the party-boat skipper, in the morning, then to the Portuguese sailor if I can. But I'll be at the meeting in time."

"Christ, I hope Streeter comes up with some answers," Emerson said. "This is out of hand already and getting worse every minute."

Aran let the man mutter on a few minutes more and then hung up. He saw the questions in Jenny's eyes and told her the things Emerson had recounted. "I'll take today to set up arrangements to interview the Sheepshead Bay captain and the sailor from the tuna boat," he said. "I'll catch an early flight out of Dover in the morning."

"Good. The Brownings invited us for dinner and cocktails," Jenny said. "Strictly casual, of course."

"Then we'll go," Aran said. The Brownings, Jenny's friends, lived in Milford. Alison was a teacher in the same school as Jenny, Bob was in electronics. They were nice, compatible and low-keyed, and he always enjoyed time with them, but actually he was going more for Jenny's sake. He'd seen the quiet worry just behind her brightness and suddenly it flung itself out at him.

"How long will you be away this time?" she asked.

"I can't say yet. Maybe I'll take you with me." He laughed. Her face stayed grave.

"Maybe I'll go. I don't feel much like swimming," she said, and came to put her head down upon his chest. He held her until she moved away, not looking at him, and started to prepare breakfast Aran made the long-distance calls during the rest of the morning and the afternoon, clearing interviews with the two men with their doctors and local authorities, pinpointing times and flight schedules. To make Emerson's four-o'clock meeting, he'd be running tight. The afternoon drew to a midpoint quickly enough and he changed clothes, waited for Jenny to finish. She soon appeared in cream slacks and a red blouse and looked absolutely edible. He used his car and they drove to the Brownings'. Cocktails were served on a small terrace of the modest home the couple had bought a year ago. Talk, at the beginning, was about the attacks, now the first-ranking national news story, but it finally turned to less intensely grim topics and everyone managed to relax. They left a little before midnight, drove slowly back to the cottage wrapped in a warm, pleasant glow. Inside, as they went to bed, Jenny turned to him with wanting, need surging up like a silent wave cresting higher and higher, waiting to break and free itself. He cleaved into her, gently, then less so, wedding flesh to flesh, gasps to gasps, and she cried out for more and more and wrapped her body around his until there seemed an unbroken Gordian knot of sensuous union. But the knot shredded finally as she screamed out in pleasure and fell away from him to lay clutching the sheets, trying to cling to that moment beyond all recapturing. Until the next time.

She turned to him, nestled into the hollow of his shoulder as a burrowing creature pushes a place for itself out of the ground. He slept then, with her, and the night wore on in silence.

The first of the cottages that lined the adjoining beach stood some hundred yards from Jenny's place. It belonged to a couple, the Mintners, who had two children, a seven-year-old boy and a five-year-old girl. Judy Elman, a local girl, baby-sat for the Mintners all summer. Judy was a serious, studious girl who liked working with children as well as she liked the extra money. On the nights when the Mintners visited in Washington and weren't expected back till late, she slept on the low cot in the front room, the door propped open a few inches because the latch was broken. This was one of those nights, and Judy Elman had finished studying her biology book and now slept heavily, the children in the adjoining room.

The next cottage was shared for the summer by Karen Ellis and whoever happened to be her boyfriend of the week, or the month. Some managed to last that long. Karen worked in Baltimore as a book designer; she was divorced and still running from that experience. The current male companion was a young lifeguard at the beach with the appropriate name of Ernie Swimmer. The cottage was a tiny place, hardly more than a large dressing room, and when Karen grew drunk and passionate, one invariably following the other, the cottage always seemed too confining and she wound up on the dark, deserted sands of the beach just outside her door. She was both exceptionally drunk and exceptionally passionate that night, so much so that, with Ernie Swimmer matching her on both counts, she literally screwed herself into a hollow in the sand. Finally, surfeited, exhausted, and quite drunk, she fell asleep in the little hollow with Ernie Swimmer laying half atop her, hard asleep, too. Ernie Swimmer was the first to wake, but it was too late then.

They came out of the sea, one single line of them at first, dripping with the water still clinging to their bodies, pausing on the wet sand, their stalked, periscopic eyes peering at the line of cottages. They waited, sensed, listened, waved their antennae in the air, and then silently moved a few feet with their sideways, crabwise movement. Another row emerged from the sea, crowded close behind the first, then another row, and the surf became alive with others, row after row crawling up onto the beach, stretching all along the curving beachfront until the sand was a solid mass of waving claws and flat, eight-legged bodies. A full moon cast a silvery patina over their shells, thousands of them now, mostly blue crabs but a sprinkling of spider and rock crabs among them. They waited, covering the beaches until there was not an inch of sand visible, and then—like a huge phalanx of some strange, armored army—they moved forward. The tremendous mass of them moved together with surprising speed toward the line of darkened cottages and behind them; still others came out of the sea until there was nothing but a solid mass of shells and waving claws.

The silent surge of hard-shelled forms moved forward, coming first to the hollowed place in the sand where Ernie Swimmer still lay atop Karen. The great mass of them moved around the two forms to proceed on toward the cottages while a hundred or so crawled into the hollow. Ernie awoke to the severe pain exploding all over his body, half-screamed as he tried to whirl. He seemed to be ripping apart at once, which was exactly what was happening to him. His back, legs, neck, and head were covered with blue crabs sinking their powerful, serrated claws into him. He slid from Karen, tried to shout again, but a claw clamped onto his mouth, tearing part of his lower lip away as another gouged into his eye. Karen woke then, tried to scream, but the sound, muffled by a dozen shells, never really left her mouth. She tried to get up, slipped on wet shells, felt the excruciating pain consuming her legs, abdomen, breasts, buttocks. For the briefest moment, she thought she was having another case of delirium tremens which she had experienced before after a hard-drinking night, but the pain told her this was different. Karen and Ernie never got out of that hollow of sand where they'd so enjoyed the pleasures of the body. In a fleeting, last moment of her life, not really aware of what was happening to her, Karen recalled that she'd had crab for dinner.

The seemingly endless phalanx of claws continued to move forward. At the Mintners' cottage they pressed in through the door that was propped ajar, hundreds and hundreds of them crawling into the front room in silent movements. Judy Elman, asleep on the low cot, felt the painful bite on her hand that dangled on the floor. She cried out, half-rose, fell from the cot with the weight of the crustaceans hanging on to her hand and arm, and was immediately engulfed in a floor of seething shells. She screamed, tried to crawl to the door over the mass of crabs. She hardly moved a foot as pincers gouged deep pieces of her, covered her with ripping, tearing claws until she lay still, staining the shells red. They swarmed on into the next room where the two Mintner children slept, a tide of killing crustaceans, as inexorable as the tides of the sea.

Down the beach, the blue-green tide surged against the next three cottages that were placed closer together. The crabs crawled up onto each other, became a small wall over which still others moved to enter the open windows of the first two cottages. In the last of the three cottages, a middle-aged woman in blue pajamas, Edna Haggerty, was still up reading by a lone lamp. Her husband slept in the next room, but Edna was having insomnia lately. She looked up from her book as she heard the small, plopping sounds from the tiny kitchen off the living room. Putting her book down, she rose to investigate. Her scream woke her husband who, barefooted, came running to see the attackers as they streamed over the windowsill and fell to the floor. He seized a broom and started striking at the crabs as Edna Haggerty, ran screaming from the little kitchen, and pulled the front door open to run out. A wall of snapping claws fell in on her, carrying her to the floor under their weight. Her screams brought her husband running. He brought the broom down hard on the swarming invaders, lifted the handle to find twenty crabs clinging to it, dropped it, and bent to clutch at his feet as claws ripped at his toes. He slipped, fell on the wet shells. He never got up again.

Aran woke suddenly, Jenny's arm across his chest. He lay unmoving, frowning into the darkness of the room where the moon filtered in to give definition to objects. He sensed something: a feel of danger, a primitive instinct still left from man's early defensive biology. He moved Jenny's arm from him and she stirred as he swung from the bed and pulled on trousers. The cottage was silent and yet there was something besides silence. He strained his ears and caught the sound: a faint, clicking noise. It was coming from outside and he went to the window, open only a fraction of an inch; he peered out down toward the beach.

"Oh, Jesus," he gasped. "God almighty." The clicking sound was suddenly louder and he whirled, ran into the front room. The window was open a few inches there and they were squeezing through. Aran snapped on the light and the dozen or so crabs on the floor halted, blinked, momentarily startled, their antennae waving wildly. He skirted them, reached the window where another dozen were just crawling in, and slammed the window down with all his strength, crushing shells, sending legs and pincers falling from smashed bodies. Those on the floor recovered and started to attack. Aran leaped onto a small sofa, tore one from his ankle where it'd sunk a claw, jumped down the other side, kicked two scuttling forms across the room as Jenny appeared in the doorway in her wispy shortie pajamas. She stared for a moment and then screamed.

"Get back," Aran shouted at her. "Put on shoes." He grabbed hold of a chair and smashed it down on four scuttling attackers, smashing their backs. Jenny had disappeared, returned with shoes and a small sand shovel, brought it down on two that had circled behind him. He took it from her, smashed it on the last of those inside the room as she went to the window. She half-screamed and shrank back from the curtain of waving claws pressed against the outside of the glass.

Aran fell into the chair beside the phone, dialed the police emergency number and heard the incredulousness in the voice that answered.

"That's right, cottage seven-four just north of Reheboth. But you'll find them all along the beach, thousands of them. Call the Fire Department. You'll need foam," Aran said. He heard the desk officer start to shout feverishly into his other connections. Aran put the phone down, put on shoes and a shirt, brought Jenny slacks and a blouse and told her to dress. She donned clothes with her eyes riveted on the window and the mounting layers of waving claws that almost obscured the window now. They clicked against the window as they pressed and tried to bite the smooth glass.

Jenny's voice held quiet terror as she murmured: "Will it hold?"

"Not if they pile much more weight up against it," Aran said grimly. "If it breaks, we run into the bedroom. There aren't that many against the side of the house."

"Oh, my God," Jenny whispered, and, over the top of the layer of waving claws and shells, Aran detected the first gray tint of dawn in the distant sky. Jenny came to him, stood against him, and he could feel the trembling of her. Or was it his own? The clicking sound of the claws striking the glass grew louder and he heard Jenny's breathing becoming tight. The sound of sirens came then and he pulled her to the other windows on the side of the house that looked back across the dunes, which were now black with the crabs. He saw the three police cars halt, the officers emerge to stand atop the dunes, one talking into a hand transmitter. The others took out their revolvers, emptied them into the crabs, reloaded, and fired again.

"Wasted bullets," Aran muttered, though he realized it was but a human reaction of fear and disgust. The grayness of dawn gathered strength, adding definition to the mass of crawling crustaceans. More police had arrived along the edge of the beach and Aran heard the sound of their distant gunfire. Aran went into the other room to check the window glass, halted, stared. The crabs had disappeared from the window. He ran forward, pressed his face against the glass where he could see down to the water.

"They're going, Jenny," he shouted, and she was beside him instantly. "Back into the sea. Look at them—thousands and thousands of them."

"Just here?" she questioned.

"No, they'll be moving back all along the other beaches. They're going, returning to the sea."

"Because of the shooting, the sirens?" Jenny questioned.

Aran paused, felt his lips draw back in a grimace. "No, I don't think so," he answered. "The dawn maybe, or because they're finished, or perhaps because it's time for them to go back." Aran listened to the heavier sound of the fire engines wail their arrival, but the crabs, with amazing speed, were already vanishing into the surf. The firemen would be too late for all but a few stragglers. Aran turned from the window to meet Jenny's wide eyes.

"They could come back," she breathed. "Anytime. Here, somewhere else, anyplace."

Aran nodded, feeling helpless.

"What's happening, Aran?" Jenny asked, and he could only shrug and feel helpless again. "What could happen? What are the possibilities?" she pressed.

"The sea could be changing. It could become a hostile place for man," Aran said slowly.

"Hostile?" she echoed.

"In every sense," Aran said.

Jenny sank down on the sofa. Her eyes stayed wide, haunted, staring out into space, and he sank down beside her, found her hand with his. He sat silently with her, listening to the muted sounds outside, sirens, shouts, engines throbbing, and the new day slowly filled the cottage with its light. Finally, Jenny detached herself from him. Moving with almost abstract slowness she went to the kitchen closet and returned with a broom. She began to sweep the dead and crushed crabs out the front door and the sun stabbed into the room as she pulled the door open. Aran went to the doorway to look down toward the sea. Only the sand met his eyes now, directly in front of the cottage. Turning to glance down to the other beaches, he saw the police and firemen hurrying in groups, clustering at other cottages. Aran closed the door, went back inside where Jenny had just finished brushing away the broken crabs from beneath the window. She backed away, slumped into a chair, and her breath came in a deep sigh.

"I'm not staying here when you leave," she said, staring at him. "I'm going with you."

"Did you think I'd let you stay?" he asked and he moved to gather her against him. "Start packing," he said. She rose, went into the other room, and began to throw things into two suitcases. Aran returned to the door, watched the activity on the adjoining beaches. The extent of the attack was discovered only as the police and firemen began checking all the cottages. The torn remains of Ernie Swimmer and Karen Ellis were found first, then the horror inside the Mintners' cottage, and finally the full horror of what had happened revealed itself. All but a handful of people in the cottages along the beaches had been bitten to death. By midmorning, the beach area was almost as full of officials and news-media people as it had been of crabs.

Jenny was packed and ready to go when Aran turned from the doorway; he got his jacket and went outside with her. She halted just beyond the doorway, her back to the sea, her eyes moving over the cottage, finally straying to the beach and the water.

"You know, I love this place," she said softly. "I've been coming here ever since I was a little girl. I've always felt as peaceful here as at home. But suddenly I'm a stranger here. Suddenly this is a place I don't know anymore, all of it a place of fear." She closed her eyes a moment as if trying to shut out sights that couldn't be shut away. "I don't know if I could ever come back here now," she said, opening her eyes to stride away, moving up to the dunes where the cars waited.

They drove to the airport in his car and they were almost there when Jenny's question speared at him.

"If the sea became that hostile place you mentioned, Aran, what would happen?" she asked.

"All that's been happening magnified countless times. Every fishing boat that sailed would have to fight for its catch. Every trip would be a kind of warfare. We couldn't win, not even with our huge commercial fishing processes. We couldn't prevail against billions of hostile creatures that really attacked. They'd shred every net dropped into the sea, menace every human that ventured onto or into the water. The sea would no longer be a place of food and comfort and pleasure. Many areas of the world depend on the sea for their living and their existence. They'd be badly hurt, perhaps more totally than we can imagine at this time. If all this is biochemically triggered, the composition of the sea itself and everything in it could change. Fish could, conceivably, become poisonous or nonedible. All the things we take from the sea could suddenly become harmful and useless to us. The huge oil tankers and ocean liners would no doubt be safe from serious attack, but they'd be simply travelers across a hostile place, like giant seagoing tanks running across enemy territory."

"But these attacks now, they seem so totally vicious," Jenny said.

Aran nodded, felt the frown digging into his forehead. "That's the thing that bothers me most about them, not only the sudden and complete reversal of behavior but the use of their natural weapons and abilities with such effect."

"Wouldn't that be instinctual, an automatic thing with a change of behavior patterns?" Jenny questioned.

"Maybe," Aran conceded. "But they're using their natural weapons in ways they've never been used before, with an applied intelligence that seems more than instinctual. It's almost as if they've suddenly taken on man's abilities to organize, plan, make the most of their natural advantages. It's uncanny."

Jenny lapsed into silence as they neared the airport. Perhaps silence was best now, Aran pondered in grim anger. He had no words of explanation and no words of comfort, not for her, not for Emerson Boardman, not for anyone. All he had was notes and he was on his way to add more. Maybe something would come together, make sense. Maybe. He swung into the airport turn-off and headed for the terminal parking.

CHAPTER FIVE

Emerson convened the meeting precisely at four o'clock and Aran thanked luck for having made it on time. Both interviews had taken longer than he'd expected and he had dropped Jenny off at the apartment of a friend after they arrived in Boston. Emerson's face showed fatigue: etched lines creasing his forehead, his eyes red from sleeplessness. The conference room was crowded—everyone that had attended the first meeting and a lot of new faces. Among them was Admiral Willard Hotchins, United States Navy, who was there expressly at the request of the President of the United States.

The admiral had steel-blue eyes in a face as stiff and unbending as his collar. The Fishing Industries Association was represented by Robert Eloins, a dour man who looked perpetually dyspeptic; and Max Rosen was there for the Maritime Unions. Two thick-waisted men were representing the National Seashore and Resort Operators League. Aran recognized Senator Coolidge from Florida, Senator Staunton from Virginia, Rudman from North Carolina, Marantz from New York, and Burroughs from Maine. Emerson rose and put the following items in front of those assembled in the room.

—Commercial fishing was almost at a standstill. Two more tuna boats had been attacked and sunk, almost all their crews lost. One was literally driven sideways onto a reef by countless tons of tuna pushing against it.

—Party fishing had ceased. Three chartered cabin cruisers out of the Florida Keys never returned to their ports.

—Beaches were closed at all the major resort areas along the entire coast. Attacks on anyone in the water continued. Sea bass, bluefish, cod, mackerel, and even schools of porgy had been identified as attacking.

—The Secretary of Agriculture had issued a statement of concern. Some thirty to fifty percent of the weekly food consumption of the seaboard states was seafood: fish, shrimp, crustaceans. The supply of beef and poultry wasn't plentiful enough to make up this deficit. The tightness of the beef and poultry market made this un-likely in the foreseeable future.

—Processors of canned seafood reported their supplies almost depleted due to panic buying and demanded escorts for fishing fleets.

—Homes and summer places along the entire East Coast were being abandoned. Real estate groups claimed that sea-front property had plummeted in value and homes were being offered for sale in panic conditions.

—Seashore business and resort operations were losing millions of dollars as people canceled reservations.

Emerson halted his report, grim-faced, let his eyes scan the group in front of him. "I could read more, detail it for you, but there's no point in that. The most important factor, of course, is being cut off from a sizable part of our food supply. We're still bringing in seafood from the West Coast, which doesn't seem to be affected."

"Any reason for that?" one of the new faces, Rosen of the Maritime Unions, asked.

"Not that we can pin down," Emerson answered. "Of course, any profound change in the organic or chemical composition of the sea would, in time, probably affect all oceans."

"Is that what this is?" Eloins of the Fishing Industries asked. Emerson turned to Leslie Streeter, and the biochemist rose.

"We think that an environmental change is the only logical explanation," Streeter said. "Between those already employed by the Fish and Wildlife Services who constantly analyze water samples and those we've added, there are over a hundred men at work analyzing marine samples. I hoped our preliminary analysis would pinpoint the answers quickly. Unfortunately, we've not come up with any significant changes in water content, biologically, chemically, or organically."

"Which all means what?" Rosen queried.

"Which means that very subtle and complex changes may be occurring that will take longer to analyze and uncover," Streeter said.

"How much longer?" Senator Marantz of New York asked.

Streeter shrugged. "That's impossible to say. It could be a matter of days, but then it could take months."

"Months?" somebody exclaimed. "God knows what'd happen by then."

"I hope it won't be anything as long as that," Streeter replied. "But we may have a subtle combination of factors causing this aggressive behavior. That would mean a great number of possible combinations of factors, perhaps even the composition of the sea itself. The molecular structure of sea water may be undergoing intrinsic changes. For example, each molecule has a defined number of heat calories and conductivity coefficient. This thermal conductivity coefficient is affected by area and the temperature difference between surface molecules and those of deeper water. It may be necessary to probe these factors."

"Hell, that sounds like years," one of the men from the Resort Operators League exploded. "We're interested in now. What are you people going to do here and now? You can't just stand around analyzing water samples. What about a net to protect the beaches?"

"Along the entire Eastern seaboard?" Emerson returned. "I'd say impossible, or at best, a matter of a year or more to build."

Robert Eloins interrupted with quiet acid in his voice. "You're really telling us, and the American people, that you don't know what the hell's going on and you can't do a thing about it," he said. Emerson's voice sounded protest but, Aran noted, his eyes registered discomfort.

"Not at all, not at all," Emerson said. "Admiral Hotchins is here to provide the temporary assurances you want."

Aran watched Admiral Hotchins rise and felt the thinly disguised condescension in the man. The admiral surveyed the others and smiled. "All this public panic is ridiculous," he announced. "It's mass hysteria."

Aran felt anger pushing inside him. "A lot of dead people wouldn't agree with that," he interjected quietly, and saw the admiral fasten him with a steel-blue eye.

"Aran Holder has been on my team, assigned to interviewing survivors for anything that might help us," Emerson explained to the admiral. "Aran's quite well-known for his scientific writings."

Admiral Hotchins grunted, turned his eyes back to the others. "I see this as a small-boat problem. A few small vessels may have to stay in port till we've everything under control, but we won't premit any serious disruption of our seafood supply," he said.

"That's already happened," Aran said. "And most seafood is taken in by a huge network of small craft."

Admiral Hotchins showed impatience in his manner, but kept calm assurance in his voice as he replied. "I assure you, we've the means to handle this thing, whatever it is," he said.

"The Navy won't let the seas be run by a few thousand fish gone crazy because of some environmental change. We'll provide an escort for commercial fishing fleets, one destroyer to a fleet. No damn fish is going to bother a United States destroyer, you can be sure of that."

"What will the destroyer do in a mass attack such as has happened?" Aran cut in.

"Why, depth-charge them," Admiral Hotchins thundered. "Blow them into little pieces, that's all."

"What about resorts, swimmers?" Senator Rudman questioned.

"We'll provide helicopter coverage of all the shore areas, coordinating with local authorities. We'll be able to spot any large mass of fish from the air and warn bathers to go ashore," the admiral answered. "With that kind of air spotting, bathers won't have any problems. We'll have this damn foolishness under control in no time at all."

Aran watched the others digest the admiral's words and stand back before the authority of his manner. It was not an act, Aran realized. The admiral believed his arrogant assumptions. Aran met Emerson's eyes and saw the man look away, speak to the admiral.

"Then I can issue a statement to inform the public of your plans and that the situation is under control," Emerson said. The admiral nodded confidently, almost serenely. There were more questions directed at Admiral Hotchins now, but Aran turned off listening, rose, and walked to the door. He slipped out of the conference to stand by the hall window and look out across the harbor. He heard the door open behind him, and Leslie Streeter emerged.

"You don't buy the admiral's confidence, I take it," the biochemist said.

"He has no idea of what we could be facing. He's a pompous ass," Aran retorted.

"Perhaps you don't agree with my approach, either," Streeter said. Aran regarded the man, decided he was sincere in his probing.

"I'm bothered by some things in it," Aran admitted. "You're looking for a change in marine biochemistry over a tremendous stretch of water with Arctic currents and tropical flows. You're theorizing that that could occur all over at once. It doesn't seem likely to me."

Leslie. Streeter's lips pushed out. "That disturbs me, too, I'll concede. Most environmental changes are localized; at first, anyway."

"And most result in more than one kind of visible effect. This is confined to that aggressive, vicious behavior," Aran added. "It seems too channeled, too virulent for a reaction to a biochemical change."

"Perhaps, but then some biochemical changes could result in just that sort of behavior, as with antimetabolic enzyme behavior."

"Yes, but there's something different about this," Aran said. The biochemist's eyes stayed on the younger man, narrowed, absorbing his remarks.

"But it has to be a matter of environmental change," Leslie Streeter said. "There just isn't any other possible explanation for it."

Aran shrugged. "Not that we know about yet," he said, unable to refute the man's certainty, yet unable to embrace it completely. Leslie Streeter turned away, walked down the hall, wrapped in his own thoughts. He would keep on with his laboratory examination of every bit of microbiotic sea life, his endless water analysis. It was what he had to do. It was all he could do. *We're all locked into our life patterns,* Aran thought. And all he was locked into was a gut feeling, he scolded himself as he took the elevator to the street.

He hailed a cab and arrived at the apartment where Jenny was staying. Her friends had gone away for a week and left the place to her. He took her to dinner, and when they returned to the apartment, she insisted he stay with her, though he'd thought of going to his folks. He didn't protest too strongly, and while Jenny showered, he sat down with all the notes he had taken thus far and went over each interview, one by one. He became totally absorbed in his search until finally Jenny came to him, her arms encircling his neck.

"You've been staring at those notes for over an hour," she said.

"I keep thinking there's something in them that I'm missing," he said. "A key, a little something, a clue of some kind. I can't find it and yet I keep feeling it's there."

"A connection?" she said wryly. He looked up at her.

"All right, a connection, if you like. I still believe in connections. There's a pattern to everything," he said.

She shrugged her disbelief. "You're too tired to see it if it is there," she said. "Come on to bed." The comment was accurate as well as appealing and he let her pull him up and into the bedroom where a large, king-size bed filled the room. "Ted and Vivian believe in the pleasure principle," Jenny remarked as he started to undress. In the cool smoothness of the bedsheets, he found her arms waiting for him, her warm wanting a soft catharsis shutting out all else, and finally he slept. When he woke in the morning, Jenny was up fixing bacon. She had turned on the radio and he listened to the morning newscast of Emerson's statement as he began to dress.

"The Department of Fish and Wildlife Services reassures the American people that the unprecedented marine-life behavior, while not scientifically explained as yet, is being carefully studied. There is no cause for undue panic. Steps have been taken by the United States Navy and Air Force, under the direction of Admiral Willard Hotchins, to insure the safety of the sea for all who use it. During the daylight hours, all shore areas will be under helicopter surveillance. Any unusual marine activity will be detected from the air. All resort and shore activities, including swimming, may be safely resumed in accordance with local advisories and controls. Beach patrols are being organized for the night hours.

"Commercial fishing fleets are being escorted by warships of the United States Navy. However, the Navy obviously cannot provide an escort for every boat in the water, so for the time being, pleasure boating and party-boat pleasure fishing are forbidden. Proper scientific explanations for these unusual marine outbreaks is expected shortly and corrective measures will be taken at once. The Bureau is fully confident that the steps now being taken under Admiral Hotchins' supervision will be more than adequate until that time."

Aran switched off the set. Emerson wasn't actually to blame for the statement. He really had nothing positive to tell the public. Going along with the admiral's arrogant rhetoric was his only course to calm the public fear. Aran went into the bathroom and let cold water shock him into full wakefulness, then returned to Jenny in the kitchen.

"Got anything to keep you busy today?" he asked. "I'm going to pore over my notes again and pay another visit to some of the people hospitalized by beach attacks in this area."

"I'll go shopping. That always helps to keep one's mind occupied," she said. She paused, her lips tightening. "I was thinking about the cottage, about not wanting to go back there," she said. "I hope you find something in your notes. I hope somebody finds something."

⚜ ⚜ ⚜

Emerson Boardman woke in Dolly's bed, rubbed sleep from his eyes. He'd stayed late with the admiral and his aides, working out details of the overall plan. Emerson believed the admiral. He wanted desperately to believe the admiral's assurances. The helicopter patrol was to go into effect at once up and down the coast, concentrating on the populous resort areas: Cape Cod, Martha's Vineyard, the Boston beaches, Hyannisport, Providence, all the New York areas, the Atlantic City and Cape May shores, and down along the Delaware coast, Virginia Beach, Hatteras, Myrtle Beach, the Georgia sea islands, and down the Florida coastline to Miami Beach, Coral Gables, and the Keys. Local police helicopters were assigned the smaller beaches in between and part of the plan seemed to work. Enough people were reassured by the sight of the helicopters to return to the beaches.

Emerson swung out of bed as Dolly came into the room in her white panties only. She sat down on the edge of the bed. "Do you think it'll work? The helicopter patrols, I mean," she asked. "Will it be safe to go swimming?"

"Why, I'd say it'd be perfectly safe in those areas being patrolled," Emerson answered. "Why?"

"I'm supposed to go swimming tomorrow on a beach picnic with the girls from my bowling league," Dolly said. "It was planned weeks ago and they've been calling me all day yesterday, seeing as how I work for you. We'd planned to go to the Cape."

Dolly's round face was already in a half-pout of disappointment and Emerson didn't want her to go into one of her pouting sessions, which she invariably did when something she'd counted on didn't come through. He didn't have to start home till noon and he hoped for an hour or two in bed with Dolly before then.

He felt better this morning, less worried and tense. He'd be able to function this morning.

"Go, by all means. The Cape is one of the major patrol areas. It'll be quite safe. Just follow the local restrictions worked out for each area," Emerson said.

"Are you sure?" Dolly frowned, looking petulant.

"Absolutely. Any concentration of fish will be spotted by the helicopters as they move inshore," Emerson said. He reached to her, let his fingers slide over her full, heavy breasts, across their small, hardly raised points. "Just to be sure, to be extra safe, why not do your swimming in one of the coves? All the attacks have been along the beaches fronting the sea. Then you'll be doubly safe. You'll have the air patrols and be in one of the coves."

Dolly's eyes searched his face. "All right, if you say so. Everybody's been looking forward so much to tomorrow," she said.

"I say so, Admiral Hotchins says so, the helicopter patrols say so," Emerson returned, leaning forward to push his face right into the center of the twin mounds. Dolly sighed and felt better. All the girls had been looking forward to a day at the Cape. She moved under Emerson, prepared herself for his panting efforts, and thought about which bikini she'd wear tomorrow.

CHAPTER SIX

Three things happened that weekend. Each dissolved the admiral's arrogance into so much empty bombast. The first day of the air patrols was quiet and uneventful. The helicopters were a reassuring sight to many as they made long, low sweeps over the shores. By later in the afternoon, a number of people, thirsting for the pleasures of swimming and the beach, went out into the water. Reports that there'd been no trouble anywhere made others more confident and the next day, Sunday, saw a good number of people returning to the beaches. Emerson was pleased, and from his home, he was in contact with Washington and with Admiral Hotchins. He knew it would take time to fully reassure the public, but the first day had gone well. Emerson wasn't a believer in omens, but he was happy to embrace this as one.

At the Cape, Dolly Wojieski and the six other girls of the bowling league held their picnic at one of the smaller beaches of a cove. Susan had brought a magnificent picnic lunch and Edie Haas had come with wine. Everything was so beautiful, calm and bright, and with the helicopters making their low sweeps periodically along the water, Dolly had been tempted to switch to one of the beaches directly fronting the sea; but she decided to follow Emerson's advice. Dolly wasn't one to switch plans once she'd decided on them and so they swam, ate, then all stretched out in the sun, Harriet Eberle pushing her bathing-suit top so low that she was practically topless, Dolly noticed. She pushed her own top down some and let the sun caress her body.

It was midafternoon when they all decided it was time for another swim. Dolly pulled her top up a little and ran into the calm waters of the cove, wishing for the fun of splashing through the surf. Some two dozen other bathers were in the water, she saw, and she struck out in a long, lazy sidestroke. Flo Rizzotta and Edie were having a race, Flo splashing too much to win. Dolly turned on her back and floated past Harriet Eberle, heard the sound of Harriet's form doing a surface dive behind her.

Dolly felt the sharp pain in her ankle, so sharp and so quick it really didn't pain at all for that first moment; and then another sharp impact on her calf, this one hurting. She cried out, tried to yank her leg up, but it refused to come and suddenly it seemed on fire with terrible, searing pain all over it. She cried out again, whirled, and looked for Harriet, but Harriet hadn't come to the surface. Then Dolly screamed as her knee felt as though it were being torn off. She saw shapes then, darting shadows, coming at her from all directions.

She heard Edie Haas screaming then, joined by Flo Rizzotta's voice, and then, suddenly, the cove was a place of screams and cries, terror let loose. But Dolly hadn't time to bother about the others. Her body was in the water but on fire. She twisted and tried to swim, but four fish seized her left arm, biting chunks from it, and she could only whirl in place and scream. Mouthfuls of water gagged her and she got her head above the surface. She saw a dozen more darting forms coming at her, others closing in behind them. They weren't swimming in from the mouth of the cove, from the ocean, she realized, but were rising up from the deep water in the cove itself. They'd been in the cove all along. They'd come in during the night, stayed silently at the bottom, and were rising to attack now.

Realization was an abstract, dreamlike thing, as though she were sitting somewhere else watching and making notes. The terrible, needle-sharp pain in her abdomen made her scream and scream again as more teeth sank into her stomach, ripping, gouging. She felt her bikini being torn off in shreds and her right breast was seized, torn off at the tip. Dolly Wojieski's tears mingled with the salt water of the cove as she turned slowly in the water, her body half-eaten away now, floating in a pool of redness. The pain was both sharp and yet dull now, as her life flowed from her and the small knot of vicious attackers, not more than twenty-five, continued to tear at her. Almost idly, she saw they were cod. As Dolly's lifeblood ran from her, as it mingled with that of the other girls and those others that had been in the cove, she thought about Emerson Boardman. With her last, conscious moments she thought about Emerson, her boss and weekly bedmate. *Damn you, Emerson,* Dolly gasped without voice. *Damn you, you stupid bastard.* Why had she even listened to him, she asked herself, when she knew he was such a stupid, incompetent bastard. Dimly, she felt her body jerk in the water as they tore more flesh from her.

What was left of Dolly Wojieski died, along with the six other girls of her bowling team and everyone else who had been in the cove. Those who'd gone swimming on the main beaches also met the same fate as, without warning, they were attacked by small groups of cod, bluefish, and haddock, clusters of twenty-five to fifty, moving out of the little coves, inlets, and bays where they'd lain on the bottom overnight, waiting. They'd struck, like underwater guerrilla fighters, whirled, darted, circled, struck again, and then vanished out to sea.

Overhead, the helicopter pilot, a young Navy lieutenant, made a slow turn and saw people struggling out of the water, to collapse on the beach. He caught sight of bodies floating in the water and the slowly spreading red stain on the sea. His eyes swept the water and failed to see any large mass of fish, no large, dark shadowy area they'd briefed him to watch for and report immediately. There wasn't anything even the size of a submarine off-shore. But something was wrong, terribly, dreadfully wrong, he saw as his stomach turned over. He sent out an urgent alarm warning to the main reception base. It was too late. The scene had been repeated all over: other helicopter spotters no more able to spot any large areas of fish moving inshore than he had. The young pilot guided his helicopter along the shoreline and all he could see, in the distance, were a half dozen fish leaping in and out of the water playfully. They appeared to be dolphins.

Later in the day, when reports began coming in from various areas, it was apparent that the pattern had been repeated all over: the attackers lying in the coves and bays to emerge in small, swift, death-dealing groups and vanish into the vastness of the sea afterward. It was but the first blow for Admiral Willard Hotchins, U.S.N.

The tuna fleet of six boats that put out from Providence, Rhode Island, was accompanied by the U.S.S. *Stevenson*, a destroyer of the John C. Butler class, rated as Escort ships, displacing 1,350 tons standard weight. The tuna fleet reached the fishing grounds and the men began throwing out chum and lines when the water for a half-mile-square radius seemed to blacken and rise up with densely packed bodies. Some of the tuna leaped, smashed against rods and lines, and some seized the rods and pulled the fishermen into the sea before they were able to let go. The tuna vessels bobbed and jiggled atop a sea that was no longer water but a seething mass of slippery bodies pressing upward, hundreds and hundreds of tons of them.

"Holy Jesus," a sailor aboard the destroyer gasped.

"Full speed ahead," the captain roared down to the engine room. "Prepare to fire depth-charges," his voice thundered across the ship's speaker system. The destroyer leaped forward through the mass of tuna, heeled over slightly, her sharp prow cutting forward, and then the captain heard the ship's propellers whirr, grind to a halt, try to spin again, and jam. Hundreds of pounds of tuna had been wedged into the whirring blades, bringing them to a complete halt, the suicidal attack once again completely effective. The U.S.S. *Stevenson* lay helpless in the water as depth-charges were fired from her in the excitement. Before the cease-fire was ordered one blew the bottom out of one of the tuna boats that was too close and she sank immediately. Others were rocking in the water as thousands of tons of fish pressed up under them. One heeled over, spilling most of her crew into the mass of frenzied fish. Two others, trying to turn and flee, crashed into each other and began to sink, their doomed crews fighting to cling to masts and cabin roofs. Some of the other boats managed to break into clear water and race away, their crews panic-stricken men with ashen faces.

Then, as suddenly as they had appeared, the half-mile square of tuna vanished, submerging almost as one into the vastness of the sea. The destroyer had sent out a distress call, but when planes appeared there was only her slender hull wallowing in the water and the half-sunken remains of the two tuna boats which had crashed. A little over an hour later, a second destroyer hove to and, with sailors armed with rifles standing at the rails, four scuba divers were sent over the side to clear the props. It took almost three hours to clear them enough to start the engines, the divers working with poles and rakes to clean away the dead carcasses. One propeller shaft had burned-out bearings and didn't work at all, but finally the U.S.S. *Stevenson* limped back to port on one prop.

The final blow to the admiral's arrogance came thousands of miles away, along the shores of Norway where the frigid waters of the Arctic push down into the North Sea. There, the *Irkutsk Christina* beat a windward path through choppy waters. The *Irkutsk Christina* was a Russian vessel, a catcher ship, one hundred and ten feet long and weighing two hundred tons. She was one of three such ships sent out by the mother ship, the huge *Novgorod,* the factory vessel that lay waiting in the open sea for the catcher ships to return with the carcasses of dead whales to be butchered on her specialized decks. But for five days, the *Irkutsk Christina* had seen no sign of a whale in the waters where whales were usually plentiful. Only a far spout on the horizon six days back had given any sign that there were whales near, and now, as they had for each day, the lookouts scanned the water and the gunner sat behind the powerful harpoon gun mounted at the very prow of the ship.

Gregor Romanko manned the sonar screen on the bridge of the vessel as the device searched the depths for whales moving along the bottom or lying quietly, their shapes outlined well enough on the screen either way. Gregor watched the screen with quiet distaste. They had already taken their legal limit during the last trip, but it seemed no one paid much attention to that. Gregor had put in for a transfer to another kind of work, but his application hadn't been answered yet. He'd had enough of this slaughter of these great creatures. He was a seaman by trade, but this was not for him. Slaughter, nothing else, was what it was. With the powerful catcher ships such as the one he stood upon and the unerring harpoon guns, the whales did not have a chance. In the old days, there was a contest made of skill and brawn, bravery and luck. It wasn't simply ruthless slaughter. Gregor often talked about his dislike of whaling with his wife, Ludmilla, as they sat at the table with their young son. Look at what was done to the right whale, by 1910 all but extinct and still hardly plentiful; the blue and the humpback now on the endangered-species list; with the sperm not far behind.

No, he'd had enough, Gregor Romanko told himself as he watched the sonar screen. It had got so he was always hoping that no moving shape materialized on the screen and he cast a glance at Captain Sorokin, who stood nearby. Captain Vassily Sorokin watched the cold waters with hands folded behind his back. He was a grim, ruthless man who drove his men and his ship hard. More than anything else, Captain Sorokin prized having the best record of kills of any catcher ship. Gregor returned his eyes to the sonar screen, watched the small shapes, minor undersea formations, appear and vanish on the echo-finder.

The day wore into midafternoon and they sighted the *Ino Maru,* a Japanese whaler, passing in the distance. Aboard the *Irkutsk Christina,* Captain Sorokin stood on the bridge as if carved out of whalebone, Gregor thought idly, only his eyes flicking across the icy sea. Suddenly, the lookout's voice broke the stillness.

"Whales, off the port bow," the shout came, and Gregor took his eyes from the sonar screen for a moment. He saw the rounded backs surfacing ahead, counted four of the great mammals swimming in a group. As he watched, the whales shifted direction, headed into the shoreline of the Norwegian coast which rose up dimly to the port.

"Right rudder," Captain Sorokin called and ordered the helmsman to "Stay after them." The captain stepped to the chart table, scanned the geodetic map of the coastline with a frown.

"They're going in farther," the helmsman called.

"Stay with them," Captain Sorokin said and bent over the charts. The shoreline was very rocky with reefs that extended far out, the charts told him. He watched the compass and took a quick bearing as the four whales continued to swim near the rocky shore. Gregor Romanko felt the throbbing of the ship as the engines pushed her in pursuit.

"Right rudder two points," Captain Sorokin rasped, bent over the chart table. "Hold steady." The lookout's voice broke the silence.

"They're going down," the call came. Captain Sorokin swore, and Gregor looked up from the sonar screen to see the four whales diving, disappearing under the water, still moving toward shore. The *Irkutsk Christina* sped forward, most of the crew lining the rails now, all eyes watching for their quarry.

"Watch for them, damnit," the captain shouted at Gregor, and he focused back on the screen. He picked up the edge of a reef and was about to call out when Captain Sorokin barked at the helmsman, his eyes fixed on the maps.

"Left rudder, three points," the captain commanded. Gregor kept his eyes on the sonar screen and suddenly picked up the large, moving shape.

"I have one," he shouted and gave the location to the captain, who immediately altered course in pursuit. Gregor glimpsed the harpoon gunner poised over his weapon and looked back into the screen. The line of the reef had disappeared now, but the moving shape of the whale traveled across the screen. He felt Captain Sorokin step closer to him, scan the screen with him, and then Gregor saw the motionless shape appear in the center of the screen. The shape grew larger, a stationary, motionless area. The captain darted back to the chart table. "Rocks, dead ahead," Gregor shouted. "Dead ahead."

He heard Captain Sorokin curse. "Hard to port," he screamed at the helmsman. "Goddamn charts. Never accurate," the captain swore. The *Irkutsk Christina* veered hard to port at full speed. She slammed into the reef exactly at the spot where the coastal chart indicated it to be. Her hull tore apart on the sharp reef, crumpling like an eggshell, and the ocean poured into her. Men and fixtures came loose and were sent hurtling across decks and cabins. Gregor Romanko, before he was torn away from his place, stared into the sonar screen to see the line of rocks he had picked up suddenly dissolve, become moving shapes, sliding away on the screen. He was sent hurtling then, across the bridge to slam into the other side, his feet going out from under him. He lay there, momentarily dazed, a small trickle of blood oozing from a cut along his temple. But the rocks had moved, he told himself. They had moved. They had never been rocks at all, he realized in shock.

He heard the command to man the boats, pulled himself to his feet, and saw that the *Irkutsk Christina* was already bow down in the water. He scrambled down the bridge ladder to the main deck where the ship's two lifeboats were being lowered into the water. He was ordered into the first boat, saw Captain Sorokin standing by until the other lifeboat was filled, and then clamber into it. The boat was rowed away from the ship. Gregor Romanko sat in the stern and watched as a column of steam hissed up from the *Irkutsk Christina* as her boilers went underwater. The lifeboats moved away from the vessel out of the circle of suction as she went down, slowly at first, then quickly, as though she were being pulled down under the water by an invisible string.

The men in the lifeboats swore, asked questions of each other, and shivered. Captain Sorokin sat stonily, his thick brows pulled low over his eyes. But Gregor Romanko stared at the water, seeing not the icy waves but the sonar screen as the motionless rocks became moving shapes and slid away. The whales had tricked them, he told himself. They had taken up positions overlapping each other, held motionless to form the outline of a reef while the first one held the ship in pursuit. The sonar screen faded from in front of his eyes, but not the image he'd last seen upon it: the rocks changing into moving shapes.

The whales had tricked them, Gregor told himself again. It wasn't possible. Whales could not do things like that, and yet they had done it. He knew what he had seen on the sonar. The whales had tricked them into crashing against the reef. The phrase repeated itself over and over in his mind, the full meaning of it more than he could comprehend. The shout of alarm broke into the silent refrain inside his brain. It was Mendavich, the harpoonist, fittingly enough, Gregor thought as he looked up to see the three huge shapes rising out of the sea. Finner whales, he saw at once, seventy to eighty feet long, close to a hundred tons each, and aggressive.

Transfixed, he saw one of the whales move toward the other lifeboat, watched the crewmen bend to the oars in a frenzied effort to get away. The whale caught up to the fleeing lifeboat in a matter of seconds, its head dipping down, then coming up under the lifeboat, lifting. The lifeboat and the men in it, like so many toy pieces tossed upward by a child, flew through the air. Some landed atop the huge back, only to slide off into the churning water, while others fell directly into the sea. Gregor saw the whale's huge tail thresh the sea into froth, the lifeboat splintered into bits of wood. He glimpsed Captain Sorokin knocked twenty feet by a blow of the tail that surely broke every bone in his body, and then the boat he was in began to move. Gregor turned to see the second of the whales bearing down on them, looking like some monstrous ocean liner covered with a thick, rubbery hide.

Instincts, not thought, moved Gregor Romanko. He dived overboard, almost into the oncoming mammoth, and he swam downward. The underside of the whale swept past him, brushed his body, turning him around and sweeping him down along its length with the current its huge form created. He didn't hear the screams of the men in the other lifeboat as the tremendous form smashed it to smithereens. The whale's tailfin moved and, his lungs about to burst, Gregor was flung to the surface and tossed into the air. He came down alongside the huge whale, the slippery skin sliding away from his hands as he clutched at it. But his very closeness to the mammal protected him from the threshing tail. He caught glimpses of his fellow crewmen, smashed, broken bodies tossed in the churning water, and suddenly the whale halted its tailfin and began to move, brushing past him with effortless speed. He dived and avoided any chance blow of the great tail, surfaced, and was alone. The huge animal had vanished into the sea.

He was unaware that a Norwegian Air Force plane flying nearby had witnessed the finish of the scene and had called in a distress signal. A coastal tanker responded and finally arrived at the spot where Gregor Romanko drifted on a piece of the lifeboat. The icy Arctic stream had all but frozen him and he was pulled out of the waters in shock. At the hospital where he was taken, the doctors could not save his left leg, but they managed to save his life. When he came out of the anesthetic, he kept repeating the single phrase, "The whales tricked us."

He was judged in severe emotional trauma as well as physical distress and taken to the psychiatric wing of the hospital. The European press picked up the story at once. They had been giving full coverage to the attacks along the American Atlantic coast and now they had a bizarre incident in their own waters. In Britain, Reuters put the story on the news wires with Gregor's repetition of the same phrase over and over and in America it was added to all the other occurrences.

To Aran Holder, it became part of a frightening mystery that grew more ominous with every report. Since Sunday morning, when all of Admiral Hotchins' bombast had exploded, Aran had been making personal and phone interviews. When the story of the *Irkutsk Christina* came through, he added it to his now voluminous notes. He continued to pore over the pages, halting only when Jenny made him do so.

Emerson called him in Monday morning and Aran saw the shock of Dolly Wojieski's death in the man's staring eyes, his gray face, and slowed speech. Aran wanted to find comforting words, but realized there weren't any and stayed silent. He knew the self-blame and guilt Emerson Boardman felt, and watching the man's eyes, he could guess at the rest.

"I told her it was all right. I told her it was safe," Emerson said, as much to himself as to Aran.

"You believed the admiral," Aran soothed. Emerson nodded and leaned forward.

"I want you to take charge of all press releases on this," he said, his fingers working nervously. "I can't handle it alone any longer, not now. I have to concentrate on coordinating all the material Streeter and the others are sending through. Besides, there's a top-level meeting being called by Washington. I've got to get together a full, detailed report for that."

The words were layered with logic, but the real truth lay somewhere else, Aran knew. Emerson felt he had betrayed not only Dolly but everyone else. It was more than he could face, and issuing press releases was a form of facing the world.

"I won't put out any more crap," Aran said, more coldly than he'd intended. "No more whistling in the wind, no matter what anyone wants."

"Washington is afraid of panic. The Pacific coast is all on edge. They keep watching and waiting," Emerson said.

"It's too late to be worried about panic. It's here," Aran said. "I keep wondering about it breaking out on the West Coast."

"Biochemical changes would ordinarily stay concentrated, for some time, at least," Emerson remarked.

"Exactly. That's one of the things that bothers me about Streeter's biochemical-change theory. I don't call the entire Atlantic seaboard and now the North Sea a concentration."

Emerson shrugged, his lips thinning. "Roy Waite still feels strongly that some undetected current flow is the cause of it."

"Oceanographers think in their terms, biochemists in theirs," Aran commented.

"Roy feels that perhaps a new, very deep current has been set loose by an underwater earthquake. Such a current, rising out of a tremendous fissure very deep in the sea floor, could be feeding new chemical compounds or organisms into the water."

"But Streeter's analysts haven't found any new organisms."

"Waite thinks perhaps they aren't recognizable yet. He feels they'd be carried freely by convection currents. He theorizes that the plankton, which as you know go down deep during the day when the sun penetrates the upper water, come back near the surface at night having intermingled with these new substances to affect in turn the larger marine life."

It would explain the tremendous area being affected, Aran realized, but he turned away unsatisfied. They were all caught up in their theories, evolving new ones as they went along, postulating possibilities while the sea seethed with purposeful violence. It didn't fit right.

"Will you take on the press job, Aran?" Emerson asked. "Just for a while. You can still follow your leads and do your work."

Aran nodded agreement, extracting another promise of complete authority in releases, and by midmorning had met with the news media and issued a statement that the air patrols would continue, but people should stay out of the water. Later that day, he took part in a meeting with Emerson and a delegation of European officials: Richard Alden of the British Admiralty office, two Dutch marine biologists, and a French oceanographer. Like the Pacific coast observers, the Europeans had been watching apprehensively, and with the attack that sunk the *Irkutsk Christina,* had flown over their respective governments. They had no new theories to contribute and they left with precious little to carry home. Certainly no reassurances, as there was nothing to give them that could do that. An agreement was made to send them copies of all American findings and they, in turn, would put their best marine experts to work on the problem. The British, Aran learned, were already running patrol boats along the coasts, looking for anything unusual.

When Aran went back to the apartment and Jenny finally, he noted in bitter amusement that the seashore resort operators and real-estate interests had already begun a campaign extolling the benefits of the sun and the salt air as sufficient reason for visiting the shore. The resiliency of the American corporate mind, he thought. But alone with Jenny, he gave vent to his own frustrations and fears.

"What is it, goddamn it!" he cried out. "What in hell is it? It's too channeled, too directed to be just a reaction to biochemical changes. Just look at how they've moved against us, with organization, cleverness, planning. We put out air patrols to spot them and it was quiet. Then they slipped into coves at night to strike in small, fast groups. And now that Russian catcher ship."

"You believe that sailor's story," Jenny said.

"Yes, damn it, I believe it. I believe it and I don't know what to make of it."

"Maybe it's phylogenetic. Maybe we're witnessing some tremendous evolutionary leap in the development of marine organisms," Jenny offered.

"Maybe," Aran said. It didn't fit right, but then nothing else did, and it was no less valid than some of the other theories that had been put forth. Certainly his own angry protests were naked, without a shred of evidence to add substance to them. He sat down with his notes again after dinner, stayed with them, poring over each interview once more until finally he went to bed, pressing himself against Jenny's softness.

"I wish I could help. I mean really help," she murmured.

"You help, just by being here," Aran said as his hand found her breast, his thumb moving slowly across the tiny point. Jenny moaned at once, turned to offer the round softness fully to him and his lips moved down, touching it lightly, then pressing harder, finding the pink tip. He pulled gently, felt the softness become firmer, form itself into a tiny point, a small, surrogate erection. Jenny's hands held him there, pressed his mouth down harder until he pulled away, let his tongue trace a thin, candent line down her abdomen, across the slow rise of her belly. She gasped, arched her back, and her long, tanned legs fell open as the petals of a flower fall open to the sun. He let his lips press down into her, a sweet soft kiss, then moved his tongue through the deep soft-wire mossy triangle. He felt his own body become electric, a trembling wanting surging through him, and then he heard her cry out as he found her moist softness, eternal anointing washing from her. As the sea washes itself upon the waiting shore, he found himself thinking, giving and demanding. Jenny as Jenny, Jenny as woman, strangely like the sea: full of dark, beckoning mysteries, a thing of surges and rhythms, a cradle of life, a place of beginnings. What was the womb but a tiny, individual sea nurturing its new life?

"Oh. Oh, God, oh, yes, yes," he heard her soft moanings and felt the warmth of her thighs as they rose, closed around his head, a sweet blanket. His hand, stroking the smoothness of her belly, felt its quick, spasmic movements in mounting crescendo, and then suddenly she was writhing, screaming, twisting against him, falling open as if by that she could draw in forever what was so excruciatingly brief. But all the ecstasy of the world encapsulated drew away from her in moments and he heard her groan of protest as she fell back onto the sheets. His caresses made her shudder in after-pleasure until she lay quietly, turning as he positioned himself beside her, hands reaching for him. It had been a beginning, not an end, and he had come to know Jenny's surging rhythms. She would rise up again in cries of ecstasy, less quickly this time, tasting of him now, savoring more slowly the silent words of the flesh. So it was, later, or hardly later at all—time not made of seconds, minutes, but of touching, feeling, pressing—until she dug hands into his back as she flowed out around him, warming, holding, closeting with that moment that was forever, eternal, and yet gone at once.

Finally he slept beside her, drained and renewed at once, and the night surrounded them with its darkness. She woke in the deep of the night, her voice crying out in terror. "They're coming in. Oh, God, their claws, they've got me." Aran woke to her scream. "They're biting me, oh, God."

He shook her, hard, saw her come awake. Her cries trailed off, but in her eyes the specter of terror remained until that, too, slowly dissolved, and she sat up, pressing her hands to her face.

"Easy, honey," Aran said, rubbing her back with his hand. "A nightmare, that's all." Jenny looked up at him, her eyes round.

"Yes, the nightmare has gone away, but what about the reality?" she asked. "Will that go away? Or will it get worse?" Once again, he could only shrug in helplessness. She lay back, closed her eyes, and Aran stretched out beside her, their bodies hardly touching now. He thought about the *Irkutsk Christina* in the waters of the Arctic current. Was it spreading? he wondered. Was it encompassing the Atlantic and its peripheral waters? Would it go on, like the ancient sailing ships, around the Cape of Good Hope and into the Pacific? Could there be an environmental change that moved so swiftly, that was so vast in its origins? Or was Jenny's offering more close to truth than he had thought? Was this some tremendous evolutionary leap in the phylogeny of marine life? Paleontology offered ample evidence of such leaps that permitted one species of life to adapt and remain while other species vanished entirely. Aran turned on his side, made his mind close itself off from further speculating, and finally he slept until the waking sound of the alarm clock.

He rose, wanting to feel optimistic, hoping for some break-through from Streeter's analysts. When he reached the offices of the Wildlife Services, Emerson met him at the door. "The President has just issued an executive order to all food markets to limit sales of poultry and beef to the consumer," Emerson said, handing him a teletype copy of the official order. Aran read it silently.

It is my unpleasant duty to inform the American people that poultry and meat products will be limited by executive order. The Department of Agriculture advises that the halt in obtaining the regular supplies of fish oils, guano, fish meal, and sea weeds has affected the production of fertilizers, a base product in the chain of farm production of meat, poultry, and many grains. The cutoff in these supplies has also affected certain chicken and cattle feeds, the processing of certain food items, and the manufacture of a number of chemical compounds.

An increase in the demand for poultry and cattle foods has also put a severe, sudden drain on available supplies. The use of chemical fertilizers is expected to relieve this problem, but this will necessitate an increase in such production. During this period, the above-mentioned food supplies must, necessarily, be limited to consumers. The government agencies involved assure me that all are working toward a speedy solution of this most unexpected and unusual set of circumstances.

Aran handed the sheet back to Emerson Boardman and gave a half-grunt. "It's happened faster than I'd expected," he said. "Anything from Streeter?" Emerson's eyes still stared hollowly, he noted.

"No, but Admiral Hotchins called. He's forming plans for Naval vessels to move out with heavy steel nets. He figures they can bring up a sizable catch. He'll present the details at the meeting I called for Friday." Emerson paused, shrugged, and sought Aran's eyes. "It's an idea," he said. "Especially if he goes into deep water. Maybe this thing, whatever it is, hasn't affected marine life away from the coastal zone."

"Maybe," Aran said, discarding the idea but having nothing to offer. Emerson turned away and went into his office and Aran glanced at the latest batch of reports: Sporadic attacks whenever bathers insisted on swimming; lobster fishermen still unable to draw up anything but shredded nets. The air patrols had spotted no large formations of fish near shore; the relative quiet was an uneasy, ominous calm. He met with newspaper and television reporters later in the day to answer their questions as best he could with no answers to give. When he finally left the office, he found a chain of people slowly marching in front of the building while others, some kneeling in prayer, formed a line across the street. A large group of spectators, none smiling or laughing, stood by and watched. A blond-haired young man with intense blue eyes led the marchers in a long circle as he called out in a clear, vibrant voice.

"These are the days of the Lord's anger," he intoned. "It is the fulfillment of prophecy, the beginning of the Lord's fury. As it saith in Isaiah: 'It shall come as destruction from the Almighty. And they that spread nets upon the waters shall languish. The land shall be utterly emptied and utterly desolate.'"

Aran skirted the marchers and went down one of the narrow side streets with words about sinners and trans-gressors and the Lord's punishment following him, the young man's voice clear and strong. Strangely, he found he couldn't scoff at anything anymore and he hurried on, glad to arrive at the apartment and Jenny's arms.

CHAPTER SEVEN

It was the following morning when he arrived at the office, in time to see Emerson downing a shotglass of whiskey, that he received the call from Herb Bixly of the *Globe*. But first, Emerson pushed the reports that had come in at him and he scanned them grimly. There had been another crab attack, this time along a line of permanent homes south of Virginia Beach. These were all large houses that fronted on private beaches and private quays. The crustaceans had come in at high tide, thousands again, and scuttled up along the beaches and over the low quays, finding entry into most of the fine old rambling houses, according to the top report he read.

"Where the hell was the beach patrol?" Aran asked.

"They were on duty, mostly local police and some civilian auxiliaries," Emerson said. "I just finished talking to the commander at the Norfolk Naval Station. It seems a number of human errors compounded things. First, the crabs emerged after the patrol had passed that section. When they were discovered, they were already into a number of the homes. In panic—automatic reaction, I guess—more time was wasted as the patrol emptied their guns at them."

"Jesus, what a waste of effort," Aran groaned.

"Some of the patrol got too close, fell, and never got up. A few others ran and called in the alarm. But, in another piece of confusion, they called the Navy at Norfolk. The Navy in turn notified the local fire departments, but it all took up precious time. When the firemen reached the area, they did get a number of the attackers with high-pressure hoses and foam, I was told, but most had already fled back into the sea. Norfolk sent out fast patrol boats, but they didn't get there in time to find anything."

Aran went into the small press office he'd been using, shaking his head at the succession of panic-stricken errors. Compared to the first such attack, less lives had been lost, but that was only because the homes held less people than the crowded summer cottages and were harder to get into. Yet some fifty-five people had been bitten to death and an equal number hospitalized. Arthur Oberlin, of the Shorefront Real Estate Association, phoned to demand that the Bureau issue some kind of positive, reassuring statement. Shorefront homeowners from Kennebunkport to Jacksonville were moving out in panic.

"I'd rather they move out and stay alive," Aran said. "I won't urge anyone to stay and risk being attacked." Arthur Oberlin screamed and demanded and Aran felt his anger rise. "You're concerned—but with property values. I'm concerned with lives," Aran snapped.

"Damn right I'm thinking about property values," the man snapped back. "Even if you bastards finally find the reasons for this and the cure, it'll take years for things to return to normal. People don't forget something like this."

Aran hung up on the man. Maybe they shouldn't forget, he had wanted to say. He groaned silently. The thought had no roots, no basis, and yet it had caught in his mind. Jesus, he was reduced to searching for any ray of hope, any stray crumb of redeeming value, he thought, and grimaced. He took a call from the Atlanta office, telling him it had been decided that all press releases should come from Boston and that they'd stopped issuing any releases of their own. Coordination, he was told, but he knew they'd simply decided to shift the burden of being able to say nothing.

Emerson came in with three of the secretaries who, speaking for all the girls, wanted to know what to do with the mountain of mail sacks filled with letters from the public—some offering theories, some demanding solutions, most simply full of fear and questions. It was decided that mail only from recognized authorities or official agencies would be answered at this time and he let Emerson work out the mechanics for handling this.

It was late afternoon when the call came in from Bixly. He'd known Herb Bixly for a number of years in a casual way. The man covered the science beat for the *Globe* and they had often crossed paths at official functions.

"You heard about Evan Taylor, didn't you?" Bixly asked.

"No," Aran said, straightening in his chair. Evan Taylor was an old subject of his, a brilliant, fascinating scientist.

"He committed suicide last night," Bixly said. "I thought it might have slipped past you with all the panic stuff you're handling."

"Jesus," Aran heard himself gasp, felt the shock waves coursing through him.

"You did that series on his work in animal communications, particularly marine life," Bixly went on. "Anything you can tell us about him?"

Aran felt his mind flying back to that time. He'd spent three months with Evan Taylor then, got to know the man quite well. "He was a surgeon as well as a biochemist," Aran said. "Then he became a behaviorist. He was an advanced thinker, a brilliant man." Aran lapsed into silence. It had been two years since he'd done the pieces. Right after they'd appeared, Evan Taylor had opened his own laboratory in the Florida Keys. And now he had killed himself, Aran thought, frowning, the realization still creating shock waves inside him. "Was there a note?" he asked Bixly.

"If you can call it that. There were two words on it. 'I'm sorry,' " Bixly said.

Aran frowned. "Nothing else?"

"Nothing else," Bixly echoed. "Well, I thought you'd want to know. Anything new officially on the real problem?"

Aran gave him Roy Waite's theory on new deep currents and Bixly hung up, happy for the item. Aran sat back, thinking about Evan Taylor. The man had always been an eccentric, tall and thin with an ascetic face and a missionarylike zeal that disturbed many people by its intensity. Evan Taylor had set up his laboratory in the Keys and surrounded it with secrecy and silence. He was into underwater communication but also into something else, Aran remembered Taylor telling him once over the phone. The frown pulled deeper as his thoughts refused to put memories into order. The suicide was almost unbelievable. He had come to know Evan Taylor well enough to know his absolute dedication to his work. He was eccentric, intense, highly keyed, and Aran could understand personal problems devouring him. But Evan Taylor would have been terribly caught up in the disastrous attacks, the unexplained marine behavior. That brilliantly curious scientific mind would have been beyond all excitement, plunging into this tremendous opportunity to study, observe, deduce. He'd have been consumed in trying to find answers. Personal problems would have been pushed aside, if only for a little while. Evan Taylor would have been able to do no less. Yet now, of all times, he had killed himself. Aran shook his head in disbelief. The choice was scientifically out of keeping with the man more than out of character.

And the note, he mused; two cryptic, strange words: *I'm sorry*. "Damn," Aran said aloud, his thoughts groping into the past. There'd been a letter from Evan Taylor a few months after he'd set up his new quarters in the Keys and now Aran strained at memory, trying to recall what it had said. But his mind was cluttered, overflowing with the present, and he grimaced and stretched out in the chair and closed his eyes. There was a technique, a system he'd developed long ago for recalling things. Never try to pull it out by itself, he'd learned. Go back to surroundings, reconstruct what happened before and around the item you sought for, mentally sneak up on it. The technique worked and he began to build pieces of the past in his mind.

The three articles had appeared two years ago. Evan had been pleased with them, had called from his new lab to offer congratulations. They had talked and Evan told him he'd hired two bright young assistants: a girl, Kay Elliot, and a young ichthyologist, John Akberg. Aran let his mind trace on, float along by itself. After the phone call he had done a story for one of the popular magazines on tissue-culture reproduction *in vitro*. There'd been a letter then from Evan detailing a number of problems he'd solved in tissue-culture reproduction and congratulating Aran on the piece. Then silence from Evan Taylor, and Aran was back to where he'd met Jenny, started seeing her regularly. That Christmas he'd sent Evan Taylor a card with a note in it. The letter he searched to recall had come soon after that and it took shape suddenly, materializing as it fitted into its proper place in time. He saw it appear before his closed eyes, the last paragraph the one he wanted to recall.

"I'm on to something tremendously exciting—marine life communication—and something more, something very much more. I've got hold of it and I'm consumed with it."

The letter had ended then, abruptly, but that was Evan Taylor's way. Aran's mind closed off its backward search-dow and stare at a sky made dull by particle-filled city ing and he opened his eyes, rose to stand by the win-air. One question persisted, refusing to leave his thoughts. Why had Evan Taylor chosen this moment to commit suicide? He would have plunged into the strange sea life behavior the moment the first reports started to appear. Had he found something that sent him into an emotional depression? Had he seen the future and been unable to contemplate it? Or, more likely, had he been under a terrible emotional strain, a personal depression, and found something that pushed him beyond despair?

The questions whirled and deserved an answer, Aran decided. He turned from the window, rested a hand on the phone. Evan Taylor had an ex-wife living in Florida, but it was unlikely she'd know anything. He sat down, got information and the number on the Keys, an isolated spot south of the Pennekamp coral reef. The phone rang unanswered for a long while and he was just about to hang up when he heard the receiver picked up. "Miss Kay Elliot, please," Aran said.

"Who's this?" a girl's voice answered.

"Aran Holder. I knew Evan, personally and professionally," Aran said.

"Aran Holder, Aran Holder," the voice mused aloud. "Oh, yes, yes, the writer. He mentioned you sometimes. Yes, he did." The voice was low, husky, and somewhat slurred, Aran thought.

"Is this Kay Elliot?" he asked.

"Nobody else. Kay Elliot, the one and only," the girl said. The slurring was definitely there, Aran decided.

"I'm calling to find out more, if I can. I don't understand it. Why did he do it?" Aran questioned.

"Evan was a very sensitive person, did you know that?" the girl said, her tone slightly singsong. "He was brilliant, the most brilliant man I ever knew. But things got to him, even little things. It must be terrible to be so brilliant, so sensitive to everything. It must be like living in a goldfish bowl turned inside out, every-thing magnified, everything bigger than it is. How about that, Mr. Holder, how's that for perception?" Aran heard her laugh suddenly, a short, wry, self-turned laugh.

"Have you been drinking, Miss Elliot?" he asked quietly. She laughed again over the phone, harder this time.

"Has Miss Elliot been drinking? Has Kay been clobbered? Have fish been eating people? Is the sky falling?" She laughed again.

"You worked closely with Evan," Aran tried. "What made him do it? What did that strange note mean? What was he sorry about?"

"Today. Tomorrow," Kay Elliot said. "Good-bye, Mr. Aran Holder." The line clicked off and Aran stared at the silent phone and slowly put it down. Was she drunk out of grief? he asked himself, and frowned at the question. That would be involved, he was sure, but there'd been something else, a strange quality in the brief conversation, a strange bitterness that had come through the girl's slurred remarks. Aran got to his feet, his lips drawing in tightly. If Evan Taylor had come on to something he may have left notes, observations, perhaps even conclusions. It was worth a try, Aran decided. He went into Emerson's office where Emerson, behind his desk, looked up at him with eyes that took a moment to focus. Moving closer, Aran smelled the sharpness of whiskey.

"Better use some breath fresheners, Emerson," he said, not ungently.

"I'll be all right," Emerson muttered. "Sometimes, when I keep thinking I'll see Dolly walking through that door, it helps."

"I'll be away for a few days. I'm going down to Evan Taylor's place," Aran said. Emerson's eyes lifted. "I might find something. It's worth looking around," Aran said.

"I want you here for the meeting Friday," Emerson said.

"I'll be here," Aran answered. He saw Emerson's attention come to an end, the man's eyes shift away. He walked from the office, caught the elevator, and hurried out of the building. The line of marchers and the intense-eyed young man were before the building again, more placards in evidence now. Aran scanned them quickly.

THE ANGER OF THE LORD
IS RAISED!

THE SINS OF MAN. SEEK
NO FURTHER REASONS

FOR THE LAND SHALL BE
DESOLATE—Jeremiah

Aran went through the marchers and hurried on, hailed a cab, and reached the apartment just as Jenny was beginning to make dinner. He stopped her, saw dismay cross her face at once. "It'll only be for a day. I have to be back Friday for a meeting," he said, quickly telling her about Bixly's call and Evan Taylor's death.

Jenny shuddered. "The Keys ... they're so low and they curve right out into the Caribbean," she said.

"I'll be fine. There hasn't been much activity reported down there," Aran answered, but Jenny looked unimpressed. "I can catch a late flight into Miami, get a night's sleep, and go down to the Keys in the morning."

"Why go down there? What has Evan Taylor's suicide got to do with anything?" Jenny asked. "What do you think you'll find down there?"

"I don't know. Maybe not a damn thing, but the whole business is bothering me. I want to see it out for myself," Aran replied.

"Another gut feeling?"

"Maybe part of the same one. I don't know."

Her face edged a pout. "I won't be here when you get back, probably," she said. "Ted and Vivian will be coming back here Saturday."

"You're going back to the cottage?" Aran asked in surprise.

"No, to my place, in Falls Church," Jenny said.

"I'll have to get a hotel room when I get back here. I could get a double," Aran offered and she shook her head.

"No, I'll be happier at my place. You're all involved in this thing and you should be, but this way you won't be having to think about me waiting around for you. You can concentrate better without me here."

"Your car is at the cottage," he reminded her.

"I'll go there first and pick it up. In the morning," she added with emphasis, and leaned her head against him. "It's best this way, even though I'll be down in Falls Church. I'll just be waiting there for you."

He pressed his arms around her. "I'll get down to you in a few days," he said. "And I'll be back Friday. Can't you wait here till then? We could have Friday night together."

She shrugged consent. "I ought to spend some time Saturday with Vivian and Ted when they get back," she reflected, and turned and helped him pack his small bag. She insisted on driving to the airport with him. Every street corner with a newsstand was clustered with people waiting for the late editions. At the airport, another line of quiet marchers bore their placards about the Lord's anger and the fulfillment of prophecies. He hurried through them and into the lobby and Jenny kissed him quickly. "See you Friday night, soon as the meeting is over," he said.

"I'll be waiting," she said. "I still wish you wouldn't go down there." She waved a hand as he started to reply. "I know, writer's curiosity. Yours is overdeveloped. The man killed himself, that's all. He had his reasons, I'm sure."

"Only he shouldn't have, not now," Aran said.

"Nobody should. There's never a right time," she replied. He hurried down the corridor to the ticket desk with her words following. They stayed with him during the flight and he wondered if he were indeed being foolish to chase down to the Keys. Yet the strange, bitter, unsober tone of the phone conversation also clung, an unsettling obbligato to the enigma of Evan Taylor's suicide. He finally dozed off during the flight, then woke when they neared Miami. When he landed, he managed to find a room at a nearby motel and was glad to fall into bed. He left instructions to be called early and slept quickly, heavily.

The morning call woke him to bright sun streaming into the room and he dressed quickly and hurried downstairs to rent a car. Before driving south, he cut across the Julie Tuttle Causeway to Miami Beach, drove north along Collins Avenue, then south, through Miami Beach Drive, and down onto Collins again. The famous "Gold Coast" was crowded, as were the other beaches. No one was in the water, but the sand was its own sea of browning bodies. He watched one of the admiral's helicopter patrols pass overhead in a long sweep, flying north past Bal Harbour. Except for the absence of bathers in the water and pleasure boats plowing the blue waves, the scene was one of calm. The vacationers at Miami seemed confident of the safety of their expensive beaches and content with the sand and the sun. Most of them probably never went into the water anyway, Aran reflected.

He went on south across the MacArthur Causeway and headed for the Keys. He halted for something to eat and to remove his jacket in the dry, hot sun. Then he sped on, but it was a little past noon when he passed Key Largo, then on past the Pennekamp reef. He halted again to check out the address and ask directions, and finally turned from the causeway onto low sand and an unpaved road. The sharp, fresh smell of the sea surrounded him and then, along the edge of the water, he saw the cluster of low-roofed buildings standing alone along a narrow strip of sand, a line of palmetto trees at one side and yaupon dotting a small dune at the opposite side.

Aran halted the car, got out, and walked slowly around to the front of the largest building, which faced the sea. His eyes scanned four very large, interconnected tanks filled with sea water but nothing else and he stepped closer to them. They were sunk into the ground, a foot or so down from the stone edges running around each. He saw closed iron gates connecting each tank, the largest one leading directly out to the sea. They were obviously designed to hold marine creatures, he noted; then he turned away and walked to the curtained glass door of the house, pressed the bell, and waited. He idly scanned the smaller, shed-like building that jutted out near the tanks, noted the line of plastic pails against one wall and a long-handled vacuum attachment for cleaning the tanks.

He pressed the bell again, waited, finally heard sounds coming from inside the house, and then the sliding glass door was pulled back. The girl stood in the doorway, a highball glass in one hand. Aran took in reddish hair, full and loose around a high-cheek-boned face with a small nose and full, red lips. She was tall with a sultry hostility in her face. A brief, white cotton halter struggled to contain deep, heavy breasts. Her bare waist was tanned, narrow, flared into long, tattered jeans. She wore nothing under the brief halter, bold, sharp points pressing hard against the fabric. Her eyes were blue and somewhat bloodshot, he saw, and they peered at him with contained waiting.

"Kay Elliot?" Aran ventured. "I'm Aran Holder. We spoke on the phone yesterday." He waited and she continued to peer at him, studying him. "You don't remember?" he asked.

"I remember. You're the writer," she said. "Why'd you come rushing down here?"

"To talk to you," he answered. "I want to know more about what happened."

Her sultry hostility remained, but she finally pushed the door open wider and turned back into the house. "Come in," she said and he followed her inside. It was a large room strewn with papers, files, folders, stacks of ledgers, and two opened briefcases. An L-shaped coffeetable stood in front of a similar-shaped sofa in deep blue. Two bottles of gin rested on the table, one empty, the other half-full, along with glasses. Kay Elliot, moving a little unsteadily, he noted, slumped down onto the sofa and he saw one ballooning breast push itself upward half out of the halter. She gestured to the bottle and the glasses.

"Not right now, thanks," he said. She lifted her glass in a mock salute.

"Welcome to *Ab Ovo*," she sang out, pulled deep on the drink.

"*Ab Ovo*?" Is that what Evan called this place?" Aran asked.

"That's right," Kay Elliot answered. Aran half-frowned, pulled on past learning, Latin lessons long forgotten.

"From the very beginning, right?" he said after a moment.

"The man's a winner," the girl said, taking another drink from the glass, looking at it, noting it was almost empty.

"Any special reason for the name?" Aran asked.

"Evan loved the classics." The girl shrugged. "And he liked mystifying people. Few around here have any idea what it means." She lifted the glass, drained it, waved it at him, and reached for the bottle.

"When did you start today?" Aran questioned.

"Start? Stop? When I got up. Or when I went to bed. I forget," she said, leaning backward with the drink, stretching for a moment. She was really a quite extraordinarily attractive young woman, Aran decided. Even now, obviously on her way to getting drunk with determination, she radiated a powerful, feline sexuality and a mind that was undoubtedly sharp. He reached out, took the glass from her, and put it on the table. She let him, watching him with amusement.

"Ready to join me?" she smiled with mocking maliciousness.

"I want some questions answered while you can still answer them," Aran said.

"That's honest, at least," she said. "I like honesty." The girl focused on him, with a little effort, he noted. "You're nicer-looking than I expected," she commented.

"You expected I'd come down here?" Aran frowned.

"Oh, no. I just try to match faces with voices. It's a little game of mine," Kay Elliot said. Her mocking amusement suddenly turned off. "What questions?" she asked harshly.

"Why did Evan do it?" Aran asked.

She reached for the glass. "Try another. I don't know the answer to that one," she said.

He let her take the glass. "I think you do," he said. Her bright blue eyes concentrated on focusing on him again.

"I was too late to ask him," she said. It was a turning-aside answer, he knew.

"I'd say you've had enough to drink," Aran commented.

"How touching. You're concerned about little Kay," she said and suddenly there was acid in her voice.

"I'm concerned about getting answers, I told you," Aran snapped.

"More honesty," she said, taking a deep breath. Her breasts almost came through the white cotton halter, small, circled points making bold imprints. She looked up at him, tilted her head to one side. "Let's spend the rest of the afternoon screwing. How's that for honesty?" she said.

"Outside of the obvious reasons, why?" Aran asked.

She shrugged. "It makes me forget," she said.

"Forget what happened?"

"Forget everything. It's the only thing that really works." She lifted her glass. "Better than this crap," she snapped. Aran's eyes studied her. All the things he'd sensed in the brief phone conversation were here, magnified, the bitterness unmistakable, mixed in with a hint of something that seemed the shadow of fear.

"What happened with Evan? What made him do it?" Aran asked. Kay Elliot lapsed into sudden sullenness, pulled on her drink. "Is John Akberg still working here?" Aran questioned.

A short, bitter laugh escaped her. "John ran. Home, to Iowa. He ran."

"When?"

"Three days ago."

"Why? Something personal?"

Her eyes grew crafty and she smiled slowly, appreciatively. "Good try. You've a bit of the bulldog in you, don't you, Aran Holder?"

"What happened? How did it happen?" Aran pressed. Her face turned cross and she took a long drink.

"I came here for answers, Kay Elliot," Aran said. "I'm going to get them, from the police, from somebody, or from you, but I'll get them." She continued to drink and glower at him and he turned, went to the door, looked back at her. Inside the glower, a strange apprehension lurked in her eyes. "I'll be back," he said, pulling the door open.

"Evan Taylor was a great man, do you hear me?" she flung at him suddenly. "You can tell that to anyone who asks you. Tell them Kay Elliot said it and she knows."

Aran decided to spear harder. He returned to the sofa. She had a wall put up around herself, around all that had happened. Protectiveness? Or something more? He had to pierce it, hit hard enough to make it break.

"Were you making it with Evan?" he threw back harshly. He saw her hand come up in a wide swing as her face flushed. He blocked the blow, caught her wrist.

"Bastard," she spit.

"Were you?" he insisted.

"No, goddamn you, no," the girl shouted. "I wish I had been. Evan was making it with his work. That's all he could think about. He was too exhausted at the end of his sixteen-hour days to even sleep well."

Aran kept his grip on her wrist. "He had to know what's been going on. What did he say about it?" he pressed. He let go of her wrist and she stepped back, her breasts pushing hard against the cotton as she took deep breaths. He watched her face close in on itself.

"Leave Evan Taylor alone. He's gone now," she said. She sat down on the sofa, faced half-away from him and drained the glass. He'd get nothing more from her now, he knew. She had drawn the wall around herself again.

"I'll be back," he said again, but she didn't answer. He walked out of the house, started back to the car, and halted to look at the four, interconnected tanks again. They were large enough to hold anything: a dozen dolphins, a big ray, even belugas or the large sharks. He started to turn to the car, halted, his eyes narrowing as he gazed out over the blue of the water. A series of upright panels that seemed to be rising out of the water formed a line about two hundred yards offshore. He stared at them for a moment, was able to define nothing else about them, and continued to walk to the car. As he started to drive away, he glimpsed the window curtain being pulled back, the white of Kay Elliot's halter flashing as she watched him go.

It had been a strange and disturbing meeting with this sultry, attractive girl who seemed on a tremendous drunk. She was holding back something. But what? he asked himself. Plain loyalty to Evan Taylor's memory? Or a kind of love? He believed her answer about not making it with Taylor. It had been too full of honest fury to be a lie. But unfulfilled love could be even stronger than the consummated kind. Love on a pedestal had to be protected even more fiercely. Was it as simple as that? Aran asked himself and felt rejection spearing at him. There was something more in her evasions and sullen silences. And John Akberg, in her own words, had run off. He had run and she wanted to screw away the day, another kind of running. But beyond all that there was the fear that kept leaping into her eyes at quick, sudden moments. And the nihilistic bitterness that underlay her drinking and her remarks. That wasn't grief alone. That was something else.

Aran swung the car up to a one-pump gas station and halted by a man leaning over an open hood. He asked where he could find the police chief. "That'd be Chief Wilson in Key Largo," he was told. Aran swore silently, swung the car around, and headed back to Key Largo, fifty miles away. The day was sliding into late afternoon when he arrived in Key Largo and found the police station, only to be told that Chief Wilson had to go to Miami. "He'll be back," the deputy said, "about eight o'clock tonight." Aran asked about Evan Taylor's suicide and was told that only Chief Wilson could release any information to him. He went, cursing again to himself at the one-horse operations of small, municipal bureaucracies. He found a diner and sat down to a sandwich of stringy roast beef and coffee that was too weak. But he managed to kill an hour. He went into a phone booth and put in a collect call to Emerson, caught the man just about to leave the office.

"I've been delayed some," Aran told him. "But I'll be there in time for the meeting tomorrow."

"Aran, I'm depending on you to be there," Emerson cried out in instant alarm. "The meeting will be closed, of course, but the newshounds will be waiting afterward. Christ, they'll fire questions by the hundreds. I'm just not up to it, Aran."

"I'll be there," Aran repeated. "Nothing from the West Coast yet, is there?"

"No verified attacks, if that's what you mean. But every kid bitten by a crab causes a local panic out there. The whole coast is edgy as hell. Did you find anything out where you are?"

"Not yet," Aran said.

"Then why don't you get a plane back now?" Emerson urged nervously.

"I'll be there for the meeting," Aran said and hung up. He checked his watch, swore quietly, and went outside. He found a movie theater just opening its doors for the evening's first show, bought a ticket, and went into the cool darkness. He sat through the movie, seeing the screen but not seeing it, his mind full of unanswered questions. It was seven-thirty when he got out and he hurried from the theater with a handful of others, mostly teenagers, and walked back to where he'd left his car at the police station. Chief Wilson had returned, he was glad to find, and he was shown into an office with metal chairs, a metal desk, and metal file cabinets. Chief Wilson was a big, overweight man with sharp blue eyes that seemed smaller than they were in the beefy face. A neatly creased uniform managed to look rumpled on his big frame as he sat back in a swivel chair that creaked. Aran introduced himself, implied that he'd come down in his official capacity as press officer for the Bureau.

"It was suicide, all right, if that's why you're asking," the police chief said.

"How did he do it?" Aran queried.

"Gunshot. Shot himself with a Winchester three-o-eight slug," the policeman said.

"I see," Aran muttered and wondered why the girl had been so unwilling to say that.

"Only he did it in a funny kind of way," the policeman added. Aran's eyebrows lifted questioningly and Chief Wilson went on. "It seems he took a rowboat from his place and rowed out to sea, sometime about midnight, according to the girl who worked for him. He shot himself out at sea in the boat."

"How did you find him? The boat drifted back to shore?" Aran asked.

"What was left of him drifted back," the policeman grunted. "He'd been bitten in half. I guess they just attacked the boat when they saw it. In fact, we didn't figure a suicide until the medical examiner found the slug in his head."

Aran felt the shudder go through him. Perhaps that was why Jay Elliot wouldn't even talk about it—the terrible, shattering grimness of it. Yet why had Evan Taylor rowed out to sea to shoot himself? A gesture of some sort? What kind of gesture? To whom, to what? He pushed the questions aside for the moment, thanked the police chief, and rose to go, pausing at the door.

"Did you know Evan Taylor personally, Chief? Did he talk to you at all about his work?" Aran asked.

"Never met the man," the police officer answered. "He kept to himself and his place is pretty isolated, as you saw."

Aran nodded, left, and returned to his car. He sped off onto the causeway, heading back to see Kay Elliot again. There was still something more and she had the answers, he was certain. Grimly, he kept thinking that Evan Taylor's death, John Akberg's running away, and Kay Elliot's constant drunkenness were all part of one thing. Had Evan Taylor come upon a vision of tomorrow that had simply overwhelmed him? If so, wouldn't he have called the Bureau with what he'd found? Aran asked into the night The man was a committed scientist. He should have hastened to communicate his findings. But he hadn't. Because he wasn't sure enough? Because he couldn't offer proof yet?

Damnit, maybe there weren't any findings at all, Aran swore silently. Maybe it was all highly personal. But instantly, other questions hurled themselves at him. Why did Evan Taylor row out into the hostile sea to shoot himself? Aran shook away further speculation, refusing to ride the wild carousel of thoughts without answers. He concentrated on his driving and sped through the darkness that had come over the Keys. He finally turned off the causeway and onto the dirt road that led to Evan Taylor's place. The cluster of buildings were shrouded in darkness, except for one light from the drawn curtains of the living room that cast a diffused, dim glow. He halted the car, got out, and pressed the doorbell. There was no answer and he walked around the side, called out, got no reply. He returned to the front door and pressed the bell again, harder and longer. There was still no answer and he tried the door. It slid open and he went inside. Kay Elliot lay on the couch, sprawled there, the empty bottle on the floor beside her.

Aran went to the girl, shook her. She didn't stir. She had passed out, he saw, and he was angry. "Damn," he muttered aloud. It'd take hours to bring her around to where she could think and function, and he didn't have hours. He gazed down at her. She looked entirely peaceful and really quite lovely. He let his eyes go to the room off to the left, saw the edge of the bed inside it, and reached down to lift Kay Elliot from the couch. He carried her into the bedroom and put her down on the bed. She still didn't stir and only her steady breathing indicated she was alive. He left her there and returned to the living room and began to look through the files and ledgers and folders strewn about. The ledgers were mostly neatly entered dates, progress records of some kind with their ordered sequence. He collected a bundle of the loose papers and files and sat down with them and began to go through each one carefully.

He had expected material on marine communication, but he found detailed, voluminous records on embryology, cell-tissue culture and molecular structure. As he pored over the material, the frown that gathered on his brow stayed. Hours passed as he continued to study the material, and he finally rose and put aside everything to stand with his lips pursed, his brow furrowed. He walked from the living room, down a hallway to where a closed door ended the corridor. Pushing it open, he found himself in a small but well-equipped laboratory. Rows of vials and test tubes lined the walls, each with labels and numbers that he recognized as corresponding with the material he'd been examining. Aran moved along the rows, recognizing tissue cultures, viruses, some dead in their glass prisons, others very much alive. Finally, his face grown grave, Aran returned to the living room and went into the bedroom where Kay Elliot still lay across the bed where he'd put her. He wanted to shake her awake, pour coffee into her, take the long, slow process of bringing her around. But it was into the small hours of the night and there was no time for that. He had to leave if he was going to catch that first flight out of Miami.

He turned from the girl's sleeping form, walked out of the house, and paused outside. The air was still, humid, the sea quiet. Everything was quiet. Except inside him. There was no quiet there, only a terrible seething he could not call fear ... not yet. But it was made of fearfulness. As he slid behind the wheel of the car, Aran Holder held dark specters inside him. He glanced back at the low-roofed buildings and the silhouetted outline of the big tanks beyond them. "*Ab ovo,*" he murmured softly and the name now was shadowed with new meaning. But he refused to let his writhing, leaping thoughts race out of control. He had to go over his own notes again. That was suddenly terribly important. He had to read them with new eyes again. Then he'd return here, for the answers Kay Elliot had locked inside herself. Only now he wasn't sure that he wanted those answers, either.

Aran sped northward, to Key Largo and Miami, and in the warm night, he felt chilled.

CHAPTER EIGHT

I t was, that very moment, a time of answers.

To some questions that had been voiced. Only to some. On the other side of the Atlantic, dawn cascaded over the little harbor of Positano on the southern coast of Italy. The low, stone quays and wooden piers were already resounding to the shouts of the fishermen readying their small, masted craft. These were the men who went out each day for *scungili,* the much-in-demand, tasty octopus, gourmet dish and village staple.

Small boys, some from the village, some from the steep hills surrounding the harbor, were already gathering. Mostly all from poor homes, they would wait for the time when the vessels returned with their catch, to beg, coax, or steal some of the tentacled delights. The scene was being echoed in every harbor along the southern Italian coastline, in Naples, in Capri, in Sorrento, Amalfi, Agrópoli, all the way down into Calabria, wherever the boats set out for octopus.

The square, whitewashed stone house sparkled in the new sun as it looked down on the harbor of Positano. At one window, Tullio Costanza finished buttoning his trousers. He could see Captain Ruffo on board, barking orders, his bald head shining like a beacon. Pannini and Spezione were getting lines and nets ready and the others moved about the deck like so many ants. Tullio Costanza turned from the window to look across the room at Simonetta, still asleep on the big double-size mattress on the floor, taking in her heavy breasts with the large, round centers that rose and fell in rhythm, the wide-hipped lustiness of her crying out even in sleep. His lips drew back as he thought about going to her, waking her with his hands clasped into the dark, mossy core of her as they had been again and again during the night. His muscles moved with the throb and vibrancy of youth, the sheer animal vigor of his thirsting, young maleness.

But there wasn't time enough now, damn, he thought, pulling a T-shirt over his thick chest, brushing his hands through dense, black curly hair. He heard the girl stir behind him and glanced again at her. She half-smiled in contentment. Why wouldn't she be content? he snorted inwardly. She had had Tullio Costanza with her last night. Simonetta would be gone when he returned at the day's end, he knew, off for the week to pick olives at her uncle's place in San Sosti. He shrugged. Fiorenza would be here. He had been with her only the night before and he smiled as he thought about her wild tossings and turnings, her low, muffled, urging screams. No gentleness for Fiorenza; the rougher the better. So unlike Camilla, her sister. He almost laughed aloud when he thought about that. If Fiorenza knew about Camilla, or about Simonetta, there'd be screaming heard all the way to Rome.

But then, he'd made no promises to any of them, Tullio told himself. All day he fished for the octopus. He was having no tentacles around him on shore. Besides, he had a reputation to uphold. Even in Naples, everyone on the waterfront knew about Tullio Costanza and envied him and his way with the *ragazze*. With a last glance at Simonetta's sleeping loveliness, her full, lush body, he slipped out the door and ran down the steps, down along the narrow streets to the quays until he reached the boat. Captain Ruffo glared at him. "Late again," he snapped. "What *zitella inacidita* was it this time?

"*Zitella inacidita?*" Tullio roared. "You wish you could be Tullio Costanza, that's all." Tullio swung aboard and swaggered to where he kept his gear in the wooden chest alongside the gunwale. He could be late, he knew. He was as good catching octopus as he was catching women. Maybe there was a connection, he often thought. He fished for the *scungili* sometimes, but he liked most to dive for them, go after the good specimens. Often, as he swam in the water, watching through his face mask, the octopus made him think of a woman. The soft, round, bulbous center made him think of a woman's breast. It even felt smooth and palpable. They could squirm like a woman, too, he laughed to himself. And change colors the way a woman changes her mind—abruptly, instantly. But he always caught the ones he wanted. In the sea and on the land.

Tullio braced his feet on the deck as the lines were cast off and the boat began to move out of the harbor. He let the soft wind caress his face. This was what it was all about, anyway, he mused, working, living, eating, screwing. You took what you wanted out of life. You took it and the hell with everything else.

The boat moved out of the harbor, out into the blue Mediterranean, and the captain let the current carry her along into the shoreline. Six other boats out of the harbor were drifting not too far away. Tullio knew every man aboard them. They all knew each other and were friends. There was enough octopus for all. He watched lines being lowered into the water, a few small nets dropped overboard. He stripped down to the swim shorts he wore under his trousers, bent down and lifted the tank onto his back, adjusted the straps, and donned the face mask. Swinging over the edge of the boat, he dropped into the water, went down at once, disappearing into the blue-green world he liked almost as much as the one on shore. It was a world punctuated by the brilliant coral formations, the orange-red anemones, and the flashes of silver shapes darting through it.

The hull of the boat made a heavy, cigar-shaped outline above him and he saw some octopuses already caught on a line or the nets, most of them the small, Mediterranean species. He dived deeper and reached the bottom quickly. It was not very deep here and he frowned behind the face mask. The ocean bottom was covered with octopuses. He had never seen so many in one spot. The catch would be a great one today, for everybody. But he wanted the tastier, larger ones and he turned and swam for the rocks where they hid among the undersea crevices. Behind him, the swarm of cephalopods seemed almost eager to curl themselves around the lines hanging down for them.

Tullio Costanza moved smoothly along the rocks, slowed as he saw a pair of tentacles protrude over the edge of a reef formation. He changed direction, headed for them, saw two more suctioned arms rise, and then the cephalopod rose fully into view. Tullio almost halted. Mother of God, this was a big one, much bigger than was usual in these waters. But he knew his octopuses—big or little they'd try to flee. Any fight they offered would be purely defensive, clinging to their attacker only to spurt away at the first opportunity.

He circled, came at the octopus from the other direction, positioning it between himself and a flat piece of rock. He frowned again at the size of the tentacles, triple those usually found here where the small Mediterranean cephalopod reigned. He waved an arm to the left, prepared for the creature to spurt to the right, where he was set to seize it. He saw the octopus change color, from a pale gray to a reddish-brown, and suddenly, it emitted a powerful jet of water and shot forward. Not to the right, but directly at him. Taken by surprise, Tullio found himself wrapped in tentacles, and pulled downward. But he'd been enmeshed in tentacles before, though not so large or so powerful as these. He was experienced. He pushed back, pulled one arm from around his shoulders, unwound another from his waist and was half-turned away from the creature, pulling at still another arm, when he gave a silent cry of pain behind his face mask as the sharp, powerful beak bit deep into his shoulder.

The pain shot an extra burst of strength through him and he pulled free of the tentacles and whirled in the water to see the octopus coming for him again. He swam backward, fending off its tentacles as it groped for him, gliding effortlessly after him. Tullio's frown was one of incomprehension. Octopuses didn't behave in this fashion, attacking, biting—not man, certainly. He dived down under the waving arms, evading the creature, and then, his eyes widening, he saw two more octopuses moving out of the rocks toward him. These were both larger than the first one, he saw in astonishment. He spun in the water, struck out for the surface, and felt tentacles wrapping around his waist. He ignored them and continued to strike out for the surface. He felt more tentacles encircling his waist, didn't waste time to wrestle them off, and then he felt the pain—sharp, excruciating—this time in his thigh. He felt a wave of nausea go through him. Octopuses could discharge a poisonous toxin, he knew, used to paralyze their prey, but he continued to fight his way upward.

He broke the surface of the water with the octopus still cling-ing to him and was about to lift his face mask off and call out for help when, his eyes widening, he saw the scene in front of him. The six small boats, stretched in a half-circle, seemed a writhing mass of tentacles. Crewmen were rolling on the decks, all but covered with octopuses and, as he looked on in horror, he saw three men plunge into the sea wrapped in coils. Most of the hun-dreds and hundreds of *scungili* were the small, Mediterranean octopuses they had always caught, but many others were two and three times larger, the heavy Atlantic cephalopod. But the small as well as the large were all biting ferociously with their sharp beaks, clinging with their suctioned tentacles as they bit again and again. None were attempting to flee, but were attacking with fury and viciousness.

Tullio Costanza glimpsed the captain of his vessel, Ruffo, at least two dozen of the creatures on him, one wrapped around his head, biting deeply into the bald scalp. Tullio watched the lines of blood moving down across the tentacles. "It is a scene from hell," he murmured before the pain in his leg came again. Now he felt almost numb. He tried to swim, lifted an arm, but found it was held tightly. Suddenly he was being pulled back beneath the surface of the water. He tried to fight, but a powerful tentacle held his left arm immobilized and he couldn't move his leg. He tried to wriggle, squirm, but tentacles held him firmly. Normally, he could unravel the suckered arms, for Tullio Costanza was a young and virile man. Hadn't he proved that often enough, he asked himself. But it was the pain and numbness in the lower part of his body that made him helpless. He saw another eight-armed creature move toward him, wrap itself around him, also, and now he was being dragged down to the rocks where he had caught so many of these creatures.

His back hit against the rocks and he saw a tentacle squirming up before his face mask, felt it catch hold and rip the mask from him. The water felt pure and cold as it rushed over his face, and then he glimpsed the other octopus detach itself, spurt around and move directly at him, suddenly deep red-brown in color. Tullio tried to struggle, but the numbness had made him weak. He got an arm free, had all he could do to push against one of the tentacles. The second octopus spread its arms out, starfish fashion, blocking out the light that filtered down from the surface of the water. Tullio, horror-stricken, saw it close in on him. It was the habit of many of the *scungili* fishermen to dispatch the small octopuses with a quick bite between the eyes and now Tullio saw the powerful beak in the center of the creature's body come down to bite him right between the eyes. It couldn't be, Tullio told himself in his last, fleeting moment of life. It couldn't be. Octopuses always fled ... just fled. It couldn't be. Only it was, and, slowly, the cephalopod began to suck away at Tullio Costanza.

Above, on the surface of the sea, the small boats from Positano drifted aimlessly, silent now, their crews pulled into the water or lying grotesquely amid nets and fish lines on the decks. In the harbor itself, at the edge of the stone quays, a shout of glee went up from the waiting youngsters as they glimpsed the small octopuses foolishly clambering up along the stones and wood pilings. They, too, knew the shy fear of the *scungili* and they rushed to seize the scuttling creatures. Their cries of pain, surprise, then fright echoed across the waterfront as the small Mediterranean octopuses sank very sharp beaks deep into flesh. Shopkeepers and passing men and women rushed to aid the youngsters, to find themselves bitten, their legs wrapped around with clinging tentacles. Many of the youngsters fell with cramps and nausea, some with multiple bites as they writhed and screamed on the quays. Other people ran from the waterfront shops with shovels, rakes, brooms, some even carrying chairs to use as weapons. They struck at the octopuses that moved with surprising speed, and pushed at hundreds more that came out of the water, scuttling to attack.

The people retreated, wielding their implements as best they could, trying to drag the youngsters into the houses. The retreat was less difficult than striking at the cephalopods, as the scuttling creatures only stayed out of the water long enough to seize a leg or an arm and sink their beaks deeply into flesh. Some people, who had been attacked by a number of the small octopuses, or who had fallen, were severely bitten, the others only painfully.

It seemed only a matter of minutes, and indeed it wasn't much more, before the octopuses dived into the water to disappear.

The fishermen in the boats offshore suffered the real attacks, the swarming hordes that bit and bit and killed all within reach. It was only later that the world learned that what had happened at Positano was repeated all along the Italian coastline south, all the way to Sicily. One craft, out of Naples, was attacked by octopuses larger than any man aboard had ever seen. Another boat, out of Amalfi, returned with one survivor, an old man who repaired nets for the others. He told of how the *scungili* had swarmed up out of the water on the lines and nets, over the boat, hundreds of them, choking and immobilizing with their tentacles, then biting deep with their beaks. He told of how he saw one seaman attempt to hide himself in an old steamer trunk just below decks, but a huge octopus with ten-foot-long tentacles swarmed over the trunk for a moment, then lifted the lid with its suctioned arms and descended over the helpless man inside.

It was the beginning—an answer to fears and questions, to wonderings and conjecture. And it seemed almost a signal. At the same time as the octopuses attacked, fishing trawlers leaving the English port of Plymouth to steam into the English Channel were suddenly surrounded by thousands of halibut, flounder, turbot, and wolffish. Nets were simply ripped away by the sheer weight of numbers and boats were pushed into each other, smashed against one another, and panic overtook captains and crews—and then the seething mass of fish vanished. It was, one fisherman said later, as if they were showing us what could be done.

Dutch herring boats out of the West Frisian islands, on the other hand, found not a herring anywhere and returned with nets empty save for a few, lone fish. Along the English coast resort beaches at Blyth, South Shields, Whitby, and Scarborough— halibut, cod, and Atlantic salmon descended upon bathers with vicious attacks, sweeping in from the North Sea. French beaches also came under attack at Quiberon, Saint-Nazaire, La Rochelle, all the way down to Biarritz. As had happened across the sea, along the coast of the United States, thousands of bathers were killed by piranha-like attacks.

By the day's end, fishing fleets from Norway to Spain reported that they had either had their nets ripped loose by masses of fish or they netted no catch at all, saw no fish whatever. The cephalopod attacks on the Italian coast were followed by fish attacks on bathers also. What had happened along the Atlantic coast of North America was duplicated: the attacks, the panic, and the helplessness of the authorities. But it had an even uglier, more ominous ring to it. To those countries—particularly the islands of Britain, Scotland, Ireland; and the low-lying countries of Holland, Belgium, and Denmark—the sea provided a much higher proportion of table food than it did to the United States. Authorities gathered their marine scientists at once for urgent meetings and knew, even as they met, that their counterparts across the sea had as yet found no answers.

It had spread, and the full impact was only beginning to be felt. It had spread, and with it, the helplessness, the incomprehension, and the corrosive touch of fear.

The cephalopods figured in one more report that day, this time across the sea off the southern Bahamas. Six men sailed out of Little Exuma on the sixty-foot ketch, *Dolores*. Being Bahamians, they weren't violating the order against pleasure boating which had jurisdiction over United States citizens only. Also, all being members of the Bahama Tourist Board, they had decided to do something dramatic to show that events really weren't all as frightening as the news media made them sound. And, moreover, the waters around the Bahamas had been singularly free of trouble. Tourism, which came mostly from the United States, anyway, had fallen off to practically nothing. Something had to be done, something to catch the eye of the news media, not just another advertising effort to encourage tourists. A sail around the Bahamas on the old ketch, which belonged to Malcolm Eleazar, who really thought of the scheme, would certainly do the trick.

They sailed south first, to round the southern end of the islands, Malcolm Eleazar at the tiller. They were just passing the tip of Acklins Island when the ketch was rocked on its side, heeling half-over, then still further. Malcolm Eleazar managed to cling to the tiller as he saw three of the others catapult over the side. Only then did he see the tentacles—tremendous, thick, suctioned arms—pulling the ketch over on its side. Malcolm Eleazar could only stare at what he saw as he clung to the tiller: the largest tentacles each at least twenty-five feet long; the soft, bulbous body pushing itself half onto the deck; and then, another octopus, perhaps a little smaller with arms each twenty feet long, emerging next to the first. Both sent out huge tentacles, wrapped them around a mast, and pulled. The ketch went over all the way and Malcolm Eleazar closed his mouth as the water swept over him. He felt himself spin back along the overturned stern of the ketch, then he came free in clear water and surfaced.

The vessel lay like a dead fish, keel-up in the water, and he was close enough to grasp hold of the rudder stem. One of the huge octopuses half-straddled the ketch at the bow while he saw the other holding two of his companions, Elliman and Turner, in its huge tentacles, strangling them as it bit deep into each man. Malcolm Eleazar clung to his hold on the rudder stem. He didn't try to swim away. He heard someone else shout, a brief cry, then a hoarse scream, and then nothing else. He continued to cling to his place. Perhaps that was why he was the only survivor. As he watched, the huge octopus slowly slid down from the overturned bow and moved through the water with small jets of thrust, suddenly streamlined and graceful. It turned suddenly, half-lifted the ketch from underneath, as if to see if there were anyone still hiding inside it, then let it drop back. It turned, spread its arms starfish fashion, and sank out of sight.

Malcolm Eleazar clung to the rudder of the ketch and wondered if he were having a nightmare. It had been less real than some nightmares he'd had. His eyes looked across the blue Caribbean waters, lapping gently against the overturned ketch, and, slowly, he pulled himself up onto the barnacled bottom of the hull, now the top of the vessel as it lay out of the water. He sat there, spread-legged, and the hot sun burned down upon him. But Malcolm Eleazar was twice blessed with luck. The *Dolores,* lifeless and overturned as she was, wallowed in a strong current. It carried her to South Bluff on Acklin's Island where the floating hulk was spotted from shore. A powerboat put out and picked him up and brought him ashore where he gasped his story into the transmitter belonging to a man who operated a citizen's band radio. Later, a United States Navy helicopter came and picked him up, flying him to Miami for a full interrogation. Malcolm Eleazar told them exactly what had happened, and the size of the octopuses. He didn't care if they thought he was exaggerating. He didn't give a damn what they thought. He cared only that he was alive. And he very much doubted that he'd ever be able to eat octopus again.

Exhausted from being up all night and the drive back from the Keys, Aran slept aboard the flight, waking only once to have breakfast, then sleeping again until he reached Boston. He heard the reports from Europe on the radio of the taxi he hailed to take him from the airport to the Fish and Wildlife Offices. Once again, though the day was hot, he felt chilled. Once again he found himself fervently hoping that Leslie Streeter would announce that his analysts had pinpointed the cause, had found changes in the marine chemistry. Once more he hoped for sound, scientific explanations. God, how he hoped for that! Aran prayed silently.

He reached the office in time to freshen up and read the official reports, which were stacked in order of arrival, those on the octopus attacks first. Grim estimates of the dead added a shriveling footnote to each report. He met Emerson in the hallway. The man's face was flushed, tiny red veins in his cheeks standing out boldly. "God, am I glad you're here," Emerson gasped. "After what's happened today there'll have to be a full statement issued. The President's sent a special representative to the meeting," Emerson said. "Did you learn anything worthwhile down at Evan Taylor's place?"

"I haven't learned anything yet," Aran said, choosing words. It was the truth. He had learned nothing. He had found only shadows. He followed Emerson into the conference room and was introduced to Ernest Shuster, the President's representative and head of the Environmental Protection Agency. Shuster was a tall man with deep-set, grave eyes in a long, lean face. Aran took a seat beside Shuster and his glance swept the others. All seemed to be guarding their expressions behind set faces, except for Admiral Hotchins. He wore an air of patient impatience. Emerson asked Eakins, the ichthyologist, to lead off.

"We've examined over a hundred different specimens, some of those involved in actual attacks, which we were able to catch," Eakins began. "We found no variations or altered aspects organically, no change in blood content, heartbeat, neurological systems. We found no changes in circulatory systems, respiration rates, no identifiable alterations of any sort. I'm afraid we must rule out anything in this sector."

He sat down and Roy Waite came next. "So far we've been able to detect no new, powerful convection currents. I still believe this to be a very real possibility. I can't offer evidence, though, at this time."

Aran watched Leslie Streeter rise, the biochemist's usual self-assurance absent. "Nothing, gentlemen," Leslie Streeter said almost brusquely. "Absolutely nothing. No chemical changes in the molecular structure of sea water, no changes in plankton or any of the other minute marine organisms. The elements contained in ocean water have shown no change in balance or presence. We took samples during different times of the day and night, just in case an upwelling might be causing biochemical changes. We found nothing." Leslie Streeter threw his hands up in a gesture of defeat.

"Has the fact that this has spread to European waters given you any new directions for seeking answers?" Ernest Shuster questioned, his eyes sweeping the room. Streeter answered for the others.

"It only compounds our problems," the man replied. "Right now I can only wonder if some new element is perhaps acting on marine life and being absorbed without leaving a trace. The possibility is remote, yet it must be considered."

Aran sat silently, listening to the sound of defeat and frustration. He thought of Jenny's theory of phylogenetic advance, of a sudden, evolutionary leap. He would have offered it once, but now he kept silent. He would say nothing yet. He felt only impatience filling him, pushing at him to get up and race out of the room, back to his notes. Not that he would find answers there, but shadows might be given shape ... and fear given new depths. He heard Ernest Shuster's voice, returned his attention to the meeting.

"With what has happened today in European waters, the President has called an immediate meeting with other heads of state on what will quickly be a very serious food problem," the man said. "As no one here can offer scientific explanations for what is happening, and therefore no solutions, not even an estimated timetable for a solution, long-range plans must be pre-pared now."

Aran listened with lips compressed. Ernest Shuster's con-cern, his looking ahead, was more than wise. The hostility of the sea would be more devastating than anyone here could yet foresee.

"Do you think it will spread into the Pacific waters?" he heard Shuster ask. "The Japanese government is very concerned."

"I still believe it's the result of a vast subterranean fissure. That would create a gyre encompassing the entire North Atlantic basin," the oceanographer answered. "If so, it'll be confined to the Atlantic and its peripheral waters."

"And if it's really a biochemical change in the composition of the sea, it will spread," Shuster finished. The silence was his reply. Aran saw the man's eyes find him. "I understand you're handling press relations on this, Mr. Holder," the President's man said. "I suggest the American people be told only that we still have no answers or explanations for what is happening."

"I doubt that'll satisfy the news media or the people," Aran said. "They'll want to know if it'll get worse."

"Tell them the truth, that we don't know. But the President is concerned that no statement be issued which will increase any air of panic. There's always time for more pessimistic reports."

"The truth but not the whole truth," Aran remarked, unable to hide the acid in his reaction.

"We don't know just what the whole truth is yet," Shuster replied, not without validity, Aran admitted silently. "Admiral Hotchins has indicated that in his belief we can control the effects of this strange marine organism behavior."

"I hope so. The admiral's efforts so far haven't been outstandingly successful," Aran returned, watched Admiral Hotchins fasten him with a hard eye as he rose to address the others.

"I'll tell you one thing. We'll get fish on the table, kelp and seaweed into manufacturing plants, and fish oil into the chemical companies," Admiral Hotchins boomed out. "While you fellows go on analyzing and testing. I'm going to send out warships, heavy cruisers if I have to, with steel nets strung between them. I'll put out a mine-sweeping operation, all the way down to ocean bottom. We'll bring up every damn fish around."

"That just might be the key statement," Aran said, and the admiral halted to glower at him.

"The sea's full of fish. They won't just vanish," Hotchins barked. "They won't evaporate. They're there."

"A country can be full of guerrilla fighters that don't vanish either. They're there, too, but not where you want them," Aran retorted. The admiral had lost none of his arrogance, Aran commented to himself. Nor had the man improved his comprehension any. He saw the disdain in Hotchins' eyes.

"Do you really think any concentration of fish can stand up to the firepower of the United States Navy?" the admiral pressed.

"No, but that just might not be the contest—brute force against brute force. I remind you that your destroyer *Stevenson* was rendered helpless and the tuna fleet made into a shambles," Aran said.

"That was a convoy operation and the other vessels were undisciplined," Hotchins snapped. "I'll admit we were surprised by the suicidal nature of the assault, but our people will be prepared for that kind of thing now. This will be very different. If there's any mass attack—fish, lobsters, octopuses, whales; I don't give a damn what—guns and depth-charges will go into action. The crews will be at battle stations."

Shuster's voice cut in. "What about the use of submarines, Admiral?" the man questioned.

"We've considered that carefully. Submarine commanders feel that the attack value of undersea craft is questionable in this problem. There's some doubt that a torpedo fired into even a heavy mass of fish would explode. It might just push right through instead. Of course, against a big, stationary target such as a whale they'd be effective. But for now, we feel that submarines would be most valuable in underwater observation and pursuit of concentrations. Subs might be able to pinpoint areas of gathering deep down under the surface where air spotters couldn't penetrate."

A murmur of other questions rose, all directed at the admiral, who went into detail on the plans to make the Navy into armed fishing vessels. Aran listened, made notes which he knew he'd need for the press conference that would surely follow the meeting. Finally, the meeting closed down with Shuster again warning that the President wanted no statements issued except official ones and even those were not to be unduly negative. Shuster's eyes met his, the man's words pinpointed, and Aran nodded slowly and kept his glance noncommitally bland.

The others rose and moved off in different directions, each alone with his failure to provide answers. Aran hurried into the small office that he used, drafted an official statement, and finally faced the crowded room of waiting news people. He gave out the official statement, then answered the questions thrown at him, detailing the admiral's plans and trying to sound positive. Feeling more than slightly guilty, he nonetheless managed to convey optimism and was somehow able to make the admiral's plans sound as though they might be successful and that he believed in them. It helped to offset the real admission of the official statement, the bitter fact that they had no explanations, no answers, no promises.

Finally, the questions and the shouting came to an end and the mob of news-media people hurried away. Aran returned to his small office for a moment, checked the last sheaf of reports once again, and then walked from the room. He passed the partly open door to Emerson's office and paused as he saw Emerson, sitting alone in the fading light of dusk, taking short, quick gulps from a flask. It won't help, he wanted to say, and found himself thinking of Kay Elliot. It hadn't really helped her, either, he mused silently, then he hurried down the hallway to the elevator.

Downstairs, the intense-eyed young man led a larger group of marchers in a quiet vigil. Aran noted that the onlookers had grown in numbers, their eyes grave, full of privacies. He hailed a cab and was at the apartment in minutes. Jenny was clinging to him before he could close the door.

"Oh, God, you're back. I was so worried, especially after the reports this morning," she said, finally stepping back. "It keeps getting more and more unbelievable." She shuddered, paused. "Octopuses now. It seems almost a crazy dream."

"You find the involvement of octopuses hard to believe?" he asked quietly.

"Yes, I guess so," she said. Aran walked into the living room with her.

"The octopus is considered by many marine biologists to have the most complex brain of all invertebrates and an intelligence superior to anything in the sea except for the marine mammals," Aran said, and saw the surprise in Jenny's eyes. "It has the most sophisticated nervous system of what we call the lower animal forms and an octopus eye is physically much the same as a human's. They've demonstrated their intelligence in captivity, figuring out some problems faster than primates."

Jenny's eyes stared into space for a moment. "Maybe every-thing thinks more than we realize; thinks more, knows more, feels more, *is* more," she murmured.

"Maybe," Aran echoed.

"And the story of that man in the Bahamas—was he exag-gerating the size of those octopuses?" she asked.

"Probably not," Aran said. "There is so much down in the sea that we've never seen, creatures of a size that we can only guess about. It's time we stopped being so goddamn skeptical, thinking we know it all. Christ, the evidence is around for us to see. Less than eighty years ago, Professor Wood, writing in the *National History Magazine,* told of an octopus cadaver found at St. Augustine, Florida, that weighed six tons. The tentacles, it was estimated, must have been seventy to ninety feet long. Hell, squid with fifty-foot tentacles aren't uncommon now."

Jenny turned away, her eyes deep, fearful. "Where will it end?" she asked. "Will it end?"

"I don't know," Aran said. "But I think this is only a beginning."

She shook away further thoughts, plunged into mundane practicalness. "I didn't know when you'd be here. I was just start-ing hamburgers for myself. You must be hungry," she said.

"Not very, but a hamburger sounds fine. I'll be going over my notes," he said and sat down before the coffeetable where his file folder rested. He pulled everything out, starting back with Candy Nolan and the big blue whale. That seemed so very long ago now. He read quickly, turning pages, scanning answers with a purpose, searching for only one thing now. He was more than halfway through when Jenny called him to the kitchen to eat, and he put them down and went inside with her. He ate out of habit more than anything else and was sipping coffee when her ques-tion intruded into his thoughts as if from a faraway place.

"Where are you, Aran?" she asked quietly. "Not here, not with me."

He let the sigh escape him. "I'm sorry," he apologized.

"No, don't be sorry. I understand, really I do. I just wondered where you were," she answered.

"I'm going back," he said softly. "Tonight. I can make that late flight." The disappointment washed into her face but her eyes held his.

"Something in your notes, isn't it?" she asked. "You think you've found something."

"I'm not sure, not of anything, not yet. I just know I have to get back there as fast as I can. I've got to follow through."

"For yourself?"

"For me, maybe for all of us."

"You're afraid. I can feel it. Something's frightening you," she said. "And I'm afraid, too, then."

He wanted to deny her remarks, but found that he couldn't summon words. She wasn't on target, not completely, yet she was close enough. "Are you familiar with something called genetic engineering?" he asked, finding it difficult to form the words.

"In a vague sort of way. It's advanced molecular biology, isn't it?" Jenny said. "It's using DNA in ways we never thought possible, changing around genes and all that sort of thing."

"It's more than just changing them around. It's been called gene surgery, genetic therapy, genetic mutation. Some believe that DNA, that molecule which is the center of each cell, controls more than simple heredity as we used to understand the term. It's thought that DNA governs memory, habits, the very cast of the mind, all kinds of characteristics we once thought were only acquired."

Jenny frowned in thought. "Haven't they been able to combine cells of different species, even using mammalian cells and putting them into different organisms using bacteria and viruses as a carrying agent?"

"That's right. The World Health Organization's Advisory Committee put it this way. 'By overcoming the usual biological barriers between species, as offered by these new methods of genetic engineering, organisms can be created and propagated which possess completely new characters.' That means a point has been reached where it is possible to create forms of life never known before on earth."

"It sounds like science fiction," Jenny said.

"Only it isn't. It's very real. It's been done, mostly in cell-tissue culture, but frogs, toads, and chickens have been grown through genetic engineering methods."

"It scares me. It scares some of the people working in it, too. Didn't a group call a voluntary halt to their work in this field?"

"Yes, but the now-famous conference in Pacific Grove, California, The Asilomar conference, decided that work should go ahead under a set of stringent guidelines they adopted, controls aimed at biohazards." Aran paused, grunted, his mouth tightening. "Controls," he said. "A word, a set of recommendations. In practice, everyone is their own boss in sticking to them."

"Why are you asking me this, Aran? Do you think this is behind what's been happening?" Jenny questioned.

"I don't know, damnit, I don't know," he exploded, surprising himself as his fist pounded the table. "Maybe I'm crazy. Maybe I'm just reaching out wildly, seeing all kinds of far-out possibilities because there's nothing else to explain it, to hang on to. All I know is that the other theories don't satisfy me. They all have holes that won't go away."

"That's why you're rushing back down there tonight," Jenny said.

"I have to know what Evan Taylor found out. There was something. I want to know why he killed himself," Aran said intensely. He saw Jenny nod ruefully.

"How long this time?" she asked.

"Not long. I'll get answers if there are any down there or I'll find out there's nothing. It'll be that simple."

"You know where I'll be," she said, and uttered a short, wry snort. "I feel as though I ought to be giving out cards: Miss Jennifer Vandam will be receiving at home." She came against him suddenly, pressed hard to him. "I'm afraid, Aran. Let someone else go down there. Tell someone else. Let them find the answers."

"No one else would buy it. I don't really buy it myself, but it's eating at me and I've got to find out," he told her. He stepped back, began to pack the small bag he'd only brought back a few hours ago. He put in fresh shirts and underwear, a new blade in his razor, zipped up, and went to where Jenny waited, leaning against the wall. "I'll call you in Falls Church, soon as I've anything to tell," he promised.

He kissed her, left with her round, fear-filled eyes going with him. He was able to book passage on the late flight to Miami. When he boarded the plane, he settled deep into his seat and slept. It was a fitful, restless sleep, yet better than none at all. In Miami, the same young woman was on duty at the car rental desk and speeded him through. He managed a glimpse at the newspapers on a nearby stand, saw that they were giving full play to the admiral's pronouncements and plans. Aran glanced at his watch as he climbed into the car, estimated the time when he'd get there. He didn't care. He wasn't here to abide by social etiquette.

He drove fast, swinging onto the Florida Turnpike as soon as he could, then crossing onto the Keys. On the causeway, he was a lone traveler with the sea on his left, the vast, black expanse of it traced by a thin path from a half-moon. There were houses along the way, dark bulky silhouettes, most only a few dozen yards from the water. All were dark, he noted, and no doubt emptied. Never populous, the Keys seemed desolate now. It was a vulnerable place, this low finger of land, vulnerable to the fury of the wind and the power of the sea, and now to the death that could rise from the ocean depths. Crustaceans swarming up here could cover the narrow, low land in minutes, he reflected. He peered forward, following the headlights as they opened the darkness ahead of him, wondering if, suddenly, they would pick out a multitude of waving claws covering the causeway. He smiled grimly at the workings of the mind and sped on.

It was silent and dark when he finally drew up in front of Evan Taylor's buildings. The big window of the main house was curtained, but a light inside slipped around the edges of the drape. Aran knocked and waited, but got no answer. He knocked again and then pulled on the handle of the sliding door. It opened at once and he stepped into the house. A lamp burned and the room was as he'd left it hardly twenty-four hours ago, strewn with papers and file folders. "Kay?" he called. No one answered. He called again, then moved forward to an open door that led to another room. He pushed it aside and saw a bedroom, her form outlined atop the bed. He stepped inside, found a small lamp, and put it on. Kay Elliot lay on the bed in slacks and a loose deep-blue blouse, barefooted, her legs drawn up, her body curled around an empty gin bottle still half-cradled in her arms. He took the bottle away, shook her.

"Kay, wake up," he said. She half-turned, more from his touch than anything else. He shook her again and her eyes didn't even flicker. Aran stepped back, removed his jacket, then his shirt. He reached, grasped her arms, and pulled her to a sitting position.

She started to topple over, but he caught her, held her there, and shook her again. She murmured, but her eyes remained closed.

"No ... drink ... give me ..." she half-whispered. Aran knelt down, pulled her forward onto his shoulder and lifted, rose with her and carried her limp form into the bathroom. He put her into the tub and turned the faucets on from the shower. Water sprayed down on the girl and he saw her body twitch involuntarily. He turned the faucets on full force and she was soaked in moments, her mouth opening, gasping, as she struggled to open her eyes. She half-turned in the tub and the blouse came open, her deep, smooth breasts falling forward. He reached down, pulled the blouse from her and let the hot water sting her flesh. She had magnificently round, full breasts, he saw, tiny pink nipples cresting each cream mound. Kay Elliot's eyes were opening and closing and she was mumbling sounds.

He shut the hot water off, turned on the cold all the way, and she half screamed. "No, stop. Goddamn it, stop," she said, her voice thick yet. She tried to climb from the tub, but he pushed her back, his hands slipping across the wet smoothness of her breasts. She was awake now, crying and swearing and shivering. He put the hot water back on again and she screamed, then he switched back to the cold only and once again she screamed. "Stop, Christ, stop," the girl pleaded and she was quivering, her eyes wide now as, slipping, she tried to clamber from the wet tub. He shut off the water and she lay grasping the edge of the tub, her eyes staring at him. He was wet, too, small trickles of water coursing down his bare back. He pulled her out of the tub, saw her go down on her knees, her stomach heaving as she began to retch. She pressed her soaked slacks against the tub, lowered her head over the side, and he straightened up and left her alone. He found the kitchen, rummaged through the cupboard and found tea, and made a strong kettleful.

She was slumped on the floor, her head against the round edge of the tub as he returned with the cup of tea. She looked up at him, tried to find anger, but was still too nauseous. He gave her the tea and she drank it, then a second cup when she finished the first. He got a third into her and finally she put her head back, a deep groan sliding from her lips. "Oh, God. Oh, Jesus," she said. He pulled her to her feet, his arm around her, and walked her to the sofa in the living room. She stood up unsteadily and caught at his arm. He pushed her onto the sofa.

"I'll bring you some towels," he said. He returned with two thick beach towels. He went into the bedroom as she pulled off her slacks and dried herself, returned with another pair of slacks and a blouse he found in her bureau. She put the clothes on as he took the tea kettle back to the kitchen; she was dressed when he came back into the living room. Her breasts, still damp, outlined themselves against the blouse and her eyes were red-rimmed but focusing clearly. She stared at him as he halted before her.

"Bastard," she said, but there was no fury in her voice, only resignation.

"Sorry," he said. "But I want you sober. I want answers, once and for all."

"I don't have any," she said sullenly.

"You know plenty. You're holding back," Aran said.

"You don't know that," she countered.

"Last night, after talking to the police, I came back here. You were passed out, dead drunk."

"Peace, it's wonderful," she said.

"I sat down, almost till dawn. I read all the papers, looked through every folder and ledger. I went into the lab next door," Aran said through tight lips. He saw her look of mixed hostility and apprehension.

"You had no right," she growled.

"I had every right," Aran said. He leaned forward. "It's not your private pain, not any longer." He saw the apprehension in her eyes become something else, a kind of inwardly turned fear. "Evan Taylor was deeply into genetic engineering. It was clear from his papers," Aran said. "How deeply? What had he learned?"

Kay Elliot stared back at him and in her eyes he saw the fear struggling with itself. "Why did he kill himself?" Aran pressed. "Evan killed himself. John Akberg ran. You've been hiding in a bottle. Why? It has something to do with what's been happening, hasn't it?"

"What makes you say that?" she returned quickly, her eyes suddenly touched with caution.

"Evan wouldn't kill himself at a time like this," Aran shot back. "There has to be a connection. Something to do with dolphins. He was working with dolphins, wasn't he?"

The caution deepened. "Why do you say that?" she returned carefully.

"Those four tanks outside are typical of tanks for dolphin work; plenty of room. But mostly because of my interviews. I went back over each one. Candy Nolan had seen dolphins leaping in the distance just before the whale attacked. So had the skipper of the Sheepshead Bay party boat and one of the helicopter patrol pilots mentioned seeing dolphins in his report. Some other survivors had mentioned that, too; a passing remark in the interviews. But when I looked for it, it made a pattern. Now you tell me, what had Evan learned about the dolphins?"

Kay Elliot shook her head, stared into space. "No dolphins," she murmured. "They didn't see dolphins." Aran felt the frown pull at his brow. She turned her eyes to him, met his stare. "We weren't working with dolphins," she said.

"What were you working with?" Aran questioned, frowning.

"Killer whales," the girl said softly. "Not dolphins, killer whales."

Aran heard his own gasp of surprise. Killer whales, he thought, his mind racing, *Orcinus orca*. Of course, he thought. They would look like dolphins to the average person, even to experienced seamen at a distance. They had the same shape, same structure, same behavior in the water. Actually, both were members of the same order, Odontoceti, scientifically called: the order of toothed whales. Dolphins were smaller members of the family, but from a distance the size would be a minor difference.

"Why killer whales?" Aran asked.

"They're more intelligent than dolphins, much more so. The Navy experimental labs have learned this, too. The killer whale learns faster, responds to more things more quickly. In fact, we don't know how intelligent they are. We can hear only a fraction of the sounds they make. We don't know what they receive, or impart, with sounds they generate in high-frequency ranges we can't hear."

She halted, but Aran caught something unfinished in her voice and probed quickly at it. "What else?" he snapped. "What else made Evan work with killer whales?"

"They're most like man. They're intelligent, think, communicate; they can be gentle, playful, affectionate; and, like man, they can kill for the pleasure of it. They have the killer instinct. Dolphins fail in that. They're just gentle creatures. Like most animals, they kill only to eat. But killer whale and man, they match in every aspect."

Aran gathered the question for a moment, asked it slowly. "Why was that so important?"

The girl's eyes were round, staring at him as she answered. "Because he wanted the compatibility of organisms, as much as was possible to achieve," she said. "He wanted to give it every chance to take. He rejected every other marine animal. The killer whale fitted."

"Evan Taylor had found a way to carry through the final steps in genetic engineering," Aran murmured, awe in his voice. "He implanted human DNA, didn't he?"

The girl nodded. "We had three females and one male. We mated them and all the females took. When pregnancy had just begun, Evan transmitted the human DNA cells, using bacterio-phages. He had satisfied himself that Nirenberg's work on the universality of the genetic code was valid, but to play safe, he used human brain-tissue cells. He'd stored them in liquid nitro-gen until we were ready."

"And the females had their calves that carried the human DNA molecules," Aran said gravely.

"Yes, all three of them, and we raised the calves. We raised what Evan had created," Kay Elliot said. Aran heard her words and with it the quotation from the W.H.O that he had repeated to Jenny ... *as offered by these new methods of genetic engineer-ing, organisms can be created and propagated which possess completely new characters.* Evan Taylor had succeeded. He had created marine animals with the addition of human DNA and his objective stood out clearly now. He sought a creature able to communicate thoroughly with man and marine life, a kind of living bridge. But something had gone wrong. Or had it really? Aran asked himself. The chill inside him had become bands of ice that pressed his breath into small, short gasps.

"What happened?" he asked the girl.

"We couldn't make any scientific announcements until we knew that the calves were growing into something different, something with really heightened abilities. It became clear soon enough, though. They learned with amazing speed, faster than any other non-human creature had ever learned. Evan decided against the time needed in developing vocal communication, trying to see if they could form words, speak in human voice range. Imitation of speech wasn't important to Evan. He was interested in understanding, comprehension. He believed that if they could understand what our words meant to us, they might in time be able to tell us what certain sounds they made meant to them. He set up a program where, each day, John and I would read to the young *orcas* from a grade-school primer."

"It worked?" Aran asked.

"One part of it worked," she said. "They listened and they understood. They knew what we meant by our words, our sounds. What is any language but a combination of sounds meaning specific things? Did you notice that line of upright panels offshore?"

"Yes."

"They used to be in the tanks. Each panel holds a number of words. By tapping a section of the L-shaped base on the panel, the right word flips up. They would tap the proper sections to answer us. It was astounding, uncanny, and terribly exciting. Everything Evan hoped for was working. The DNA had joined, fused, become part of the killer whales. They were new creatures." Her face suddenly darkened and Aran saw her hands tighten and curl around the edge of the sofa. "Then it happened," she said, and lapsed into silence.

"Go on. What happened?" he prodded.

"They were a little over a year old and one morning they were gone, all of them. Evan was shattered. The living evidence of all his work was gone," Kay said.

"How?"

"They had watched us work the levers for the tank gates. They were low, where they could be easily reached from the water. They simply opened the gates during the night and left. Evan was certain they'd come back. They had a home here and they shared a humanness."

"But he was wrong," Aran said.

"He was right, but not for the reasons he thought. They didn't return until a year had passed. By then, Evan had us tow the panels offshore where they are now and he left a plea on them. We'd go out each morning to check the panels for an answer, some communication. After a while, Evan began to wonder if the genetic implant had held. There is a question on the mortality of cell lines."

"I'm familiar with it," Aran cut in. "But they did come back, then."

"Yes. One morning we found a message had been tapped out on the panels," Kay answered. "Man must die."

Aran's eyes mirrored the shock he felt as he stared at the girl, the meaning of the words reaching out to shatter the consciousness. "Man must die," he repeated. "Nothing else."

She shrugged. "Was anything more needed?" Kay asked. Aran found no comment, could only stare at her. "Evan rowed out to them. They swam near in wide circles, but they moved away. He went to the panels, put another plea on them. They came in closer, looked, and sank beneath the water. It was their refusal to say more."

"When was this?"

"Just a few days before it all started exploding, the very first of the attacks," Kay said. "And a year after they'd left us."

Aran felt his brow wet with perspiration. "Do you know what you're saying?" he asked, and realized that she knew only too well; the question was really asked of himself, and he pressed his lips into each other. "Evan knew, didn't he? He knew what it all meant," Aran murmured. Kay didn't answer. There was no need for answers.

He sank down on the couch beside her. It was unbelievable, and yet he believed every word of it. It was more than the mind could absorb all at once, the ramifications beyond sensible, reasoned acceptance. But it fitted, all of it, explaining and fitting where nothing else did. It accounted for the gaps, the out-of-focus parts of all the other theories that had been advanced, all those little things that had bothered him. It explained why no biochemical changes in the composition of the environment had been found, why no organic structural changes were detected, why no new, deep current movements had been found. And the total, monstrous meaning of it was only beginning to burn through him.

"Why did they turn on man? What did Evan say about that?" Aran asked.

"All in the DNA, he said, their own and man's, all there, the seed of everything, even inherited phylogenetic memory."

"Jung, the collective unconscious," Aran heard himself murmur, reflecting on Carl Jung's theory that each individual's unconscious mind contained the inherited experiences of the entire human race.

"Yes, only not just a human thing," Kay said, picking up his reference at once. "Something there in every species, a blueprint of yesterday as well as tomorrow, all part of the chemical storehouse of DNA. But with most species it's been inactive. We know enough about the structure of DNA to know that it can close off certain codings inherent in it. With Evan's genetic implant, something happened—a chemical reaction, a fusion of some sort—so that the new organism retained everything it had plus the new characteristics it never actively possessed before."

"They remember now," Aran mused aloud. "The collective experience of all marine life with man, an active, conscious remembrance. All of man's ruthless, heedless exploitation of the

sea and everything in it, all the catching and slaying and disregard for species, all of it now come together in focus." Aran
halted, felt his breath drawn in. The concept staggered, yet it was
there—in the vicious, channeled attacks, the intelligent countermoves, the organizational tactics—all planned, directed, led.
They had acquired the genetic code of man's mind, his mental
processes and abilities for organizational thought, while they
retained their own advanced sensitivities and specialized organs.
They could communicate with their fellow marine creatures and
understand man. A living bridge, Aran echoed silently, and a living indictment now capable of striking back.

He swallowed, drew in another deep breath, his throat suddenly dry. "Good God," he murmured. "Was that why Evan
rowed out to sea to kill himself? Was that the meaning of the
gesture and the note?" he asked.

Kay's eyes filled with sudden anguish, her lips worked,
forming words before the sounds came. "He didn't go out to
commit suicide, not in the usual meaning of the term," Kay
said. She swallowed hard, fought to hold back tears that had
come into her eyes.

"After the attacks began, after everything really started
to explode, they came back, sometimes just the three of them,
sometimes with others. They'd swim around the panels, leaping out of the water, diving away. Sometimes they came in the
day, other times at night. We could hear them, then. They were
taunting us, gloating, laughing at us in their way. One night they
came when Evan and I were here in this room, talking. He was
a man riddled with guilt and strain, his nerves raw with inner
tension. I saw him get up, go to the closet where he kept his rifle,
and begin to load it. He was going to kill them, he said. It was
the only thing left to do. He only hoped it wasn't too late." She
paused, struggled with herself for a moment, then went on. "I

begged him not to go out there. It was useless. I understood what he was going through. I felt it, we all did. But not as Evan felt it. I kept pleading with him as he got the rowboat and put the rifle inside it, but he refused to listen. There was a moon and I could see clearly enough from the beach."

"Did he try to communicate with them?" Aran asked. She nodded.

"I saw him work the panels, but they just kept swimming in circles, leaping out of the water. Maybe they sensed what he intended to do because they kept moving quickly. I stood watching, saw Evan row away from the panels, toward them, then stop and sit quietly. Suddenly he brought the rifle up and fired. He kept firing at them but missing. They dived away, were too quick for him."

"They attacked then," Aran interjected.

"He stopped firing first. I saw him stand up in the boat and hold the rifle out and then I saw their fins, coming at him from all sides." She halted, pressed her eyes closed. "He stood, not moving, then slowly he brought the rifle up, turned it on himself, used the last bullet in it."

"He chose that way rather than being torn apart," Aran said. She opened her eyes to him.

"I think it was an offering," she said softly. "He offered his life to them." Aran stared at her.

"If so, it didn't work," he answered.

"No, they were enraged. They attacked, smashed the boat to bits. I ran then, back into the house. John Akberg had gone to Key West for some supplies. He found me when he came back. I started drinking then."

Evan got to his feet, went to the window, and pulled the curtain back to stare out at the sea—so calm, so close, so vast. This was a planet of water, seventy-percent of it the seas. It was really not man's domain. The planet really belonged to the denizens of the seas. Yet man had made the waters his, just as he had the land. Or he had until now, Aran realized bitterly. He had misused the seas as he had the land—with arrogance, ruthlessness, total conceit. Jenny's words drifted into his mind. *Maybe everything thinks more than we realize, thinks more, knows more, feels more, is more.* Maybe it was always so, he reflected, and now, in those vast waters, there was something perhaps more than man's equal.

He turned from the window, the full magnitude of what he had learned still only beginning to take form. "You're coming back with me in the morning," he said. She continued to peer out at the sea as she nodded slowly. She spoke without looking at him.

"There's a guest room down the hall. You can sleep there," she said. He went to her, put his hand on her head and she turned around, wide eyes at him.

"John Akberg ran away. Evan killed himself, maybe as an offering, maybe just in fear of a worse death," Aran said. "The question is academic now. Why did you stay on here, drinking away the days?"

"I worked closely with Evan. I was a part of most all of it. I can't escape knowing that. How many people have been killed already because of what was done here? Where will it finally end? I guess I just decided to wait here for whatever would come."

Aran nodded and understood. She had her own kind of courage, her own sense of payment, perhaps more than the others had. He left her, took his bag, and went down the hall to the square room. There was a bed to one side, a dresser opposite it. He didn't turn on the light as he undressed to his shorts, then stretched out on the bed. The air was heavy, full of moisture, and exhaustion pulled at him, yet he couldn't sleep. He lay in the silent darkness and felt very small, very alone, very uncertain. The sound of the door opening intruded into the silence and he saw her enter, walk to the edge of the bed. She was naked, he saw, magnificently beautiful, her breasts deep, full, her hips wide, womanly hips, the dark triangle full and lush. She lay down on the bed beside him, unsmiling, no coy attempts at enticement, her eyes deep, grave.

"I'm out of booze and I can't stay alone without it. Not here, not now," she said simply. She shrugged and the bitterness was in her voice again. "Courage has its limitations, at least mine does," she said. She pressed herself against him, her hands upon his chest. "Please hold me," she said very softly. He pulled her head against his shoulder, felt her smooth breast push into his side. Suddenly they were as the last two people on earth, keepers of shared secrets. The absolute totality of it all, the shattering possibilities that lay ahead welled up inside him, not unlike a roaring wave exploding against the shore, and he knew the searing despair she had already embraced. It would be a temporary refuge, of course, but perhaps there were only temporary refuges left. His lips found her mouth, opening to him at once, her tongue darting out in desperation. His hands that had already brushed the smooth, deep breasts, now held them, caressed them, and he heard her low, moaning sigh.

"Yes, oh, damn, yes," she murmured, and pushed herself onto him. The feverishness of her desperate wanting was a contagion of the senses. His mouth opened to pull upon her breasts that she pushed down onto him, sweet suffocation, primal offering beyond refusal. He welcomed her, as he had never welcomed a woman before, joining with her not simply as lovers, but as fugitives from tomorrow. Her wild, thirsting eagerness flowed over him and he tasted of her every part, the firm, smooth breasts, the gasping, wet lips, her neck, shoulders, strong, young chest, the faint line of blond hair that traced a path down along her abdomen, across the convexity of her belly, and down into the deep, dark-tufted triangle. She was abandon itself, demanding more, wanting more, answering his lips and his tongue with sharp, gasped cries of ecstasy, returning his every caress, his every touch with her own. She was sensuality, carnality, possessed by and possessor of all pleasures, the Circean cup made flesh, and Aran heard his own cries mingling with hers, everything entwining, intermingling: sounds, lips, tongues, bodies, all thirstings fused as they sought to cling to more than flesh and blood could hold.

The small room became a world, a place set apart, an arena of gasps and cries, heavings and thrustings, a place in time that was theirs and theirs alone. But finally the night showered blind ecstasy, spun and exploded, and he cried out with her as they flowed into and around each other, and clutched at, eternity in a moment. "Oh, stay, stay with me," she cried out, pressed hands behind his back, holding him hard into her, prolonging moments. He felt her convulsive movements finally slow, the senses reluctantly bowing, and slowly, he sank down beside her.

They slept in exhaustion, as they had made love, entwined, pressed around each other, until the dawn filtered through the window blinds. He woke, lay still for a long moment, taking in the lush beauty of her and remembering the night. It had been a thing apart from all else, he knew. Their sharing had been complete, that refuge he had suddenly wanted as much as she had. It had been a very special thing of its own, encompassed by the terrible knowledge they shared, and now it was time to go on. He rose, woke her gently, and she raised herself on one elbow, looking lushly beautiful as a Rubens painting.

"It's time, Kay," he said. She glanced at the light of the dawn, nodded, and swung from the bed. While she went into the other bedroom to dress, he pulled on shorts and trousers, put a call in to Emerson's home. The voice, thick with sleep, replied after a half-dozen rings.

"Call a meeting, Emerson," Aran said. "For this afternoon. Everybody." He heard Emerson's voice sharpen at once, start to question him. "Just call the meeting," he said and hung up. He washed, dressed, and waited outside for the girl. She came out carrying a small bag, wearing a deep-blue dress with white piping around the collar. Her eyes scanned the sea around the line of upright panels. "I always look to see if they've come back. I'm sure I heard them one night but I was too smashed to go out and see," she said. He turned with her, climbed behind the wheel of the little rented car. As they drove away, he glanced back at the buildings.

"*Ab ovo*," he murmured, the meaning no longer shadowed but all too clear. From the beginning, the very beginning of life itself, the new life Evan was creating. Aran pressed down on the gas pedal, sent the car skidding away.

CHAPTER NINE

The conference room held a tomb-like silence. They had listened without interruption, to Aran, first, as he put it all out before them, closing all the unexplained gaps, pinpointing and fitting together all that had happened. Kay had spoken then, detailing Evan's work, explaining the technical aspects of the genetic engineering as it had been done. Now Aran's eyes swept the silent figures that stared at him. Admiral Hotchins broke the silence first.

"Damn, I can't believe this," his voice boomed out. "You're telling us that three damn fish with some new genes are responsible for all that's been happening?"

"Not fish, Admiral, marine mammals," Aran said. "And maybe a lot more than three. I'd say almost certainly more." He glanced at Kay Elliot sitting beside him.

"The three genetically engineered males were ready to mate when they escaped," she said. "I'd guess they would have sought out females at once, made it a priority. If so, there could be anywhere from ten to fifty, maybe a hundred more out there now."

"All carrying their new genetic characteristics?" Shuster asked.

"We have to assume so. There's no reason to believe it wouldn't be transmitted," Aran said.

"It all fits," Leslie Streeter said, his voice tired. "The theoretic possibilities for this have been accepted for some while. Now it's no longer theory."

"But turning the whole damned sea against man? Organizing the other forms of life in the ocean?" Hotchins protested.

"Marine mammals were always part of two worlds, a living bridge between life-forms. Now that's been carried further. They can think as man thinks. They can understand and communicate with man and they can communicate with their fellow marine creatures. We're so damned self-centered, so arrogant, that we think we've got some exclusive on communication. Well, we don't. All animals communicate. Marine life is full of communicating sound, the stuff we call language. There are many forms of communication other than language as we know it, methods far more subtle and sophisticated and equally effective."

"You make it sound as though they're leading some kind of revolution," Hotchins growled.

"That's exactly what it is," Aran snapped. "It's the classic form of it. Take a mass of people, downtrodden, exploited, misused—organize them, direct them, show them how to fight back, and you have only one result. That's what's been done countless times on land. They're doing it in the sea. The enemy has been named down there and its name is man."

Ernest Shuster's voice cut in. The President's representative had remained pensive while listening till now. "Then you expect it will spread into the Pacific," he remarked.

"I expect they've only begun," Aran said, and saw Shuster's perpetually grave eyes grow deeper, more troubled.

"Everything that's been said in this room today is to be held in absolute secrecy," Ernest Shuster said. "None of this must get out until the President has had a chance to confer with the cabinet and other heads of state."

Admiral Hotchins boomed out an impatient roar, slapped the conference table with the palm of his hand. "All right, let's assume all this is true. Christ, from the way things have been going it seems so," he conceded. "Then we'll put an end to it. We've got the power, the means, and the brains to handle it."

"I understand your cruisers with steel nets didn't bring up much of anything," Aran remarked.

"That was only our first try. We'll get them," the admiral snapped. "The first thing is to keep all small craft in port, all over the world. We'll use only the big stuff—freighters, warships, ocean liners if we have to. Goddamn, there's no amount of fish that are going to do anything to a fifty-thousand-ton liner."

Aran felt his hands clench. He wanted to take hold of the man, shake the arrogance from him. "No, sir, I don't imagine they can. Or they will," he said. The admiral caught the unstated, his eyes narrowing.

"Meaning exactly what?" he barked.

"Meaning, sir, that you underestimate their strength, their numbers, their abilities. Given the time they escaped, they've had a year to organize, prepare, make plans. You underestimate what you people call their options."

Ernest Shuster cut in. "What do you see as some of those options, Mr. Holder?" he queried.

"They could be content with simply making the sea a totally hostile environment for man. The big vessels could move with their oil and cargoes, but they'd be the only ones that dared enter the sea. Every seacoast would be a place of danger—constant, unending danger. Every trip onto the seas would be a trip into enemy territory. Or, they might make the sea into a place of constant guerrilla warfare. Guerrilla fighters don't attack powerful forces head on. They strike in their own ways, but they cause havoc. That's what they've been doing so far. Or they might simply stay away from any attempts to net them. They could do it if directed, led, organized. They can see us a lot easier than we can see them. I'm sure you know what that immediate impact would have on a nation such as Japan."

Shuster nodded, his lips drawing back. "And to every other nation. I doubt that agricultural and meat production could be increased fast enough to handle it," he said. Aran was about to speculate on his real fears, the potential for massive, aggressive action, when the admiral interrupted.

"You know what I think? I think that's all a crock of shit. It's all hysterical. Holder, here, has been so shocked by this genetic engineering business that he can't think straight. They've shot their main guns. The attacks on bathers, the crabs making shore raids, and now the octopuses striking—it's all part of the same. That's it, that's all of it. That's their thing, one or another variation. They don't have any weapons. They can't do anything more."

"They don't have your weapons," Aran said. "They have their own, numbers beyond counting, strengths we can only imagine if organized, given purpose, unified."

"*If*," the man snorted. "I'm not talking *if*. I'm talking hard fact, real strength, air patrols, long-range reconnaissance, fire-power, huge mine-sweeping style operations. I'm talking about blasting the hell out of anything that attacks, and a dozen—no, two dozen—seek-and-destroy squadrons to hunt down every damn killer whale they spot. I'm talking about showing anything and everything who's boss." He leaned forward, his jaw thrust out. "And if that intelligent direction is there, if it's really so damn intelligent, it'll be smart enough to know that the revolution is finished, the party's over."

Aran started to gather answers, to say, "No, you're unseeing, uncomprehending, locked into your little human games. It won't be that way at all, not at all." But he heard Ernest Shuster's voice cut in.

"I'd say that we must go along with Admiral Hotchins' professional, experienced analysis. We possess tremendous technological knowledge and weaponry. We'll use it to safeguard our interests. But what we've heard here today is awesome. When this threat is eliminated, the governments of the world must address themselves to the absolute control of further genetic experimentation." He turned to the admiral. "You will initiate all appropriate action to re-establish the safety and control of the seas at once," he said.

Aran sat quietly, holding protests inside himself. It was no use to argue further now. He could only offer speculation, draw possibilities. It was not enough against the admiral's confident rhetoric. Hell, maybe the stiff-necked old bastard was right, Aran admitted silently. There was always the off-chance. He laughed bitterly at his sudden clutching out at hope. Human, so very human. Hope, that essence that refused to be imprisoned by reason. Did the DNA hold a chemical for hope? he wondered. The conference had ended, and the others were standing, talking in hushed tones. Also except the admiral. He was detailing his plans to Shuster with clarion anticipation, the President's man nodding with complacent satisfaction. Leslie Streeter came up to Aran, his face still drawn and strained.

"You were right all along," he said. "You sensed we weren't on to it. But I can't be as pessimistic as you about it."

Aran shrugged, unwilling to debate his fears now. Streeter looked at Kay Elliot. "You must write a paper on this, my dear," he said.

"Of course," Aran heard her say and wondered if Streeter heard the bitterness in the two words. The biochemist turned, went on with the others as they drifted toward the door. Emerson disappeared into his office, Aran noted, closing the door behind him. He felt the girl watching him and turned to see her clouded, troubled eyes.

"Any guesses?" she asked, knowing he'd understand at once. They shared the awareness, the terrible comprehension that still escaped the others, that would be beyond such as Hotchins and Shuster until it was too late.

"Not yet," he answered. "You worked with them. They were always more intelligent than we realized, weren't they?"

"Much more. More intelligent than anything in the sea, except maybe the huge sperm whales, but we've no way of knowing that. More intelligent, more like man." She paused. "Too much so."

"And now, a new, genetically engineered mind, two kinds of intelligence fused onto instinctive wisdom, power, cunning," Aran said. He paused, felt his lips drawn in. "There's no way of knowing which way they'll go. Not yet. But they'll tell us."

He took the girl's arm and steered her back to the small office where he'd put her traveling bag. "I'll have to find you a hotel room," he said.

"No. I'm going back."

The words, uttered without emotion, startled him and he turned and searched her eyes. "There's no need anymore for that," he remarked.

"No bottle, if that's what you're thinking," she half-smiled. "Believe it or not, I wasn't much of a drinker until Evan's death. But I think that part is over now for me."

"Then why go back? You've told about it now, Evan's work, your part in it. It's over, now."

"Is it?" she asked and her eyes held his, a terrible sadness floating deep inside them.

"You can't be a stand-in for Evan Taylor. You can't take on his guilt," Aran said.

"I don't have to. Mine is enough," she returned. Aran heard the door to Emerson's office open as Kay started to pick up her bag. He turned as Emerson Boardman's rounded form appeared in the dorway, and Aran caught the odor of fresh whiskey at once. Emerson had been into his flask. The man's eyes, small and reddened, sought on Kay Elliot, held on her.

"I'm sorry your boss wasn't here," Emerson Boardman said, and suddenly, his face growing red, "so I could shoot him myself."

Aran felt the shock spearing into him at the man's words and the venom in his glare as he faced the girl, then whirled and walked away. Aran's eyes went to Kay Elliot, saw neither anger nor shock in her face. "I'm sorry," he started to apologize.

"Don't be," she said, cutting him off.

"He's upset," Aran offered.

"He's right," she returned. She met the question in his eyes. "That's not why I'm going back," she said.

"Isn't it?" he speared. She sank down into one of the chairs, weariness suddenly flooding her voice.

"I have to go back, don't you see that? It's my way of doing something. It's the only way I have."

"How will going back there do anything?" Aran thrust.

"I think they'll keep coming back to the lab. We don't know what they'll do, but they'll keep coming back to those panels on which they can communicate with man."

"Why?"

She frowned, pulling on thoughts. "Why do caterpillars follow each other in circles for days? What strange mechanism makes birds fly thousands of miles to a particular spot? Why do lemmings rush over cliffs in some kind of migratory madness? Something makes them do what they must do. I think they'll keep coming back. It's a special place for them, a place of origin.

They've been back often enough to prove that much, and once since Evan's death—at least once."

"How do you know the original three are there? You said yourself there might be fifty more by now."

"They'd still be the leaders. They'd be the ones to return to the lab. So long as someone is there who was a part of their beginnings, they'll come back. I'm sure of it. They'll come back to taunt, to gloat, to flaunt their power and freedom."

"They could come back to kill," Aran said. "Or forces they've set in motion could move on their own—the crustaceans, the octopuses. You're completely unprotected there on that low land."

"That's my risk, Aran. I want them to come back. It's our one avenue of contact with them. That has to be kept open. That just might be the most important thing left in the world."

He stared at her and saw the need to redeem guilt, but so much more. She had hold of a truth, an ominous, bitter foreboding he could not deny, not to her, not to himself, not to the world. The deep sigh escaped him, sourness in his mouth. "Be careful," he said. "Don't take chances. If you feel something is wrong, get the hell out of there. I'll keep in close contact."

"Yes, that's important. I'll call you if they come back," she said. She reached up, brushed his cheek with her lips. "Thanks for understanding, about everything." She hesitated. "I'm not sorry about last night. I hope you're not."

"No, I'm not. It was a special night," he said.

"I'm just sorry my name isn't Jenny," she said and he felt his eyes widen. "You mumble in your sleep," she added and she smiled. He realized, suddenly, that it was maybe the first time he'd seen her really smile. It was a warm smile, even though there was a sadness in it. Kay Elliot turned, hurried out of the building, and he watched her go. He wanted to feel sorry for her, but he could only feel respect. He'd give it a few days, he told himself, and then insist she pack up and leave there.

He got his bag and walked from the little office, taking a turn in the corridor that avoided his passing Emerson's office. He was becoming more and more disappointed in Emerson Boardman's self-pity. When he reached the street, the solemn marchers and their placards were still there. They had established some sort of vigil on the corner, a kind of open-air prayer meeting and he hurried past, silently wishing them success.

He sought a hotel nearby, found one a few blocks south, a slightly run-down place, dim and faded, a mustiness to it. But the room they showed him, facing the street, was clean and airy enough. It would be but a place to sleep, anyway, and he took it, paying a week's rent in advance. Afterward, he went out and bought a small, portable radio and had something to eat. When he returned to the room, fatigue was pulling on him and he sat down, then called Jenny before his eyes grew more heavy-lidded. She answered at the first ring, her voice curling in excitement at once.

"Did you find anything down there?" she questioned. Shuster's warning about secrecy leaped up at once. He trusted Jenny completely, yet there was always the accidental remark, the chance slip-of-the-tongue.

"I can't talk about it now, not over the phone. I'm under official silence," he said.

"That bad?" she asked.

"Maybe," he said carefully.

"When can you come down here?" she asked quickly.

"Tomorrow, if I can. By the weekend, I'm sure," he said and felt her disappointment wriggle across the telephone wires. "It'll be like old times for a little while," he offered. She'd know what he meant. When they first started going out he saw her only on weekends when he drove down from Washington.

"As soon as you can," Jenny said. "And be careful." He promised her caution, blew her a kiss, and let her click off first. He undressed, went to bed, and surprised himself by sleeping soundly. In the morning, he snapped on the radio as he showered and dressed. Europe reported most of the action, more attacks on swimmers all along the coastlines and the authorities closing beaches, issuing rules—an echo of what had been done here. When he arrived at the office, newsmen were waiting. They'd received word about the special meeting yesterday and wanted reasons for it. He told them it had been called because of a breakthrough that turned out to be in error at the last moment. His explanation was accepted with reservations and he wondered how long Shuster's secrecy lid would stay on. He called the man later in the day, at his Washington office.

"It's very much on yet," Ernest Shuster said. "In fact, the President has decided not to take the Cabinet into his confidence yet just because of possible leaks. The fewer people that know, the less chance for trouble."

"Don't you think the people have a right to know what they may be facing?" Aran asked.

"The President—and I agree with him—feels that they may not be facing any more than they have already if Admiral Hotchins is right in his analysis of the situation. It's been decided to give the admiral time to carry out his operation. The success of it would end this immediate situation and give us a chance to tell the public the truth about it in a climate free of hysteria and panic."

"What about other governments?" Aran asked.

"The President is holding back on that, also, until the situation becomes stabilized. NATO forces, and a token Russian force, are working with Admiral Hotchins to combat the present immediate threat. Everyone considers that more vital than explanations at the moment."

Shortly after Aran ended the call, he saw Emerson. The man made no mention of his vitriolic outburst the day before, but his eyes seemed smaller, the pupils contracted, and Emerson Boardman's face twitched nervously as he spoke.

"I've arranged a direct line with the admiral's command quarters. We'll get immediate reports on how the operation is proceeding," he said. One of the typists came in with a container of coffee and Emerson gulped at it.

"Why don't you take a few days off?" Aran offered.

"And what, go to the seashore?" Boardman shot back bitterly. "Stay home with Emily? Jesus, no. You know all she does is talk about what a tragedy it was about that nice girl who worked for me." Aran saw Boardman's hand shake as he raised the coffee container to his lips. He knew nothing about Boardman's wife, his personal life, and yet he knew more than he needed to know now. Emily Boardman was taking her own revenge in her own way. Revenge, Aran grimaced. It was a human characteristic. Or had been, he corrected himself. He turned, left Emerson Boardman, and gathered all the reports that had come in and sat down with them. The attacks swept down from the British Isles and Denmark to the coast of Spain. Reports had been heavy during the first part of the day, tapering off toward sundown. The British Navy had virtually ringed the British Isles with a protective barrier. They had adopted a defensive policy while the French patrolled up and down their coasts. Scattered cephalopod attacks continued to come in from the Italian coastline, mostly on small craft that stubbornly continued to leave port.

On this side of the Atlantic, the newspapers had caught on to Hotchins' massive sea-air operation and were giving it full play. At the day's end, Aran took one of the geodetic maps from the file room, all the day's reports, and retired to his hotel room. He began to circle the spot on the map of each report, numbered it, and gave the corresponding report the same number. He continued to do that the following day, carefully noting the time as well as the location of each report. During the next day, he continued to meet with newspeople, fending off probes. They didn't lean too heavily on him, though. They were busy following the admiral's operations and he was grateful for that. Fewer attacks were reported on the other side of the Atlantic, because, as had been done here, the European governments had prohibited boating and the people had fled the shores. Later in the day, Hotchins issued a statement attributing the drop in attacks to the success of his patrols and, in Emerson's office, Aran snorted at the claim.

"Why not?" Emerson asked. "He's got at least a thousand ships with the NATO forces, plus air coverage."

"Patrolling the Atlantic, the North Sea, part of the Arctic, the Mediterranean, and the Caribbean. That's roughly forty million square miles of water," Aran snapped. "I'd say the patrols were something less than tight."

That evening, Aran put a call in to Kay Elliot, his apprehension mounting at once as the phone rang a half dozen times before being picked up. "Sorry, I was back in the lab, cleaning up some things," she said.

"Everything quiet down there?" Aran asked.

"They haven't shown," she said. "I'd hear them, even at night with the windows closed. You become tuned in for certain sounds, the way a mother hears her child's cry." He heard her wry half-laugh. "Not altogether inappropriate, is it?" she said.

"Call me the minute they show," Aran said. "And keep being careful."

"Thanks," she answered, her voice crisp and flat. The phone clicked off and he sat down with the map, added the day's reports, then finally undressed and slept. At the end of the first three days, he sat in Emerson's office over the results of Hotchins' operation. He read down the list—words that, to him, said so much more than they appeared to say. He plowed through official rhetoric to encapsulate the important facts:

—European waters: Coastal attacks continued by small, fast forays, eluding air-patrol detection, just as had been so effectively done here.

—Fishing: Twenty convoys of fishing trawlers and eight strictly Naval operations had been conducted off the British coast, in Danish waters, and along the northern French coastline. They hadn't netted a hundred fish.

—Atlantic sightings: There had been forty-eight individual air sightings of sizeable fish concentrations on the surface. Naval squadrons were sent to the areas in immediate pursuit under forced draft. In each instance, the concentrations dispersed and disappeared minutes before the warships reached the scene, often in direct sight of the approaching vessels. By the end of the third day, sixteen ships put into port with burned-out bearings, boiler problems, and overheated engine-room equipment. Orders were issued to cease full-speed pursuit of air sightings.

—The tragedy involving H Squadron: One of the admiral's search-and-destroy forces, Squadron H consisted of six destroyer-escorts of the Evans Class. Four hundred miles off Cape Hatteras, they spotted a tremendous congregation of tens of thousands of fish: mackerel, carp, flounder, and tuna. The fish covered the water in a loose circle at least a half-mile in radius. The squadron commander, Captain Herbert Callander, ordered a massive attack, plowing full-speed into the center of the fish with his vessels. Orders were carried out at once and a concentrated depth-charge barrage laid down by the destroyers. The barrage blew pieces of fish high into the air, showering the sea and the ships with blood. They also blew in the hulls of two Tang Class submarines that had been under the depth-charge barrage, killing almost all of the eighty-three officers and men aboard each undersea boat.

The Navy's immediate investigation into the tragedy was pieced together through the stories of the few submarine survivors and the official statements of Captain Callander. The two submarines had been in pursuit of the concentration, moving along under the mass of fish, to observe more than to attack. The destroyer squadron had sonar in operation that should have detected the undersea craft. Preliminary conclusions pointed to the fact that the dense layer of fish between the surface craft and the submarines had blocked out the sonar systems, preventing detection of the underwater boats.

—Killer whales: There had not been a single sighting of killer whales.

Aran looked up from the report and met Emerson's uneasy gaze. "Bad luck," Emerson said. "Accidents are part of any new operation, I guess."

"The submarines?" Aran echoed. "No, not bad luck, not an accident. They made it happen." He saw apprehension and reluctance in Emerson's eyes, laced with a hint of fear. They could have just vanished, as they did with the other task forces," Aran reminded him. "But they didn't. They stayed surfaced, formed that dense layer over the submarines they knew were moving along with them. Directed and organized, they saw the destroyers coming and stayed. They knew just what would follow."

The reluctance in Emerson Boardman's eyes had dimmed and now the fear glowed more brightly. Aran leaned toward him. "They've had Hotchins' forces chasing all over the damned sea, wearing out ships, men, and equipment They appear and vanish. They're using classic guerrilla-warfare tactics in answer to his operation," Aran pressed.

"He's made the adjustment," Emerson answered. "You really think they can keep this up?"

"As long as they like. They've millions of spotters, their own network of communications, one we can't break into. They can see us moving in their territory long before we can see them. They can pick and choose their spots for anything."

"Then you think this is what they'll keep doing," Emerson said.

Aran shook his head slowly, almost sadly. "No, I think they'll do a lot more," he answered. Emerson eyed him unhappily, his face suddenly darkening.

"Shit, I agree with Hotchins," Emerson exploded angrily. "This is it with them, this guerrilla warfare of yours. This is all they can do and we can throttle that in time."

Aran met Emerson's angry glare. "I hope you're right, you and the admiral. God, I hope so," Aran said, and walked out of the office. He gathered the sheaf of reports, put them in his briefcase, and went back to his hotel room. Meticulously, he noted each one on the map. Later, studying them, he could not yet make out any pattern. There were too many variables involved and it was late when he stopped analyzing, trying to draw patterns, tie in unrelated reports. He went downstairs and out into the night to find a nearby diner, where he sat over coffee and a half-eaten sandwich. The round-faced waitress commented on his preoccupation and he smiled with her at himself. "I'm not really an absentminded professor," he told her. He ordered a second coffee and drank it slowly. When he left, he walked directly back to his room, got there in time to hear the phone ringing, and answered it, to listen to Jenny's voice holding concern and a hint of petulance.

"I thought you'd come down by now," she said.

"Soon, I promise," he apologized, and told her of the hectic pace of the days. He felt a flood of wanting sweep over him at her voice.

"No more trips to the Keys," she said. "I don't like you down there. It scares me." Aran smiled to himself, was touched by her caring. She would understand Kay Elliot, he mused, out of those depths of sensitive caring that were part of her. "You still can't tell me anything more?" she questioned.

"I will, when we're together," he said. It wasn't a putting-aside answer. He would tell her then. If he still had to, he reflected. If it hadn't blown wide open by then. They—that huge, new intelligence out there—they'd see to that, he was certain. They wouldn't continue the guerrilla warfare. He thought once they might, but not any longer. There was too much craftiness, too much cunning at work in the watery depths. And too much hate. They wanted a greater victory.

When Jenny hung up, he undressed quickly and fell into bed and thought about greater victories. How much did they want? he wondered. How much had they become like man? Perhaps that was the answer. How little did they care about anything except their own wants now? He turned on his side, closed his eyes, and forced sleep to finally come.

CHAPTER TEN

The mid-morning sun was brilliant in a virtually cloudless sky the next day. Almost fifteen hundred miles east of Florida, the water over the mid-Atlantic ridge sparkled and became a bright cerulean blue. The RT-33 long-range tactical reconnaissance plane flew high over the water, when suddenly the pilot, Lieutenant James Wittee, noticed the color of the sea change. A tremendous, uneven area became a dark blue-black.

"It looks like an oil slick," the lieutenant murmured.

"Too big," Ed Flynn, his co-pilot answered. "I'd say some kind of sea growth. Maybe from the Sargasso."

The lieutenant sent the plane down in a steep descent, heading for the area that darkened the sea ahead. As he pulled up, leveling off just over the water, his eyes grew wide. "Good God Almighty," he breathed as the darkened area took on detail. "Fish, millions of them."

He sent the plane into a steep bank, came around, and made another pass over the area. Ed Flynn frowned as he stared out of the window at his side. From the lower altitude it seemed as though the entire sea were covered with them. "Look at that, will you, they're swimming in a gigantic circle, every damn one of them," he intoned. The plane banked again, flew along the outer edge of the huge mass of fish when Ed Flynn's voice rose. "They're going faster," he said. "Holy God, they're going faster and faster. Will you look at them go!"

"Call it in," Lieutenant Wittee yelled. "Quick, call it in! They're acting like they've gone crazy or something."

"Maybe they have," Ed Flynn said, snapping on the transmitter. "That'd sure fit everything that's been happening." He spoke into the sending set, gave position, described the size of the concentration, and the behavior of the fish. "That's right, in circles, swimming like hell in a huge circle, faster and faster, millions of them."

James Wittee's voice broke in. "They're going down, Ed. Look at them. They're going down while they're circling." He banked again, leveled off, stared down, saw the speed of the circling fish continue to increase again, faster and faster until there was only a whirling, spinning, furious wheel of bodies. He watched it sinking, staying together as it descended beneath the surface, sucking water in after it until there was a tremendous whirlpool—and then nothing but the huge blue-black hole in the sea which slowly closed in on itself. He watched, incredulously, as the sea became one gigantic whirlpool that finally vanished and then there was nothing, only the sparkling blue water.

He exchanged incredulous glances with Ed Flynn, then sent the plane winging off to the west. They had called in the sighting, for whatever it was worth. They'd let the brass play with it.

The report of the strange sighting reached the office soon after Aran finished a morning press conference. He frowned at the paper, put it aside, and prepared a release on the extent of the Fish and Wildlife Services investigation into the phenomena. Emerson had wanted it put out as an example of the thoroughness of the Service's efforts. Finished, Aran picked up the report again and read it over. It made no sense—bizarre behavior indeed. But then it had all seemed bizarre at first, yet nothing had been without purpose, planning, and objective. This strange behavior wasn't aimless either, he wagered. His brows pressed together; the pilot's estimate at the size of the concentration was astounding, perhaps a million fish. Of course appearances could deceive, especially from the air. Yet there had to be hundreds of thousands. Aran took the report with him into the chart room at the end of the corridor, pulled out the mid-Atlantic chart, and scanned it slowly. The furious, whirling wheel of fish the pilots had reported took shape before him on the chart and his brows continued to press down.

He sat down at a square table, took a sheet of paper and the chart, and began to put down columns of figures. He tugged at his memory, dragging up velocity and density ratios, possible combinations of water speeds and currents. He was playing games, he knew, making educated guesses and applying mathematical formulas to each. It was perhaps an idle exercise, and yet the tremendous concentration and the strange whirling wheel hadn't been a pointless appearance. That was the only thing of which he was certain. It meant something and he bent over the sheet of paper and the chart, became immersed in juggling formulas, only dimly aware that everyone else had gone out to lunch.

Harry Cohen was not a happy man. Perhaps he should have been, but he wasn't. Nothing was right, he murmured to himself. He had money, plenty of money, two homes, all the material comforts anyone could want, and nothing was right. Even his bathing trunks didn't fit right, pulling at him as he moved in the beach chair. Behind him, the big hotels of Miami's "Gold Coast" rose into the air: the Fountainebleau, the Doral, the Eden Roc, the Deauville, the long line of them that faced the beach and the water. Tonight their dining rooms and cabarets would be jammed with the comics of the Broadway-Catskills-Miami circuit, making jokes about the fish problem. They incorporated everything into their routines. Maybe it was all to the good. Laughing always helped. But now the fabulous hotels were quiet. Everyone was outside sunning, or in air-conditioned rooms sleeping. His eyes roamed across the cabanas that were packed with people, and even the narrow strip of beach was jammed with browning bodies. It was strange, he mused, how now that they couldn't go into the water, there were more people out on the narrow beach than ever before. It was as if they were drawn to the water now that it was forbidden, that suddenly they were aware of the tang of the salt air and the warmth of the sun.

Harry Cohen looked down at his own deep tan, his skin firm, with good muscle tone, and his hair, grayed, still thick and full. His glance drifted to the nearby beach chairs where Sarah was stretched out, glistening with suntan lotion. She was still a good-looking woman, Harry noted, the extra weight she'd put on over the years adding an earthiness to her—bigger breasts, fuller thighs, a bolder curve to her belly. His lips tightened. So why didn't he enjoy her more now in bed instead of less? Harry Cohen asked himself. It was a question he'd asked himself often enough. It was really her fault, he'd told himself equally often. Though now, sometimes, he wondered.

But Sarah had complained too much and then demanded too much, there was no question about that, he reminded himself. Soon after they married she began complaining about the sixteen-hour days he put in at the plant. She complained that she hardly saw him at all, and when she did his mind was on business. Of course, he could never make her understand that in the garment business you lived, breathed, and sweated for the business or it didn't succeed. He was married to the business—she used to say—so he could sleep with the business. But he was usually too tired to care, anyway. Of course, when he came home early and fresh, on rare occasions, she never denied him. Sarah knew her duties as a wife.

And she also reveled in the mink coats the business bought her, the around-the-world trips and the big house at Sands Point and the fancy schools for the kids. She complained about never seeing him but she enjoyed the results of his work. Harry Cohen's face became pained as he thought about the kids. A lot of good those fancy schools had done them. They'd grown up spoiled, full of strange ideas. He'd taken Jacob into the business only to have constant arguments with him. The kid just didn't understand that it was a game of dog-eat-dog, cutthroat competition, stealing an idea here, borrowing one there, cutting corners to get to the market first with a new line. He wanted to run the business like a gentlemen's club. But he was learning, despite himself he was learning. And Ellen, on her way through a second bad marriage, Harry snorted. His eyes moved across the crowded beach, found Ellen talking to two young men who couldn't take their eyes off her and that handkerchief of a bathing suit she wore.

His glance moved back to where Sarah lay with her eyes closed, trying to become browner than brown. Sleep with the business, she had told him. He'd done the next best thing, finding a succession of willing and eager young models over the years. They were all liaisons that began with limitations firmly established. Except with Sandy Dumont, the last of them, and the only one who'd ever got to him as more than a weekend's entertainment. Goddamn, even that hadn't fitted right anymore and he had broken off with her, too. She'd become demanding, too, bold, even calling him at home once. It had been all Sarah's fault, he reflected, his eyes still fixed on his wife's body. She had never understood that he'd done it all for her, all the sixteen-hour days, the consuming drive, the total energies given to the business; all for her and the material comforts it brought her. She should have been able to understand that, he told himself. His face tightened. A goddamned psychiatrist he'd met at a party had told him he'd done it all for himself, for his own need of power, to prove himself. He'd rejected that *sheisskopf*'s ideas then, would have no part of them. Yet now he wondered. It was one more thing that didn't fit right.

And next week—the buyers were coming down and he couldn't even take them out for a week's fishing. He had a seventy-five thousand dollar boat that he couldn't use because of some goddamn crazy fish. He cursed silently, shook his head. Sarah stirred, and the swell of her breasts rose up from the top of the pink bathing suit. He wondered if maybe he could put things back on the right track with Sarah, after all these years. She'd been fifteen years his junior when he married her and she was still a young woman. Maybe he ought to take her back to the hotel, throw her on the bed, and start screwing her until she was exhausted. He felt as though he could do it, too. A week down here, away from the business, always renewed his energies. Unfortunately, in two weeks he always felt like rushing back and screwing his competitors.

He let his glance travel across the beach, down to the water. The lifeguards sat on their high perches, but spent their time talking to girls. There was no one in the water to watch. Harry Cohen's glance traveled idly out from the shore to the sea. The horizon seemed to move and fade away as a tall wave obscured it. He watched the slow roll of the sea, saw it rising. His eyes stayed on it, idly transfixed. The water seemed to be rising higher. It was a strange optical illusion, he told himself. It looked as though it were rising and rising, a huge wave that now seemed to tower in the water.

He was half-smiling at how the mind and the eye play tricks when he heard someone shout and he blinked. The wave continued to rise in front of him. Someone else shouted and then he heard a woman scream. He tore his eyes from the wave and looked across the beach. People were slowly stirring, opening their eyes, gathering themselves. He glimpsed Sal Shortman of E-Z-Clothes sunning himself with Herb Aronson, the thieving little bastard of a designer. His eyes went back to the sea, expecting to see only the quiet blue of it. But the wave was still there, only higher now, and he started to get to his feet, frowning. Some people, those fully awake and closest to the water, were starting to run. Harry Cohen stared as if hypnotized at the sea as it seemed to rise on end. Sixty feet, he guessed, no, more like eighty. Eighty feet of water, pushed by thousands and thousands of tons.

Suddenly it blocked out the sky, started to curl at the top edge. Suddenly there was nothing but the towering wall of water. *"Sarah!"* He heard the cry tear from his lips and she sat up and looked at him. The beach was a mass of suddenly struggling, falling bodies and screams and something else now—a terrible roaring sound. His eyes stared at Sarah as she turned and saw the mountain of water starting to come down. She screamed, looked back at him. Suddenly there was so much he wanted to tell her. Mostly, he wanted to tell her that it hadn't been all her fault. Maybe not all anybody's fault. He started toward her, but a half dozen bodies fell in between. Someone crashed into him, knocked him sideways. The air was dark now, the sky blotted out, and then the huge tidal wave crashed down. Harry Cohen's eyes glanced up along the beach, all along the other beaches. The wall of water extended as far as he could see. He tried again to reach Sarah and suddenly he was struck, lifted, sent hurtling into the air on a wall of water. He felt himself being turned end over end, the water filling his mouth, his lungs, and then he became one more of the thousands of people that the great wave picked up as it rolled across the beaches of Miami.

Harry Cohen was already dead when the towering mountain of water, eighty feet high, crashed into the line of hotels, crushing in windows and fronts as though they were made of cellophane and cardboard. Some of the great structures crumpled forward as the wave ripped away concrete blocks like a giant hand. Everyone in the lobbies was sent hurtling, killed almost at once. Bodies from the beach were flung into fourth-floor windows and water swept into the lower floors, pulling out anyone in the oceanfront rooms. The wall of water extended up to Bal Harbour and down to the University of Miami's Fisher Island Station. Pushed by a fetch of fifteen hundred miles, an astronomical per-square-foot pressure, the huge wave was followed by still another, not quite as big but massive in its own right. The beachfront of Miami Beach was ripped apart, the great hotels broken and battered, the tremendous rush of towering water pushing high tides that swamped the marinas and homes of the small islands behind the beach strip, sweeping unprepared residents into their rushing waters.

When the second wave finally receded, fires had begun to burn from the snapped gas mains and only those who had been on the upper floors of the hotels, or deep in the interiors, survived. The rest of Miami Beach was a smashed, broken, wasted place, a place of total carnage and a strange silence. Thousands and thousands of bodies and twisted beach chairs littered the scene and more were being washed up out of the sea that still boiled along the shore. The luxurious hotels, their lower stories smashed and crumpled, rose up over the beach now like huge, gaudy tombstones. It was not until later—much, much later—that the extent of the disaster was fully known.

That very moment, Aran Holder was racing from the chart room of the Fish and Wildlife Services into Emerson Boardman's office, his face strained, flushed. He waved the sheet of paper with the report of the strange sighting on it, almost hurled it at Boardman. "A tsunami," he yelled. "They're setting off a tsunami." Emerson stared at him, reluctant to believe what he heard. Aran shoved the sheet of paper covered with calculations at him. "I've been figuring it over and over and that's got to be it. I make it hitting somewhere on the southern Florida coast, Miami Beach probably. Call them down there. Maybe there's still time."

There wasn't, of course, and Aran knew he'd been right the moment the operator told them the phone service into Miami was out. He stared at Emerson for a long moment, then turned and slowly walked back to his office. He sat down heavily behind the desk and silently cursed his ineptitude and knew that he would forever wonder if, had he been able to calculate faster, reached conclusions even a half-hour earlier, thousands of lives might not have been saved. He thought about Admiral Willard Hotchins and wondered what the man would have to say now about weapons.

Slowly, Aran began to write out the information sheet he knew the news media would be clamoring for within the hour. A tsunami was a shock wave caused by the sudden displacement of a huge amount of water deep in the bowels of the sea. They were usually caused by an undersea earthquake or volcanic eruption but any giant disturbance could cause them. Once set off, natural forces did the rest. They moved through the sea in the form of low waves, deep down below the surface in deep water. Often ships above were totally unaware that a tsunami was rolling past underneath them. They moved along the sea depths at fantastic speeds, usually four hundred miles an hour. As they neared a shore and the water became shallower, they began to rise, like some subterranean monster emerging from the deep, sweeping away everything in their path until they crashed upon a shoreline with the devastating power of the ocean behind them.

Aran went into the mimeograph room and had hundreds of copies of the fact sheet run off. They were all used within the hour. But it wasn't until later that night that the full reports began to come in. Preliminary estimates totaled thirty-six thousand people drowned or otherwise killed along the length of Miami Beach. Over a hundred dead in Key Biscayne, which had caught the edge of the tsunami and resultant shock waves. The upper tip of the tsunami had simply washed over part of Little Bahama Bank and all the small islands and cays of Bimini. Estimates of dead there were still unavailable.

It was past midnight when Aran returned to his hotel room. Ernest Shuster had phoned, telling Emerson to call a meeting for the following day at noon. Not only Hotchins would attend but General Albert Higgens, Chairman of the Joint Chiefs of Staff, and Daniel Brady, Secretary of Defense. Aran undressed, lay on the bed, and realized he was too drained to speculate any further. But one question had been answered for him this day. They wanted everything—domination, rule. Just like man.

Aran slept soundly, exhausted, and dimly he heard the ringing sound. It was hours later, hardly dawn, and he sat up, gathered thoughts and realized it was the phone. He picked it up and heard Kay Elliot's voice and snapped awake instantly.

"They were here last night," she said. "I heard them."

Aran felt his jaw muscles grow taut. "The tsunami," he breathed. "They had to come back after the tsunami."

"I guessed they were responsible," Kay said. "When I heard them outside I knew." Aran almost laughed bitterly. Their actions were hardly different than man's in this, too. Victory always had to be savored. For them, Evan Taylor's laboratory was a direct path of triumph.

"Are they there now?" he queried.

"No, but they'll come back, late in the day. That's their pattern. They come at night, then return the next day," she said.

"All right, now you stay indoors and watch for them. I'll be at a meeting here that starts at noon. Call me here the minute they show. I'll get a plane down there right away. Maybe I can swing a Navy jet and be there in two hours. Just call me the minute they come back."

She agreed and he hung up, excitement racing through him. He lay back on the bed, but didn't sleep again; instead he rose and got dressed, had coffee, and went to the office at nine.

Emerson had a television set turned on as he entered.

"Brought it from home," Emerson said. "The President's going on at a quarter to twelve." Aran nodded and made no comment, for none was needed. There was no other way now. It was past time for the truth.

CHAPTER ELEVEN

The President of the United States addressed the people at precisely fifteen minutes to twelve that morning. He had previously conferred with the heads of state of several European countries. The hue and cry following the Miami Beach disaster could no longer be contained by platitudinous comments. Besides, European governments were asking questions. No weather station or seismographic monitor had picked up any indication of an undersea earthquake. He did not go into the biological details, a gesture to the National Academy of Sciences. That would come out in time and the backlash on research and experimentation would be bad enough then.

A "vast new intelligence" was operating in the oceans, the President told the world, the extent of its aims and its power still "beyond assessing." But unquestionably, he emphasized, man faced a hostile environment in the sea, a threat that could profoundly affect man's life. He went on to quote optimistic evaluations of military leaders and the very troubled fears of experts on world food problems. He ended with a statement of his own confidence in the technological superiority of man, of his faith in man's intelligence, weapons, and abilities to cope with this new and strange danger.

The revelation, and the supplemental press releases that accompanied it, was also necessary to support the Presidential order to evacuate all coastal areas. Fear of further tsunamis, and of the unknown, required wholesale evacuation, the order stated.

Major cities with deep harbors, and therefore not directly fronting onto the sea, were exempted. The reasoning was that though
a tsunami hitting at New York, for example, might cause serious
harbor damage, the geography of the area would prevent the terrible loss of life unprotected coastal areas would experience. The
National Guard was called out in each of the coastal states from
Maine to Florida to assist in the evacuations. Other troops were
strung out along the shorelines on a twenty-four-hour sea watch.

The announcement set off argument and a quiet kind of
panic with many people flatly refusing to evacuate. Feverish
activity spiraled through the scientific community, and beneath
everything, a sense of shocked, uncomprehending fear. The
Pacific coast had still not been touched, but they knew now that
it was but a matter of time and the waiting was perhaps worse
than attacks. The Japanese began an immediate effort to protect
their low, storm-prone coasts; and at noon, only a few minutes
after the President finished his short, grim address, the meeting
began in the conference room of the Fish and Wildlife Services.

Ernest Shuster ran the meeting, at his right, General Higgens
and the Secretary of Defense. Aran found himself sitting across
from Admiral Hotchins. "You gentlemen possess specialized
knowledge," Shuster said, addressing the room. "I want your can-
did opinions on how to fight this threat. You are the biochemist,
Mr. Streeter. Can we mount a chemical attack, something that
would kill any undersea life near?"

"A poison?" Streeter asked. "It could be done. The material
exists. But it would be irretrievable. We couldn't get it out of the
water later."

"Could it be contained in a given area?" Shuster asked.

"No. Water molecules circulate continually. Substances
absorbed by a group of water molecules in one area have turned
up thousands of miles away in others. We'd have to let loose

tremendous amounts of terribly strong chemicals. We'd kill the sea as well as everything in it."

Shuster turned to Waite, the oceanographer. "Can we use currents to trap large numbers of them?" he asked. "Perhaps the killer whales we want?"

"The possibility is remote. They can make use of existing current flows much better than we can. Of course, if they do so, we might possibly be ready and net them in the currents. It'd be an off chance at best," Waite answered.

Shuster turned to Eakins. "As chief ichthyologist for the Services, what do you think about attacking them through genetically sterile strains?" he queried.

"I'm familiar with the work done along those lines in insect control—flies, bees, ants," Eakins said. "Sending out sterile males who mate with females who then produce infertile eggs. In time, the species dies off, or is reduced to a harmless level. No such work on a comparable scale has been done with marine life, but there is evidence that infertility programs might succeed on a limited basis."

"Why limited?" General Higgens cut in.

"With insects, sterile males cannot compete equally with fertile males. Perhaps the female has some way of detecting the difference or maybe the male behavior isn't the same. In fish, a similar element may enter into it. Unfortunately, any such approach would be an extremely long-range proposition."

"And we haven't time," Shuster said. Aran saw the admiral lean forward.

"We're back to my position on this. We must move on them with massive atomic bombing, a saturation pattern, area by area," he said.

Aran replied in a clipped voice. "You'll make the seas radioactive. You'll do more than Streeter's chemicals could do."

"There's some question as to how long radioactivity would remain," Hotchins snapped.

"Yes, two hundred, five hundred, or a thousand years," Aran flung back. "You'll turn the seas into a more hostile environment for man than *they* ever could, maybe much more than the seas as rain and wind draws up water molecules, radioactive ones, and deposits them all over."

"Goddamn, there's no other way. Conventional bombing won't be total enough," the man shouted. "I say go after them, blast them out of the water, and worry about the radioactivity afterwards. I've confidence that our scientists will come up with a way to decontaminate the water later."

"Bullshit," Aran exploded. "All you give a damn about is winning a battle and you'd destroy three-quarters of this planet to do it."

"Goddamn, there's no other way," Hotchins shouted. Aran started to answer, hesitated, unwilling to hold out the slim promise that lay inside Kay Elliot's phone call. But this was a time for any promises, slim or otherwise.

"There might be a way," he said, and saw General Higgens and Secretary Brady lean forward. "If we can make contact with them, with the original three genetically engineered leaders." Aran paused, and saw Hotchins listening, his eyes sharp. He glanced at the others in the room; saw hope, uncertainty, fear in their faces. He spoke quickly, recounting everything that Kay had told him about the pattern of their return to the waters in front of the lab. When he'd finished, he sat back. "It's worth a try. They can communicate. They understand. Christ, that's certainly been proved. Maybe we can get to them, find a basis for further communication. Those first three would be priceless if they could be brought back into captivity."

"You think that's possible now?" Shuster asked.

"I don't know. Probably not. But they're an unknown quantity. I think we can reason and communicate with them," Aran replied. Shuster's eyes went around the room, waiting for responses. Leslie Streeter was first to speak up.

"Good God, it's worth trying," the biochemist said. "The alternatives terrify me." Aran knew the surprise showed in his face as he heard the next voice comment.

"I'll go along with that," Hotchins said. "If they come back to the place we ought to contact them." Aran met the man's eyes, making no effort to hide his gratification. "Now, you said that Miss Elliot was going to phone you if they show again today," Hotchins said.

"That's right. If she does, I'd like a Navy jet to get me down there as fast as possible," Aran said.

"No problem," Hotchins said, getting to his feet. "I'll go and make the arrangements for the plane. I suggest that this meeting be ended until we see if there are any further developments down in the Keys."

"Agreed," Shuster said, rising. Hotchins was at the door already, but paused to glance back at Aran. "I'll be at the Navy Club here. You'll call me there the minute you hear from her, right?"

"Right," Aran echoed. The others drifted from the room and Aran sat alone, reflecting on how the human organism is a thing of constant surprises. He had never expected Hotchins to agree so readily to the idea of trying to make contact with the killer whales. Perhaps the man knew, inside himself, that all his weapons were of little use against this mammoth force. Aran put his head back against the top of the chair, sat quietly, and Emerson returned in a few minutes.

"General Higgens and Secretary Brady have gone out for a bite with Shuster," Emerson said. "They'll be back afterward to hear if anything's happened. I guess we just wait now."

"And hope," Aran said. Emerson left him alone in the room and Aran closed his eyes, squirmed down in the chair, and surrounded himself with stillness. He half-dozed, waiting, occupying a dim world between being awake and being asleep. Later, he heard Shuster's voice in the hallway outside, the muffled tones of the Secretary of Defense and General Higgins melting in with Shuster's mutterings. He closed out the sound and continued to wait The room was half dark when he stirred himself and sat up. He glanced at his watch. It was nearly five o'clock, the day wearing down to an end. He rose and started from the room when one of the receptionists waved at him.

"Long-distance for you, Mr. Holder," she called. "In your office." Aran moved like a spring snapping, exploding into activtiy, diving into the small office and snatching up the phone.

"They're outside," she said. "Swimming and leaping near the learning panels. I'm using the field glasses."

"How many?" Aran asked.

"Six maybe," Kay's voice answered. "But Enos is one of them. So is Seth."

"Enos? Seth?" Aran frowned.

"Evan named the three we genetically engineered after the sons of Adam—Enos, Seth, and Jared. Enos has a large white spot on his head and Seth has an unusually tall dorsal fin. I'm sure Jared is with them."

"All right, let them know you're there. Keep them there if you can. I'm on my way down," Aran said. He slammed the phone on its cradle and called Hotchins at the Navy Club. While he waited, he swore impatiently until he heard the man's steel-like voice, and told him of Kay's call.

"They showed up, did they?" Hotchins echoed. "Good. You wait there. I'll call you back."

"Have you a plane ready?" Aran asked.

"Yes, everything's arranged. Just wait for my call there," Hotchins said and the line went dead. Aran put the phone down, slumped into the chair behind the desk. The minutes went by, became a quarter of an hour, and his fingers drummed steadily atop the desk. He got up, paced the room. What the hell was holding up Hotchins? He swore silently. He jumped when the phone rang, and scooped it up. Kay Elliot's voice cried into his ear, half-sobbing.

"Why did you lie to me?" he heard her say. "You said you want to try to reach them."

"I did. What are you talking about?" He frowned.

"I think there was a chance. It might have worked," she sobbed. "But that's gone now."

"Damnit, you're not making sense," Aran snapped.

"The planes, the goddamn planes," the girl cried into the phone. "I had to dive for cover myself. They came out of nowhere, three of them, Navy jets, firing round after round of rockets at them."

Aran felt ice coating his skin. Kay continued to sob into the phone, but he was hardly listening now. His jaw had clenched and his lips were drawn back in rage. Hotchins' surprising agreeableness was suddenly so very clear. He'd seen the chance to strike at the three leaders and had rushed to do so. He hadn't gone to arrange a plane for Aran at all but to dispatch jet fighters which had then waited for his second call while airborne. Kay's voice cut into his angry thoughts.

"I'd nothing to do with it, Kay," he told her. "Believe me. I didn't know it was happening." She fell silent for a long moment, then came back on again.

"And you know what's most ironic? I don't think they hit any of them. I saw the killers dive down as soon as the first rocket hit the water. The fighter pilots laid down a crisscross pattern, but

I think they were hitting only water. I watched after they flew away. I didn't see anything floating on the surface."

Aran heard her hang up, put his phone down, saw his knuckles white on the receiver, and forced his fingers to loosen their grip. He made himself wait in the small office that suddenly seemed a cell, a place of entrapment, and he cursed Willard Hotchins again and again. Finally, he heard the receptionist greeting someone, muffled voices, and he yanked the door open. Down the corridor, Hotchins was just going into Emerson's office. Aran was after him, down the hall in three long strides. He burst into the room. Shuster was there, and General Higgens, and the Secretary of Defense. Emerson sat behind his desk. Aran's eyes speared Hotchins and he stepped back as he felt his hands clenching into fists, afraid he would lash out at the man's arrogant face.

"You bastard," Aran hissed. "You stupid, lying bastard."

"Now, now, Mr. Holder," Shuster cut in and Aran turned on him.

"Did you know what he was going to do?" he barked.

"Admiral Hotchins informed us while we were having lunch," Shuster said.

"I saw a chance to nail them once and for all, the very ones we want, and I took it," Hotchins said. "My boys laid down a tight barrage, I'm told. There's every chance they did the job."

"They didn't hit anything but water," Aran said, turning back to Hotchins. "And you wrecked the one chance for making contact, for maybe finding a way out."

"Crap," Hotchins spit out.

"Maybe, and maybe not. It was worth a try. It was our one chance."

"The chance to blast them was worth more," Hotchins returned.

Aran shook his head slowly. "Now there's no way out," he said. "No way out."

"Goddamn, there's a way out—my way," Hotchins said.

"You just can't understand, can you?" Aran answered. "You can't understand that all your ships and planes and bombs won't do. You've weapons and you can't use them because they'll do more harm than good. They have you boxed in. They have trillions and trillions of soldiers, to use your terms. You know about expendability, sacrificing men and ships to gain an objective. They can expend millions and not even feel it. They have power to set all kinds of forces in motion."

"They haven't got a goddamn thing we can't handle. They've shown us all they can do."

"No, oh, Jesus, no," Aran said. "There's so much we don't even know about. A research ship caught onto a living object twelve hundred feet down, something that was large enough to take a three-foot iron hook, bend it and escape. A few years back, a Swedish or Danish ship caught an eel larva. We know that eel larvae have a definite proportional relationship to the adult eels. This larva, if it followed the proportions of all other eel larvae, would become an adult eel ninety feet long."

"We'll take anything they can throw at us," Hotchins growled.

"Yes, maybe so, but not their strength, not the power they have when channeled and directed. That tsunami was only an example. Christ, maybe it was a warning. I wanted the chance to try to reach them, maybe find out something that would help us." Aran paused, felt the rage spiraling up inside him again. "You couldn't let me try," he said. "You couldn't hold back."

"That tsunami was their big thing. They took us by surprise with that, but that's done with. Everyone is busy preparing precautionary measures against more. They can set off as many as they damn well please now. The results won't be the same."

Aran turned away from the man, let his eyes scan the others there. Hotchins' words were there, in each of their faces—the inability to grasp the awesome power they faced. Or was it simply man's inability to grasp his own limitations, to see beyond himself? Perhaps man had ruled too long. Certainly, he had ruled poorly, his domination totally self-serving. Aran turned and walked from the room. He went back to the hotel and sank down on the edge of the bed and called Kay Elliot. Her voice, as she answered, was calm now.

"I'm sorry," he said. "Please believe me. I didn't know it was going to happen."

"I believe you," she answered.

"They haven't shown since, of course," Aran asked.

"No. But they're out there. I can feel it," Kay Elliot said. Aran turned the words in his mind. Maybe she did sense it. And maybe she only imagined it. He didn't comment on it.

"I want you to get out of there," he said. "You'll be evacuated by morning, anyway. But you leave now. If they're still near, they could hold you responsible for the attack. You said they're quite capable of making distinctions, personal conclusions."

"I'll be all right," she said.

"Leave," Aran insisted. "Right now. Get away from there. There's no more point in your staying there."

"No, I guess not," she said, a soft sadness in her voice. The phone clicked and went dead and he knew she had simply hung up. Aran turned to the map he'd so carefully marked that lay on the small end table. He'd continue to mark it. Disgusted and angry as he felt with Hotchins and the others, he still could do no less. He had to continue to try to find a pattern in their moves, something that might help defeat them. He was man. Survival was stronger than guilt and shame. He turned to the map, sat down with it, and began to make his markings, working until he fell back onto the bed and slept.

Kay Elliot let her hand rest on the phone for a moment, then walked away from the instrument to gaze out the window. Darkness was less than a half-hour away and the water was smooth and empty. Her eyes scanned the surface for signs—the tall dorsal fins cutting the water effortlessly. But there were none. The first gray trails of fog were drifting in from the south. She watched them take on depth and grow heavier, saw the main fog bank in the distance. With the night air, it would roll in to blanket the narrow strip of land. She turned from the window, thought about Aran Holder's insistence that she leave. In his eyes, there was no point in her staying any longer. He was understanding, sensitive, but he could only understand so much. He hadn't been a part of it, that time of discovery, of trust, of a special bond that seemed to have been wakened.

She half-smiled to herself as she remembered. Killer whales, even those not genetically engineered, had often proved their astounding sensitivities, the extent of their intelligence. And at first no one could be sure if the gene therapy had really taken hold so she worked with Enos, Seth, and Jared as though they were just three more young male *orcas*. She, more than anyone else, worked with them each day, swam in the tanks with them, fed them, gained their trust. Evan was occupied with planning tests and putting down results, and John Akberg never quite established the rapport she had with them. The Navy, and others who'd worked with killer whales, had discovered that they made a clear distinction between human males and females.

They played less roughly in the tanks with her than they did with John or Evan. As they swam with her, let her cling to their backs, they always seemed to exercise an added measure of what she could only term gallantry. And then, one day, Enos pushed her against the side of the tank and rubbed his body along hers, something he had never done with Evan or John. His tremendous strength became tremendous gentleness; then, one day soon after, he swam against her again, turned, and offered his erect organ to her to stroke. At first, she'd thought it was a visible sign of the genetic engineering at work, but later Evan had told her that it had happened to other young women who'd worked closely with killer whales. But she'd been nonetheless touched, somehow humbled, and when he did it again a few days later, she understood his gesture. Unquestionably, he knew that to try to mate with her was impossible, that he would injure, perhaps kill her, so he offered the only possible sign of his feelings.

Later, as he and the others learned to communicate more through the word-panels, he had once tapped out the word love. But, as he grew older, and as the genetic engineering began to exhibit itself more and more in his quick responses, she noticed he had become less gentle in the water with her. All three had begun to exhibit ugly moments, sudden flarings of temper; particularly Enos when she tried working with him. Rejection? she wondered now.

But, up until the day when they left, he had trusted her: the bond one she could feel, sense, see. And now they probably thought she had betrayed them, had called the planes to kill them. If she left now, they would be certain of it. She didn't want that. A foolish, perhaps even selfish, indulgence, but she didn't want to leave as a betrayer. She didn't want to flee in apparent fear and guilt. They were new creatures, with new, fused sensitivities, made of recombinant DNA molecules. Maybe they were tomorrow. She wouldn't leave as betrayer. She'd stay the night and go in the morning. They'd see the light, see her form moving inside the house. They would see and they would know she hadn't fled in fear as a betrayer.

She turned the lamp on, suddenly aware that she was sitting in the dark. The fog had come, pressing itself against the windows. But the light would glow—diffused, yet visible—and she went into the kitchen to fix herself something to eat: a can of beans and some sausage. Later, she bagan to pack all of Evan's notes in neat cardboard boxes. She worked long at the task, finally finished, and started to pack her own bags, but she halted, suddenly tired. She made coffee, went into the living room with it, and sank down on the couch. The fog had lifted somewhat, only streaks of it floating past the window like threads of some giant scarf. It was quiet, terribly quiet, when suddenly she heard the sound, the unmistakable splash of water as a powerful form dived into it. Another splash sounded and she put the coffee down, rushed to the door and opened it, and stepped outside.

Kay Elliot's scream pierced the silence as the pincers seized her leg. She saw the crabs, six of them, but tremendous specimens, each at least three feet across. They'd been waiting, obviously, and the one with its pincers dug into her leg suddenly pulled. She screamed again in pain as she fell backward to the ground. Another pincer seized her arm, and then she felt a third clasp onto her other leg. The pain was agonizing, their claws cutting deep to the bone. Suddenly she felt herself lifted. They were carrying her, taking her across the narrow strip of sand and into the sea.

"No," she screamed out. "No, don't." She tried to twist away, but the effort made her scream in pain. It was useless, anyway. She was held in vise-like grips that scuttled her slowly sideways into the sea. She felt the water now, pushing up against her legs. "No, no, please. Oh, God," she cried out again. "I didn't call them. I didn't. I stayed here. Don't you understand? I stayed to tell you that." A wave slammed into her mouth, made her gag, choke. The huge crabs moved deeper into the surf. God, Kay thought incongruously, they must have come from the very depths of some unexplored ocean trench. She tried to twist free once more, then felt the bone in her arm snap. She sobbed in pain, but the water was filling her mouth now as they began to swim with her, carrying her down. Her chest grew tight as she tried to hold her breath. She was underwater now, and then, unable to breathe, her lung capacity used up, she gasped out and the water rushed into her mouth. Life dissolved, too fast, the senses fading into nothing. They were taking her back to the sea, she realized with her last, conscious thought. They'd been instructed. They were returning her to the very beginning.

CHAPTER TWELVE

A ran called Kay Elliot the next morning. He let the phone ring a dozen times before he hung up. He waited a half-hour, called again, let it ring longer this time, and once more there was no answer. She had left, he told himself. Perhaps she'd listened to him and left last night. He put the phone down and felt a strange uneasiness. He'd wait for a call from her, he decided. She'd stay in touch, while this was all still unresolved. She was too involved to just disappear.

He went to the office, toyed with the idea of giving Emerson his job back, put the thought aside when he saw that Emerson Boardman was simply unable to cope with the deluge of mail, requests for information, and the continuing news-media pressure. He stayed on, the morning going quickly in the tension and pressure, the constant phone calls and requests for information. It was late afternoon when he realized he hadn't heard from Kay Elliot This time he put in a call to Chief Wilson at Key Largo. The Police Chief would have been in charge of evacuation proceedings for the northern half of the unprotected Keys. The man remembered him and he asked about the girl at Evan Taylor's place.

"No one there," the police chief said. "My men went there, found the door open. They called out, waited, but the place was deserted. They didn't have time to hang around and they didn't make a search. There didn't seem any need for that. She must have left in the night."

"Yes, probably. Thanks a lot," Aran said and put the phone down. But the uneasiness pulled at him again. No, more than uneasiness—a sense of dread, a grim foreboding. The damn feeling would stay with him, he knew, until he found out she'd left and was safe. Once again he cursed Willard Hotchins. For some reason, Kay Elliot felt safe from attack. He hoped she was right. He would have brooded more about it, but the reports that started to come in swept all else from his mind for the moment.

The British Naval forces detected it first, their sonar picking it up. The French along their Atlantic coastline confirmed it with their sonar. A Spanish cruiser over the Iberian Basin picked it up next—another confirmation.

The British sent their report out at once: deep movements of large concentrations of fish leaving the North Atlantic, moving south. They had picked up only a few, at first; then others, smaller groups, swimming swiftly, purposefully. The French ships picked up the same groups and then others. The sonar detection went on all through the night. American ships began picking up similar movements, all the way from Greenland down the mid-Atlantic ridge. Aran gathered each report as it came in, forgot about returning to the hotel to sleep, catnapped in between reports in the office. The others left and he was alone, taking the reports from the teletype as they came in.

Naval vessels of the South Atlantic fleet began to report in with the same sonar findings. Aran took another map from the chart room, began to mark on it, and soon he had a series of three channels, each five hundred miles wide, outlining the movements of the fish. He sat down and stared at it. From the British down to American vessels patrolling east of the Falkland Islands, the swift-moving bands of fish were recorded on the sonar systems. They were far too deep for air detection, but reconnaissance planes sighting killer whales reported in—four groups of whales, leaping from the water and diving back again. Aran took the position of the sightings, marked them on his map. Each one followed in one or another of the three channels he had outlined.

He went downstairs, found an all-night diner and had coffee and a roast beef sandwich, and returned to the office. The teletype had spewed out more reported sonar findings. He added them to his map, finally sat back, and a slow, icy chill crept over him. He let a wry sound escape him. It was altogether appropriate, he reflected. It was almost morning, he saw by the clock that faced him on the wall. Hotchins would be up now, trying to analyze what the mass of sonar findings meant. He'd have contacted Shuster already, perhaps. They would appear meaningless to him, a strange migration suddenly set into motion. He'd be sending ships out, positioning them to move quickly in any direction and that was good enough. Willard Hotchins was an experienced military man; he'd make countermoves, prepare for contingency actions. He'd have his fleet on alert, the Air Force at ready. He just wouldn't realize what they were doing. The enormity of it just wouldn't reach him. Willard Hotchins was locked into his structured thought processes, professionally and biologically. He was man.

Aran sat back in his chair and felt an overwhelming sadness. It had begun and there was little chance it could be stopped. He stared at the map he had marked and outlined. These past days, he'd let his mind speculate, his imagination run free, but he hadn't considered this. But it was all there in front of him now, in the sonar readings multiplied times over, in the pattern that came through. He wasn't wrong. But maybe he was wrong in the sadness he let engulf him. Wasn't this a world of miracles? Hadn't man himself pulled off a few of his own? Maybe there'd be one more, one last miracle for mankind. Maybe there was a way it could be stopped.

He heard the front door open and rose and stood in the hallway as Emerson came in. He saw the surprise in the man's eyes as they focused on him. Emerson Boardman always arrived early, he knew. He smiled at Emerson. "What the hell are you doing here?" Emerson asked.

"Watching the beginning of the end," Aran said. "Can you reach Hotchins?"

Emerson nodded.

"Reach him. Get him here. Shuster and the others, too," Aran said.

"Are you all right?" Emerson Boardman asked him, eyeing him sharply.

"I'm fine," Aran said, turning, and closed the door of the small office. Emerson's question had triggered his thoughts and he dialed Kay Elliot once more at the Keys. The phone rang on until he hung up. She hadn't phoned him. It wasn't right, it didn't fit, and the grim foreboding pulled at him again. Had she gone into hiding when the police came to evacuate her? Was she still there, not answering the phone, waiting, watching, hoping to make contact? Damnit, he had to know. He had to go back down there and see for himself. He glanced at his watch and guessed that by noon the others would be there. He could leave by midafternoon, be down at the Keys by dark. But first, he had another call to make. He dialed, waited, then heard Jenny's voice come through, soft and quiet.

"Did I wake you?" he asked.

"No, I was awake. Oh, God, Aran, I've been waiting for you to call, listening to what's been happening. When I heard the President, that talk we had before you left for the Keys flooded back over me. It all started there, didn't it, with a genetic implant?"

"It all started there," he said. "And I have to go back down there tonight."

"No. No, Aran, oh, no," she cried out at once, fear seizing her voice.

"I have to," he said. "That girl I told you about, the one who worked with Evan Taylor, I'm worried about her. She was down there alone and I haven't heard from her or been able to reach her."

"Let the police look for her," Jenny said.

"No, she might be avoiding them so they won't evacuate her," he said. He told her about Kay Elliot, what she was like, that kind of guilt and courage she had. He told her everything except about that one night. There was no need for that. It had been a thing apart, no intrusion on Jenny and him. "Kay Elliot was deeply involved in all of it," he said. "She could be very important to tomorrow. I want to find out if she's all right."

"Don't go there, Aran," Jenny cried out again. "You've done enough."

The map on the desk seemed to move as he stared down at it. "Enough?" he echoed into the phone. "Maybe, only enough isn't enough now." He paused, shook off reflections. "I'll come to you as soon as I leave there," he said. "I want to be with you, more than you know."

"I'm afraid, Aran," Jenny said. "Don't go there."

"I'll see you soon," he promised and put the phone down gently. The office was busy now, everyone was in, and the teletype continued to clatter out more of the same reports: sonar detection of groupings of fish moving south, coming into the three main streams from all parts of the sea. British and Italian vessels picked up a steady movement through the Straits of Gibraltar now, from the Mediterranean into the Atlantic. Aran sat in his office, ordered coffee, and sipped it slowly and waited.

Shuster arrived first, then General Higgens and two of his aides. Hotchins came in soon after. Aran faced them in

Emerson Boardman's office as the Secretary of Defense arrived. "Goddamnit, Holder, I hope you've got something worthwhile. There's a hell of a lot of something going on out there," Hotchins growled.

"What do you think they're doing, Admiral?" Aran asked quietly. He held the map he'd marked under one arm.

"Some kind of migration, maybe," Hotchins said. "Maybe they're making a massive switch of species from one sea to the other. I've put every ship available on duty. I've got a line stretching down the mid-Atlantic basin around to Cape Town."

"They're going past you, on south," Aran said.

"I know it. We've sonar reports from the Falkland Station on it. Frankly, I don't know what the hell they're doing yet," Hotchins said. "They're not making any attacks anywhere and they're moving in relatively small groupings so they're not trying to set off any tsunamis."

"No, they're not doing any of those things. But those small groupings put together must make ten or twenty million, I'd guess. They're every kind there is, you know. Tuna, cod, herring, bass, flounder, sardines, everything, being drawn from all over. This is only part of them, just the beginnings," Aran said.

Hotchins' sharp eyes bored into him, the man's mind tuned in, waiting. "They're swimming south into the Antarctic, gentlemen. They're the first lot on their way." Aran put the map on Emerson's desk and spread it out. "They're funneling into three groups, spread over some five hundred miles each. This center group will go straight down into the Weddell Sea, the one on the left will turn off and go around Graham Land and Palmer peninsula. I'd guess they'll move inshore at about the Polar Plateau. The right funnel will go into Mackenzie Bay or maybe the West Ice Shelf."

Aran paused, saw Hotchins' eyes starting to widen, his mind beginning to catch hold of the shape of tomorrow. Aran gave him credit for keeping fear out of his stare. "They'll dive low and begin to gather under the ice," Aran said. "Tens of millions, then twenties of millions, then hundreds of millions. They'll create warmth, increase the water temperature suddenly and rapidly. Between the massive increase in water temperature from below, and a steady upward pressure of thousands of tons per foot, the Antarctic ice shelf will both melt and split open to melt more quickly by itself. If only half of the Antarctic ice shelf is melted, the seas of the world will rise one hundred and twenty-five feet by conservative estimates. That's roughly half the height of the Statue of Liberty."

"Every harbor in the world will be underwater," Hotchins breathed. "New York, Boston, London, San Francisco, Tokyo, Shanghai, Le Havre, Bremen, every damn one of them."

"And the coastline of every landmass in the world will be submerged," Aran said. "Many places will vanish underwater altogether. A good part of Florida and many other coastal states will disappear. If all of the ice shelf melts away, all of Florida would vanish."

"My God!" It was Shuster's voice, intoning the two words in the silence of the room.

"Or a variation of the Ewing-Donn theory on glacial formation might hold here," Aran said. "An open Antarctic, largely freed of ice, would be washed by warm Pacific and Atlantic currents in the sea while buffeted by polar temperatures and winds. This would send staggering volumes of vapor into the air and the vapor would become blizzards of unending ferocity over the American and Eurasian continents and, eventually, to the forming of a new ice age. But one thing is certain. The face of this planet will change. They are reclaiming it for the sea."

"They've got to be stopped," Hotchins gasped. "I'll order strikes directly at the Antarctic waters."

"And help them loosen the ice shelf, make it easier for them," Aran snapped. The man's eyes hardened for an instant, conceded error, and he turned to the map on the desk. He drew his finger across the lower portion of it.

"Here," he said. "A line of Naval vessels straight across here firing depth-charges and a steady barrage of delayed-fuse shells. In front of them, continued air coverage dropping delayed-fuse bombs. I'll put it into action at once. We'll work in relays, shifts, between our forces, the Russians, the English, everybody. We'll start. We're closest and can get into position quickest." He paused, probed Aran's eyes. "It's got to work. It's got to slow them down at least. We'll use every bomb and depth-charge and sonic explosive we have."

"It may," Aran said. "But I think they'll just send more up around the other way around Australia. I don't think you can stop them. They're too many, just too many. And once they get under the ice shelf in real strength, you're helpless. The rest will be just a matter of preparing for what will happen."

"Goddamn, I'm going to try with everything I can get hold of. They won't get through in force, not this first time around," Hotchins said. He whirled, took Higgens by the arm, pulling him along as he rushed from the room. "You get hold of the Russians, Air Force and Navy. Brief them. I'm flying down there to take command on the scene," Aran heard him say. "I'll have my staff ready to work out the operational details with them. Christ, there's no time to waste."

Aran watched the man disappear down the hall. Willard Hotchins wouldn't have enough bombs to stop them, he reflected. There weren't enough in the world, neither nuclear nor any other kind. But Willard Hotchins might just be able to slow them down. He had the tactical knowledge and the drive to use it to the greatest advantage. He might dent this first onslaught enough. He might buy a little more time for man. There was a place for arrogance, perhaps. Only it wasn't arrogance any longer. Willard Hotchins wasn't talking about "goddamned fish" any longer. He wasn't even talking about using nuclear weapons. He saw now that you can't save today by destroying tomorrow.

Aran walked out of the room, the troubled foreboding more personal, closer than tomorrow. He hurried downstairs, went to his room—shaved, showered, and changed—and got a cab to the airport. He managed a seat on a nonstop to Miami, reflecting that he was becoming a regular on this run. He slept the way down, felt refreshed when he climbed into the rented car, and sped south and onto the Keys. Night had come down to envelop the deserted stretch of land. He'd had to stop and show identification and give his destination at two roadblocks before he got onto the causeway. When, finally, he rolled to a halt before the buildings of Evan Taylor's laboratory, he saw that a lamp burned in the living room. He pushed the door open, called, and went inside. There was only silence and he felt coldness moving along his spine.

He walked into the bedroom. Kay's suitcases, two of them, were open atop the bed. Both were partially packed and one of the dresser drawers hung open. She had obviously been packing, he frowned, and his spine was now encased in ice. He stood before the suitcases, playing at reconstruction. He turned from them, went into the living room, and spied the mug on the coffeetable. He picked it up. It was more than half full of cold coffee. She'd been packing, stopped to have coffee, and then something had happened. She'd put the mug down and gone outside. He retraced steps, halted at the doorway, felt for the outside light, and turned it on. The soft sand to the left of the house was streaked with long, sideways marks. He knew the sight of them: crab marks. But these had to be gigantic ones. Aran grimaced as he knelt down to the sandy soil. A half dozen dark, dried spots stained it. He wet his finger with his tongue and pressed down on one of the spots. His finger came up red.

He rose, half-ran down the sand toward the sea. The long, sweeping streaks were there, disappearing into the water. Aran halted, saw torn pieces of the white cotton halter, more dried, dark stains on the sand, and one sandal. He stood at the edge of the water and stared out to sea. It was almost a full moon, he noted, the sea brightened, each wave touched by silver. The long row of upright panels floated serenely a hundred yards from the shore. But he knew what had happened to Kay Eliot now. Not the details, only the answer. She had stayed, hoping for something better from them. But she'd been wrong. They offered nothing more than man had given them: ruthlessness, uncaring cruelty, slaughter. Man had made no distinction between cows and calves with his harpoons. He had put no premium on gentleness. They'd do no less now. *Damn you, Kay Elliot. Why didn't you leave when I told you to?* Aran cried inwardly.

He turned, walked back to the house, put away the coffee cup and the half-packed suitcases, and sat down in the living room. He had checked the doors and windows, closed everything, and now he stretched out on the sofa and slept—drained, emptied, and afraid.

It was still dark when he woke. He sat up, listening. The sound came again, not filtering through his subconscious now, but clear, unmistakable—the splash of water, the flat thud of a heavy body striking the surface of the sea. Aran went to the window, peered out at the moonlit Atlantic, and saw the big form gracefully sail into the air, come down again with a cascade of shimmering spray. They had come back. Why? he asked himself.

There was no one here any longer. They'd seen to that finality themselves. He stepped to the door, opened it and went outside, and suddenly had his answer. He'd left the headlights of his car on, the beams shining directly out to sea. They had seen them, or others had, and sent messages and they had returned. Had they expected John Akberg, perhaps? Or were they confused, seeing the headlights as some kind of signal? Probably the latter, Aran decided.

But suddenly he felt the excitement rushing through him, spreading into his arms and legs until he almost trembled. They were here, and he had to try to reach them. It was perhaps a last chance for this world as man knew it. Perhaps it would be a failure. Perhaps they would only leave. Or, more likely, they would close in to kill. Yet he had to try, Aran knew. Those miracles again, he thought. One more, maybe, just one more. Kay had explained the pattern of their appearances and now he stepped forward, silhouetting himself in the glare of the headlights. They had stopped leaping in the water now and were silent, but he could make out their dorsal fins circling. They were peering in at the silhouetted figure, confused, uncertain. It was what he wanted, to insure their return. He moved quickly away from the headlights, stepped into the house and closed the door, and turned out the small lamp. There were no more sounds from the sea and he lay down on the couch again, and slept till the sun crept into the room through the sides of the drapes.

Aran rose, found coffee and some sausage in the refrigerator, and made himself breakfast. He turned on the radio. The airwaves were filled with accounts of the tremendous international air and sea strikes across the length of the lower south Atlantic. Massive concentrations of marine life had been detected massing in the area, the official announcements explained, and Aran smiled wryly. It had obviously been decided that the real reason for the all-out attack was best kept from the public as yet. He couldn't disagree with their thinking. Panic and fear were already close to mass hysteria. It wouldn't take much to create chaos.

He finished the meal, went outside, and scanned the water. They were not there yet, not surfaced, at least. According to Kay Elliot's account of their patterns, they'd return late in the day. Aran felt dryness suddenly in his mouth. The prospect terrified him. He walked to the back of the far building and halted before the rowboat there. His face drawn tight, he began to prepare for later, or perhaps not until darkness had fallen again. He began to prepare to give himself a foothold on life. Perhaps that was as much as anyone could expect now. That's why he had to try, to go out there and face them. He was no hero. He was simply man, fighting to survive. It had come down to that, the full circle. And perhaps he was more fortunate than most. He knew the face of tomorrow.

He rummaged through the workshed, found enough of everything he needed, and he prepared carefully. Finally he pulled the rowboat down near the water's edge, put the oars in it, and went back to the house and cleaned up. He showered, dressed in trousers only, and lay down on the couch and picked up the phone to call Emerson.

"How bad, or how good?" he asked.

"They're running low on bombs. And there have been a number of air crashes. The men are exhausted," Emerson said. There was more hanging in his voice.

"Go on," Aran prodded.

"Roy Waite's on the carrier with Hotchins. He's afraid we could be triggering an underwater quake with the amount of explosives we've dropped in one line across the mid-basin," Emerson said. "Hotchins has ordered a slowdown."

"Surprises never cease," Aran returned.

"He stationed a line of sonar-detecting devices on merchant ships ten miles south of the bombing line," Emerson said. "The number of fish getting by has gone down a lot."

Aran turned the import of the findings over in his mind. The attempt might have been blunted. It wasn't impossible. He'd prophesied as much. But the victory was fragile. They had too many: too many in numbers, too many ways, too many of everything. How many had got through—a million, five million? They'd be heading for the ice pack to gather beneath it and wait for the others that were sure to come. A cadre of the *orcas* would be with them, directing, leading, herding.

"Ill be in touch," he said into the phone, then hung up at once and wondered if his remark hadn't been a new high in optimism. He lay back, half-slept as the day wore into the afternoon. The sound outside made him sit up—a car motor coming to a halt. He was at the door instantly, staring out, not believing his eyes as she stepped from the car and came toward him.

"Turn around, Jennifer Vandam," he said. "Get back into that car and leave."

Her eyes were dark with shadows. "No," she snapped. "No way." She stepped into the room past him. "I dreamed last night. Or maybe it wasn't really a dream. Maybe it was intuition, a sixth sense. But I knew you'd be here yet." She paused, her eyes becoming harder. "I want the truth, Aran. I'm tired of listening to half-truths on the radio and knowing there's more. I want to know what and why. I want whatever tomorrow there is with you. We had planned on tomorrows, if you remember."

"I remember," he said. He sat down with her, told her all she wanted to hear, and then the rest that waited. Fear circled her eyes when he finished.

"Don't, Aran. Please don't," she said. "There must be some other way."

"I've got to try, Jenny," he said. Kay Elliot's words came to him and he quoted them. "This might just be the most important thing left for the world," he said. "Without their direction, without their special, genetic engineering, nothing would have begun. They made it happen. They can make it stop. They are the sons of the new, genetically engineered Adam. I've got to try to reach them, to find a meeting place with them."

"What if it's too late? What if they'll only respond one way now?" she pressed.

"I've only a chance," he said, and would say no more. "How did you get past the roadblocks?" he asked.

"I told them I was coming down to work with you," she said and he made a face and half-turned away. The dusk had come to steal the last of the day from the room, darkening it abruptly. He sank down onto the couch and felt her lips find his, sweet honey remembered. He lay back with her, holding her gently. It was a time for gentleness, for the closeness of being more than thirsting, for holding in quietness and closing out the world. Words were unimportant, unneeded. But then he and Jenny had never needed words that much. He moved finally, sat up, and she followed.

"Please go, get out of here," he tried once more.

"To where? To whom?" she asked simply. He heard the sound, stiffened, listened: the slap of water echoing into the room once again. He was outside in moments and Jenny followed. He turned her to the car she'd driven up in and pushed her toward it.

"Get inside it. Wait there if you insist. If I don't come back, you press that gas pedal and get the hell out of here," he told her gruffly. He hurried from her, saw one big form in a short arc through the air, cleaving the water as it came down. He walked to the rowboat, pushed it from the beach, and grasped the oars at once. He rode over the first wave that came in. The moon brightened the sea, giving everything bold relief, and he rowed out to the long line of upright panels. He seemed entirely alone in the water silvered by the moon, and then, suddenly, the triangle-shaped dorsal of the killer whale appeared. He saw one, then another, finally counted six of them slowly circling the area. He heard the water stir close to the edge of the rowboat, and looked over to glimpse the octopus gliding alongside. It raised one huge tentacle out of the water, at least twenty feet long, he guessed. Lazily it hooked over the gunwale, then pulled back and settled down beneath the surface of the water.

One of the *orcas* suddenly shot forward, closer, an astonishingly swift darting spurt, and Aran glimpsed the large white patch on its head. That would be Enos, he recalled silently, as the whale moved away. It had come in to look closely at him, he knew as he maneuvered the rowboat alongside the upright panels, now taller than they'd seemed from shore. He saw the L-shaped base to each with the words imprinted on each base, sectioned off. He leaned forward and the sharp smell of oil rose into his nostrils. He had soaked the wood of the boat in it, pouring three oil drums over the craft during the morning. As though he were playing a giant xylophone, he hit the L-shaped part of the panels with his fist, watched the matching word spring UP on the upright sections of the device. He'd scanned the selection, chosen quickly.

STOP KILLING, he punched out, then pushed the boat back from the panels. Two of the *orcas* darted in at once; one was Enos.

NO. They hit the base section of the panel with their noses, first one, then the other; they whirled in the water, streaked past him, turned again. He moved to the panels, used an oar this time.

WHY? he struck, retreated again. Enos moved in alone, the great bulk as silent and swift as a wraith.

MAN BAD, the whale punched out on the panels. This time the killer whale backed away a few feet, waited, and Aran moved in, scanning the words on each section of the base.

Using the oar again, Aran chose the single word: WHY?

Almost instantly, the powerful form moved forward, came down so hard on the panels the entire structure shook. MAN KILLS, Aran read under the moonlight. He felt his jaw muscles tighten as he chose his reply. The great marine mammal could crush him as a child crushes a paper cup, he knew, yet he had to answer without fear. FISH KILL, he punched out, and drew the boat back from the panels.

The *orca* shot forward, slapping his huge head down hard on the water, obviously angered. He grazed the edge of the boat as he hurtled past, circled, was joined by two others, obviously agitated. Aran glanced ashore, knew that Jenny was clutching the wheel of the car, watching, being slowly torn apart inside. The one Kay had called Enos suddenly shot forward, crashing his snout down on the base panels and then whirling off. Aran saw the words punched out on the panels. FISH KILL TO EAT.

Aran moved forward, struck out with the oar, quickly and decisively.

MAN MUST LIVE.

The *orca* hurtled forward, very upset, slammed down on the panels. ALL MUST LIVE, Aran read, and the huge mammal raced around the boat, almost swamping it. He saw other dorsal fins starting to move in. The communication was coming to an end, he realized. Desperately, he struck at the panels again, punched out the question: WHAT DO YOU WANT?

He pushed back from the panels and once again, moving with angry speed, Enos darted along the panels, bringing his snout down hard on them. Aran saw the words appear on the trembling uprights. ALL MUST LIVE, and then, following them,

MAN KILLS. Aran cursed silently. They had answered him, with cold-blooded, implacable convictions—and the communication was ended, over once and for all.

The dorsal fins were moving in a swift circle now and Aran could feel their anger. They had understood him, had used the limited vocabulary of the panels to answer. They were thinking creatures, intelligent, perhaps brilliant, and filled with hate. They had returned here, drawn by the headlights, confused, wondering, and had waited to see. Now they would kill him. How he came here to work the panels, to try to reach them, was unimportant now, he realized. Perhaps they would wonder about it later. But now he was one more to be slain.

Aran felt the boat rock, watched the tentacle appear, cling to the side of the gunwale. He leaned forward, gathered up the long steel cable he'd found and attached to the bow. He drew a book of matches out of his pocket, lit them and tossed them into the stern of the rowboat as he dived overboard. The heat swept over him as the oil-soaked rowboat exploded in a sheet of flame. He swam under it, directly beneath it, and it made a spectacular pattern over his head as he pulled on the steel cable, directing it to shore.

It was burning fast, but he'd soaked it through. It'd last till he neared the beach. He swam under it as the tide pushed it shoreward, clutching the steel cable to keep it from veering off. He saw the hurtling forms circling frantically, enraged, yet unwilling to come near the leaping flames. He swam out of the fire's circle, surfaced for a moment to gulp air, retreated back under the boat. Two of the *orcas* darted in, whirled and withdrew, flinging themselves high into the air in rage. He was but a few dozen yards from shore now, the water becoming too shallow to stay under the boat, the heat starting to penetrate the shallower water to him. He struck out, letting go of the cable, swam furiously for the shore, surfaced for air, and struck out again. Glancing back, he saw them coming after him, converging like so many torpedoes fired from a warship. His feet touched bottom and he stumbled forward, caught himself, ran through the surf now, splashing and showering spray. He heard the sound of the leap, half-whirled, saw one of the killer whales in the air, hurling itself after him. Aran dived to the right as the huge form shot through the air to crash onto the sand of the beach.

He ran now, heard Jenny's scream, saw the *orca* thrashing on the sand, moving itself back into the water. Jenny screamed again and he glimpsed the tentacled form on the sand, moving toward him from the right with surprising speed. He heard the car engine roar and then saw Jenny send the car leaping forward, skidding to a halt as he yanked the door open and dived inside. She gunned the engine as the tentacles swirled up along the fender, slipping, then catching with suctioned power. She floored the accelerator and he heard the rear wheels of the car spin in the sand, catch, and they were roaring forward. He saw the tentacles slip away and disappear.

"Keep going," he yelled at her. "Get onto the causeway." The instructions were unnecessary, he realized as he glanced at her drawn, drained face. They sped through the silent darkness, onto the deserted causeway. Their lights picked up processions of blue crabs crossing the road and the car skidded and bounced as it hurtled over them, numerous columns all the way along the causeway. Jenny drove as if in a trance until they reached Key Largo, where he had her stop at the police station. She halted the car then, sat with her hands clenched around the wheel, staring into the darkness.

"They're monsters, aren't they?" she asked. "Beyond reaching."

"They're more than we know, something beyond us," he said.

"What happens now?" she asked. He shrugged. He was back to not knowing. He got out, found Chief Wilson on duty, and the police charity-drive boxes yielded enough dry clothes to make an outfit

"Did you hear?" the police chief asked. "The bombing stopped them."

"That's good news," Aran said, and caught Jenny's quick glance at him. He took her arm as they left the police station, and she clung to him all the way to Miami. They caught the early flight to Boston there.

CHAPTER THIRTEEN

otchins was there. He had grown into an old man—a tired, weary old man. Emerson didn't bother to hide his flask any longer, Aran saw. Shuster's perpetually grave eyes seemed to have grown deeper until now they were as two dark holes in his head, cadaverlike.

"We did stop them, most of them," Hotchins said wearily. "We were down to national stockpiles of ammunition. So were the Russians. The English had nothing left." His eyes lifted, met Aran's glance, and there was defeat in them. "But you were right. They were coming in from below, around the other side of the Antarctic shelf. Australian sonar began to pick them up. So did the Japanese ships. Then our icebreakers stationed off the Ross shelf began getting them on their sonar. We haven't enough ships to cover all the approaches. We've no idea how many are moving in."

"You were bombing a massive diversionary force," Aran said in the admiral's language. Hotchins nodded, almost idly.

"Naval specialists in the Antarctic stations are looking into possible ways of getting at them under the ice shelf," Shuster said. "Without helping them by destroying the ice, as you pointed out," he added with a nod to Aran. He drew a deep breath and went on. "The President has brought in the Army Corps of Engineers to draw up a comprehensive plan for the use of land areas that will become the reduced coastline of the United States. Frankly, we're fairly lucky. Estimates show a good part of Japan will be totally underwater. For the moment, it's been agreed at the top level, internationally, that the prognosis be kept from the public for a while yet."

"It'll come out. Too many people will have to be involved in the preparations to keep it quiet," Aran said.

"How much time is there?" Jenny asked.

"That depends entirely on how much temperature rise they can generate and how quickly the ice shelf will melt," Aran said. "It could take a long time, plenty long enough for the world to make orderly preparations." He paused. "Or it could happen more quickly than we can estimate. So many factors are beyond our knowing. The added mass of water, changed temperatures and currents, sudden clashes of cold and hot streams—all these might trigger vast undersea quakes that could change the face of the earth even more."

"I want to hide someplace," Jenny said softly. No one replied. It was Hotchins who exploded suddenly, whirling in his chair, crashing a fist onto the table as he shouted at Aran.

"Why, goddamn it, why? You made contact with them. You said you communicated with them on some damn machine. Did anything make sense about it? What the hell did we do to them?"

"What haven't we done to them?" Aran answered. "We've exterminated the right whale. We're on our way to wiping out the sperm and the blue. We've overfished so many areas that we've killed off whole species. We've polluted their environment, contaminated the place where they live and breathe and exist with oil, chemicals, radioactive wastes. We overfish, overkill, overdo everything. We've no regard for anything but ourselves. Every living creature exists for us. And we're continuing to do it. We do it on land, too, but the sea has its own power and the creatures of the sea have weapons nothing on land possesses."

"Those are all your words," Hotchins said.

"They said it, not the way I'm saying it, but their way. Maybe better. Man must live, I told them. Everything must live, they answered, every creature has its rights. I asked them what they wanted and they repeated the same answer. Everything must live. Not just man, not just man's ruthless greed, everything. We're not fighting fish. We're fighting the awakened phylogenetic consciousness of an entire species. And we did it to ourselves with our own DNA molecules."

"Do we just wait and try to prepare now?" Jenny asked.

"It won't be that peaceful. I imagine they'll have a number of unpleasant surprises for us yet," Aran said. The phone jangled, a harsh interruption. Emerson picked it up, listened, and his mouth opened. The sound of his breathing filled the room. He put it down without a word to the caller and turned to the others.

"It's out," he said. "It broke in Japan first. Hysteria has swept the country—riots, people fighting each other for no reason. There's been a mass rush to leave the country and their army's been called out to help keep order. People are swimming, rowing, sailing, and paddling out to ships anchored in Tokyo Bay. The London Stock Exchange has announced it is closing for the time being. The New York Stock Exchange has halted all transactions. The President is considering ordering martial law before the full impact of it reaches here."

"Maybe they won't have to melt that ice," Aran said softly. He rose, held his hand out to Jenny, and turned to the others. "I'll be at the hotel if you want me," he said. "I've a few days paid up still."

"And I'll be there with him," Jenny said. "Until we're too tired to do anything, especially think."

Aran kept his grip on her hand as they left the conference room and went down in the elevator to the street outside. He halted there, the line of silent marchers with their placards directly in front of them. The fair-haired, intense-eyed young man still led the group and those watching still looked on with grave, unsmiling eyes. Aran stopped in front of the sign the blond man carried and scanned the roughly scrawled lettering on it.

> "And I will cause the arrogancy of the proud to cease ... they that spread nets upon the waters shall languish."—Isaiah

He saw a terrible sadness in the depths of the intense blue eyes. "You've heard the President's announcements," Aran said. "And you still believe this is Biblical prophecy come true?"

"Can you not believe it?" the young man asked and Aran felt Jenny's hand tighten around his.

"But man has brought this to pass, on his own," Aran said.

"Has he? How work the Lord His ways except through His creatures?" the answer came. Aran felt Jenny tug at him and turned. He went with her and she stayed close against him as they crossed the street.

"Maybe," he heard her whisper. "Maybe he's right."

CHAPTER FOURTEEN

I t happened at almost exactly the same time in two places three thousand miles apart. Scientists spoke of unexplainable organic reversals. Churchmen said the Lord is Merciful. Perhaps they were both right.

The Hendriks had a home just south of Virginia Beach on the waterfront. When the initial hysteria had subsided, they borrowed a U-haul truck and drove to the home they had evacuated to begin permanently removing furniture. Their good friends and neighbors, the Rawlins, went along to help them. The task was painful and consuming, emotionally and physically. No one paid attention to Tommy Hendriks, aged eight, and Billy Rawlins, one year younger. They wandered away from the adults, found themselves standing along the beach by the small dock where the Hendriks rowboat was still tied up.

"I'm not afraid to go out there," Tommy Hendriks said, pointing to the sea.

"That's what you say," Billy retorted.

"I'd go out there any old time and go fishing, only my folks won't let me," Tommy continued.

"Baloney," Billy said. "You're scared out of your pants."

"You're the one that wouldn't go," Tommy shot back.

"Try me," Billy dared. The rivalry wasn't new between them. It extended into almost everything. "Chicken," Billy added.

Tommy turned and ran back to the small shed just back of the sand where fishing tackle was stored. He came back with two

poles and some dried clam bait. Billy watched him, a little appre-
hensive now. Tommy brushed by him and went to the rowboat.
"You coming, big mouth?" Tommy said.

"I'm coming," Billy snapped, and climbed into the rowboat.
He even cast off the mooring line. He rubbed his hands against
his jeans when Tommy wasn't looking, and wiped the perspiration from them. Tommy handed him one pole and some of the
dried clam bait which grew moist almost at once in the water.
They rowed a few dozen yards offshore, at the point of the low
wharf where bass used to congregate. Tommy caught two stripers
and Billy three yellowfin groupers. Mrs. Hendriks fainted when
they returned with the fish.

"There was nothing to it," both boys said, shrugging. "They
were biting good."

And across the Atlantic, in the shadow of the Neapolitan
harbor, Antonio Ricci walked barefooted with his grandfather
along the low, rocky beach. Antonio, barely seven, didn't listen to all the talk about danger at the beach and the old man
listened but didn't care anymore and so they walked together
before breakfast, before anyone was up. Antonio saw the small
cephalopod scuttling after shrimp that lodged in the water-
filled crevices of the rocks at low tide. Automatically, he ran
to catch it, but missed his first lunge. The octopus turned and
fled for the water, but Antonio didn't miss the second time
and scooped it up and carried it home. It hung as if dead,
which it soon was, in the usual octopus defense behavior out
of water.

Like a prairie wildfire, news of the two incidents spread.
Others gathered courage and followed suit. They found only
normalcy in the waters of the sea. It had passed. Like a terrible
nightmare, it had ended. There were other confirmations. The
Navy picked up sonar readings of large masses of fish leaving

Antarctic waters and Maine lobstermen found fat crustaceans quietly trapped inside lobster pots near shore.

The news caught up with Aran at Falls Church, at Jenny's place where they'd gone after the hotel. He'd left the number with Emerson, who called as the strange reversal seemed beyond question.

"Shuster and some of the others are afraid," he said. "They keep wondering if we're being conned into some tremendous tragedy. You made contact with them. Have you any explanation? Could they have just changed their minds, their attitudes? Or was it really just some kind of weird temporary behavior in the first place?"

"I'll think about it and call you," Aran said. He hung up and saw Jenny's eyes watching him. "Let's drive to the cottage," he said, and she went with him without questioning. He told her of Emerson's queries, and when they reached the coast, he stood with her at the water's edge.

"In his papers, Evan Taylor noted that he had misgivings about the mortality of cell lines out of tissue cultures," Aran said. "Strangely, abnormal or malignant cell lines seem to possess much longer life-spans than normal cells. Therefore, the DNA passed on through viruses or bacteriophages could simply have died with the death of the cells out of the tissue cultures he used."

"The genetic engineering only held for a limited period," Jenny echoed.

"That's right. Or, it could be undergoing a temporary change, a halt to its own chemistry. We don't know. It's all so full of unknowns and unexplored variables."

"But they are out there, someplace," Jenny said, her eyes scanning the water. "Something genetically engineered, a new organism on this planet, is swimming out there and we don't know when it will or if it will erupt again."

"But we've been warned," Aran said. "It's not man's planet, his exclusive territory, they've told us. Everything has a right to live. Everything must eat to live and they accept that. But we must stop our heedless slaughtering, exterminating whole species of our fellow creatures, polluting the seas, the land, the air—living with absolute disregard for anything except our own wants. Maybe, if we stop that, this won't happen again. But I think they're out there watching, waiting, giving us that second chance, that last chance."

"Something's giving it to us," Jenny said. He put an arm around her as they slowly walked back along the top of the dunes. They saw a car stop, three men clamber from it, stretch, and begin to bring out their equipment.

"Goddamn, it's going to be good to get out there and sink a hook into some of those big blues again," one said.

They halted, Aran and Jenny, and watched the three men go down to the water, dragging an aluminum row-boat with them. He felt Jenny shiver and held her close. There was little else to do.

" … and a great and strong wind rent the mountains, and broke in pieces the rocks before the Lord; but the Lord was not in the wind; and after the wind an earthquake; but the Lord was not in the earthquake; and after the earthquake a fire; but the Lord was not in the fire; and after the fire a still small voice."

I Kings 19:11